A

GREATER
GLORY

A
GREATER
GLORY

JAMES SCOTT BELL

BETHANYHOUSE
MINNEAPOLIS, MINNESOTA 55438

Published by Bethany House Publishers
A Ministry of Bethany Fellowship International
11400 Hampshire Avenue South
Bloomington, Minnesota 55438

Printed in the United States of America by
Bethany Press International, Bloomington, Minnesota 55438

ISBN 0-7394-3616-3

JAMES SCOTT BELL is a Los Angeles native and former trial lawyer who now writes full time. He is the author of several legal thrillers; his novel *Final Witness* won the 2000 Christy Award as the top suspense novel of the year. He and his family still reside in the City of Angels.

Jim's Web site is *www.jamesscottbell.com.*

Books By James Scott Bell

Circumstantial Evidence
Final Witness
Blind Justice
The Nephilim Seed
The Darwin Conspiracy
Deadlock

THE TRIALS OF KIT SHANNON

A Greater Glory

Books By
Tracie Peterson & James Scott Bell

SHANNON SAGA

City of Angels
Angels Flight
Angel of Mercy

Law can discover sin, but not remove.

—MILTON, *Paradise Lost*

Part One

1

THE SHARP RAP ON THE DOOR jolted Celia Harcourt to wakefulness.

She'd been dreaming, and the knock came just as an ax had fallen on her neck. In the way of bad dreams, Celia had awakened just before the awful moment when death's cold hand gripped her. For a second or two she did not know where she was. It might have been Baltimore again—terrible Baltimore.

But no. Another knock on the door, more insistent this time, reminded her she was safely at home in Los Angeles.

Celia rose from the sofa, trying to recall the hour. She often napped in the afternoons; not by design, but from seeming necessity. At age forty-six she was not in the best of health—never had been, really, not since the fever at age seven—and the warmth of the Los Angeles day could easily prod her to sleep.

A third, impatient knock. Celia opened the door and saw the strangest clergyman she had ever laid eyes on.

"Mrs. Harcourt?" He was a tall man with a large head. Deep creases furrowed his brow, and his minister's collar seemed to squeeze his neck, as if it were more punishment than vestment. He smiled, showing somewhat crooked teeth tinted a dull shade of yellow.

"I am Dr. Rasmussen." He removed his black felt hat. "From the church."

"Oh," Celia said with a relieved sigh. "You're from Hill Street Methodist."

"Yes," Rasmussen said, nodding eagerly.

"Won't you come in?"

Celia was glad the maid had completed her rounds this morning. The first floor was dusted and the sitting room was ready for visitors. In only a week the house would be full of family and friends, all in celebration of the marriage. Celia could hardly contain her excitement these last couple of months.

"May I offer you some tea, Dr. . . ."

"Rasmussen. That would be very nice, Mrs. Harcourt."

Celia rang the servants' bell. Ginnie appeared at the door and curtsied in her somewhat girlish manner.

"Tea, please," Celia said. "For two."

"This must be a time of great anticipation for you," Dr. Rasmussen said.

Celia sat in a chair opposite the minister. "Oh yes, it is, for Mr. Harcourt, as well. But most especially for Louise."

"Ah yes. Your lovely daughter. Is that her in the photograph?" He was looking at a likeness on the table near the window.

"Yes." Celia gazed at the image of her nineteen-year-old daughter. "She sat for it only last month. She wanted her father and me to have it, you see, because she was leaving our . . ." The last words constricted in her throat.

"How well I understand," Dr. Rasmussen said. "Oh, how well. Your only child?"

"Yes," Celia managed. The thought that Louise would soon be absent from the house she had grown up in, been happy in, was the only hitch in an otherwise joyous occasion.

"But you remember the saying, don't you?" Rasmussen asked. "You'll be gaining a son."

Celia put on a polite smile. It was only right in the company of a minister. "Thank you."

"By the by," the minister said. "Your daughter's intended . . ." His voice lifted and his eyebrows raised.

"John?"

"Yes, John. What is his line of work, if I may ask?"

"He's going to be attending Yale, studying law."

Rasmussen nodded once, slowly, and smiled again.

"Please excuse me, Doctor, but I cannot recall if we had an appointment. Are you assisting Dr. Lazarus with the wedding?"

"Dr. Lazarus, yes," Rasmussen said. "I am new to Olive Street, as you may know."

"I beg your pardon?"

The easy smile disappeared like a scared mouse, then fought its way back to Rasmussen's face. "I mean Hill Street, of course! The bishop has a way of shifting us around so. You understand."

She didn't, really, but was always willing to give a man of the cloth the benefit of the doubt. It was her way of showing forgiveness for what they had done to her. But all that seemed a lifetime ago, back in Baltimore, during the dark days.

Ginnie entered with the tea service and poured for the two of them before scurrying out.

"Dr. Lazarus has asked me to settle just a few questions for the church books," Rasmussen said. His large fingers wrapped around the entire teacup, ignoring the handle. It seemed a little odd to Celia, who had come to be one of the more respected hostesses in the city. Why, he gripped the cup like a dock worker. Perhaps he had emerged from a rough background, as she had.

"Church books?"

"Yes, we like to memorialize all of our events as a permanent record. You understand, I'm sure."

Again, the understanding escaped her. But she wanted everything to be as smooth as possible for Louise. "Certainly, Dr. Rasmussen."

"If I may make a few notes?" He reached his right hand inside his coat, holding the teacup like a ball in his left. Presently he removed a pad of some sort, which was rather worn at the edges, and a pencil. He placed the teacup on the saucer and prepared to write.

"John," he said. "And how do you spell his last name?"

"W-H-I-T-N-E-Y."

The minister's eyebrows rose as he jotted. "The Whitneys, eh? Congratulations, Mrs. Harcourt. They are quite the prominent family."

"And John is such a marvelous young man," Celia said. "It is like a fairy tale, really. A handsome prince for a lovely princess."

"How sweet," Dr. Rasmussen said. "Are you very close with the Whitneys?"

"Beginning to be," Celia said. "I daresay they are every bit as sad to be losing their son as we are to lose Louise."

Tapping his lip with the pencil, the minister said, "I presume the Whitneys, knowing them as we all do, have satisfied themselves with the pedigree of their soon-to-be daughter-in-law?"

A lump formed in Celia's stomach then, and for a brief moment she felt that she should leave the room immediately. What was the reason for all these questions? Surely the church did not have a need to know about the personal background of the families involved. There was something not quite right about this. Yet this man was a minister of God. Surely he—

"Hello!" Truman's jaunty voice broke her reverie.

"My husband," Celia announced. "Truman, this is Dr. Rasmussen, from the church."

"Ah!" As always, her husband greeted the stranger as a hale fellow, well met. That was his personality, so different from her own. She was the gloomy one, always trying to be sunny. Truman was the sun itself.

The minister rose, shook Truman's hand, then reached for a silver watch in his vest pocket. Glancing at the time, he said, "I am afraid I must get back to the church. My apologies. Perhaps we will see each other again before the happy event."

"Won't you stay for supper?" Truman asked.

"Thank you, but no. Duty calls." Rasmussen slipped his watch back in his coat pocket and started toward the foyer. Celia followed, the faint uneasiness she'd felt earlier melting away with the return of her husband. Truman Harcourt placed his arm around her shoulder and kissed the top of her head.

The minister paused near the door and exclaimed, "My hat!"

Before Celia could turn to retrieve it for him, the minister bolted back to the sitting room.

Truman Harcourt held his wife's arm. "Is everything all right?"

"I think so," Celia said cautiously.

"We haven't met this one, have we?"

"He's new."

"I'm sure all will be well." Truman drew Celia closer, resting his cheek on her hair. "My dear, this is going to be the most joyous moment of our lives. I'll make sure—"

"There we are," Rasmussen said, returning with his hat. "I will take my leave." He bowed, somewhat awkwardly. Then, without waiting to be let out, he grabbed the door handle. "Good day." Without further word, he was gone.

"He was in quite a hurry," Truman remarked. "Rather brusque for a clergyman, don't you think?"

Celia did not know what to think. "Why do you suppose the church would want . . ." She stopped herself, thoughts rumbling into her head without order or restraint. "Truman, he didn't know John's name."

"What?"

"Isn't that odd if he . . ."

"What is it, dear?"

"The church. It has a telephone, doesn't it?"

"I believe so."

"Ring them, will you?"

His eyes sharpening with concern, Truman went immediately to the Bell box on the wall, lifted the earpiece, and cranked the ringer. After a moment he said, "Give me Hill 5237." He looked at Celia as he waited, then: "Dr. Lazarus? Yes, Truman Harcourt here . . . Very well, thank you. My wife and I were just entertaining someone from your staff . . . No, this man's name was Rasmussen, Dr. Rasmussen. A rather tall fellow who . . . You don't?" Truman glanced again at Celia, this time with alarm. "Well, then, I think there has been some mistake . . . No, no need to apologize. Thank you for your time."

Truman replaced the earpiece in its cradle. "What do you suppose?"

Celia did not want to suppose, but her mind and heart did so anyway. And then it hit her, suddenly, like waves against the bow of a small ship. Trouble, yes—all of it . . . Baltimore . . . Louise. That was why this fellow had come. He was no minister.

"Blackmailer," Celia said, breathlessly.

"I am sure there is—" Truman stopped and cleared his throat. "There must be some explanation. I shall—"

Celia cried out. Her hand covered her mouth.

"What is it?" Truman said.

Celia pointed toward the paneled window in the sitting room that looked out to the garden. "Louise's photograph," she whispered. "It's gone."

2

FROM HER SECOND-FLOOR OFFICE at 238 W. First Street, Kit Shannon looked down Broadway, a street seeming to change right before her eyes.

When she had arrived in the city in the summer of 1903, the avenue bore the quaint marks of a township emerging from frontier roots and lazy hacienda ways. One could still find long patches of dirt in the asphaltum strip back then, pockmarked by horse hooves and footprints, by rainfall following dry Santa Ana winds.

Now, nearly two years later, the thoroughfare running through the heart of Los Angeles was a picture of urban exhilaration. Skeletons of new buildings rose into the sky like great sculptures. Horses and buggies still dominated the street, but gasoline-powered automobiles were becoming a more frequent phenomenon. The sputter and bang of horseless carriages filled the morning air like gunfire at a Fourth of July picnic.

And people everywhere—moving, always moving, as if afraid to stop lest they miss that promise of fortune, the hope of a better life that seemed the chief lure of the City of Angels.

That lure was one of the consistent subjects of the *Los Angeles Times*, housed in the building at the southeast corner of Broadway and First. Kit felt as if she could reach out the window and touch the forbidding stone edifice and indeed remove the letters of its signature sign: *All the News, All the Time.*

Kit turned from the window, a wisp of her auburn hair sweeping over her Irish green eyes. Hands placed on her hips, she looked at her assistant, Corazón Chavez, who sat with pencil and pad, taking dictation.

"And furthermore," Kit said, continuing her oration, "the influx of charlatans and mountebanks needs to be of greater concern to our civic leaders, especially those in the offices of the district attorney and police."

She paused, watching Corazón's feverish attempts to capture the words. "I can write this myself, Corazón."

"No," the young woman with the silky black hair protested. "I do not learn the shorthand without practice, yes?"

"You're doing wonderfully. I only hope the *Times* will print this." Her arguments were more in keeping with the progressivism of the Hearst newspaper, the *Examiner*. But Kit was *persona non grata* there after her triumph in the Hanratty murder trial. Hearst and his editor had been against the policeman, Ed Hanratty, from the start, manufacturing a sensational story to gain more circulation. They hid witnesses and tried to bully Kit out of defending an innocent man. So the *Times* was the only major news organization left. The smaller papers, like the *Express*, had little influence. And the sensationalist *Gazette* was beneath her dignity. It wanted scandal, not reform.

"General Otis is such a booster of the city," Kit continued to muse. "He is sometimes willfully blind to what is happening around us. Vice and greed and confidence games. Ooh, I like that. Write that one down."

"Vice?"

"And greed and confidence games. There lurks in the shadows of our grand buildings and magnolia trees an element of corruption. As a good people, a progressive people, we must be ever vigilant to root out this pestilence—"

"Ah, these words!" Corazón said.

"Am I going too fast?"

"I will keep up!"

"And I will double your salary."

"Miss Kit! There is no need—"

"Our Lord said the laborer is worthy of his hire."

Corazón became thoughtful. "I will not argue with our Lord," she said.

Kit laughed as the door to the office cracked open, tentatively.

"Yes?" Kit offered to the woman who peered in.

"Are you Miss Shannon?" the woman asked.

Kit nodded. "Please come in."

The woman was middle-aged, though her eyes looked older. Earl Rogers, the city's most famous lawyer and Kit's early mentor, had always told Kit to assess a client's eyes before anything else. They often told more than the client's words. These eyes seemed to do that. A fearfulness filled them.

Corazón rose and offered the woman a chair.

"This is my assistant, Corazón Chavez," Kit said. "If you are here on a legal matter, I would like her to stay and take notes."

The woman seemed tentative for a moment—Kit thought her the sort who would be tentative about everything—and then nodded. She was wearing a rich chocolate-brown satin dress. The bodice had a beautiful ecru-colored front with an under blouse featuring a high collar and an embroidered pattern of pastel flowers. Her hat was stylish and feathered. In short, she was what Aunt Freddy, Kit's dear departed great-aunt, would have called one of the city's "well-appointed women."

"I am Mrs. Truman Harcourt," the woman said. "I didn't know who else to come to."

Kit said, "I will certainly offer any advice I can."

"I am so . . ." Mrs. Harcourt's voice trailed off into a barely audible moan.

"Please, Mrs. Harcourt, take your time. And remember that whatever you tell me will be held in the strictest confidence."

That seemed to be a great relief to Mrs. Harcourt. Her shoulders relaxed somewhat.

"The law protects people's private lives, does it not, Miss Shannon?"

"In some cases, not in others."

"What others?" Mrs. Harcourt's face furrowed with concern.

"Criminal matters, for example," Kit said. "Someone who is a material witness to a crime will have to expose relevant information, whether private or not."

"What about in matters that are not criminal?"

"Again, the circumstances will tell."

"What is the law concerning libel?"

Kit folded her hands patiently. "Libel is defamation of character in written form. The basis of the action is that it is an invasion of a person's interest in their good name. Is that your concern, Mrs. Harcourt?"

The woman looked down at her gloved hands, which trembled ever so slightly. "You *did* say that all would be held in confidence?"

"That is a promise," Kit said.

Then the woman looked up again, and her face reflected depths of apprehension that seemed bottomless. "All right," she said. "I will tell you everything."

Kit nodded, recognizing that a Rubicon had just been crossed inside Mrs. Truman Harcourt. What she was about to say was going to be of great import.

"My name, before I became Mrs. Harcourt, was Celia Normandeau. Does that name mean anything to you?"

Somewhere in Kit's memory, the name did sound familiar. But she was not at all sure why. "I may have heard it."

"It is the name of a well-known Baltimore family." Celia Harcourt paused and took a deep breath. "And a notorious one. I was the cause of that."

"The Normandeau murder case," Kit said quickly.

Celia Harcourt nodded. "Then, you do remember."

"Only vaguely. It was, what, twenty years ago?"

"Almost to the day."

"I would have been only five years old. It seems to me, though, that I read about it later."

"They turned it into an ugly nickel novelette. It was quite the scandal back then." A thin veil of anger fell over the distraught face of Celia Harcourt. "I was just eighteen when I met Clyde Jefferds. I will admit I was prime for such as he. I was in rebellion against my parents, my church. When Clyde came into my life, talking so smoothly—and oh my, he was handsome. We were going to be married, see the world together, he said. It was all so romantic."

She spoke the last words without emotion, as if reading a dry crime report taken by a police officer. "I shamed my parents. When I told Clyde I was with child, I still remember the horrified look on his face. He was no longer handsome. He told me he had no intention of marrying me, that his feelings had changed. He had found another, he said, and that was the breaks. I remember him uttering those words exactly. 'The breaks,' he said.

"Naturally I could not tell any of this to my mother or father. They would never have understood. Nor my church. It was a cold, stiff religion they preached. My only hope was to convince Clyde that he had to take the honorable course.

"I went to him at night. I went with a derringer. Not to shoot him but to frighten him. To show him I was in earnest. And I found him there with her. The other woman."

As if reliving the scene, Celia Harcourt's eyes took on a distant gaze. Kit listened closely and noticed Corazón wasn't writing a word, so caught up was she in the story.

"When I saw them like that," Celia said, "and saw the look of anger—no, of hatred—in Clyde's eyes, I was stunned beyond anything I had ever felt. At some point I had the gun in my hand, and at some point Clyde came toward me. And then the gun fired, and Clyde fell. That was all I remembered.

"At the trial the woman, her name was Bromiley, made a rather unsympathetic witness. That was what saved me, I believe. That and the fact I was carrying my child, my Louise. The jury, I am quite sure, did not want to see an orphan brought into the world. And so I was found not guilty."

Kit said, "What was the reaction in the community?"

"It was swift and severe. My parents disowned me. The minister of my church publicly denounced me. In fact, I was the subject of a number of sermons in the city on the wages of sin."

Kit felt her heart aching for this poor woman. To have parents and church and community turn against her, and she not even twenty years old. Many a girl had come to a bad end in similar circumstances, forced to sell body and soul on the street, and Kit had known more than a few coming of age in New York and also in Los Angeles. Prostitution was an urban pestilence everywhere.

"I thought of suicide," Celia Harcourt said just above a whisper. "But then I thought of my baby. I knew I could not do it. Somehow, I felt God was watching me still. I ran away from home and ended up in a shelter for destitute girls in Newark. It was there that I heard the Gospel spoken of as one of forgiveness and love. Like the woman caught in adultery, I was told that I could receive mercy. I vowed to sin no more.

"I got work at a dry-goods store in Newark. It was there that I met my Truman. He was a clerk. For some reason known only to God, he fell in love with me. Even after he knew my whole history. It cost him his family, too. We ran off to a justice of the peace, then came west, to Denver, where Louise was born. Eventually we moved here, where Truman has made a name for himself in the land business."

"Yes," Kit said. "I think I have heard the name Truman Harcourt. My great-aunt Freddy may have mentioned it once or twice."

"He is the only father Louise has ever known. I have never told her of her real father. She thinks I ran off with Truman in a romantic elopement that estranged us from our families. I don't know what I should do if she were ever to find out. . . ." A sob came softly to her throat.

"Is that your concern?" Kit asked. "Is that why you are here?"

"Yes, Miss Shannon." Celia Harcourt took another deep breath. "Louise is to be married in a week to Mr. John Whitney."

Kit nodded. "The Whitneys are well-known in Los Angeles."

"And well regarded. If they knew about Louise, about me, I am certain they would not allow this wedding to take place. It would mean the ruin of my only child's happiness. It would ruin Truman, too, here in Los Angeles. Of that I am sure. Oh, they can't know, they can't!"

"Do you have any reason to think they will learn of it?"

Fear returned to Celia's eyes. "I believe we are going to be black-mailed," she said. She proceeded to tell Kit about the visit of the man calling himself Dr. Rasmussen. By the time she was through, she looked completely spent. In a weakened voice Celia Harcourt said, "Can you help me?"

In truth, there was little Kit could do. She was a lawyer, yet nothing of a legal nature was at issue. This imposter, whoever he was, had not contacted the Harcourts with a demand for money. The blackmail theory was just that—a theory. Nor had a crime beyond petty theft been committed. The district attorney would not care in the slightest for a case about a missing photograph. John Davenport, the D.A., had his sights on larger game.

Yet something inside her told Kit that she *could* help, though in a way not yet clear. It was, she was sure, the whisper of God, which Kit had determined always to obey. With her financial independence secured through Aunt Freddy's bequest, Kit could take on cases selectively, the ones she felt God wanted her to pursue. This was beginning to feel like one of those.

"Let me see what I can find out for you," Kit said.

3

AFTER CELIA HARCOURT LEFT THE OFFICE and Cora-
zón began writing up the notes of the meeting, Kit strode across
First Street. The day was cool, and nimbus clouds hovered over the
city like soggy shirts hung on a line. Kit walked past the pull carts
of the dozen or so newspaper carriers awaiting the noon edition of
the *Los Angeles Times* and entered the building General Otis had
designed to look like a fortress, complete with a rapacious eagle
perched on the uppermost tower.

Kit felt the presence of Harrison Gray Otis everywhere, knowing
his story well. It was the stuff of legend, a legend Otis was more
than happy to extol.

He had drifted west after the Civil War, and after a number of
business ventures failed, he arrived, in 1882, in Los Angeles. He was
forty-five years old and penniless. In desperation he sought a part-
ner, Henry Boyce, and bought into a four-page newspaper called
the *Los Angeles Daily Times*.

A few months later, Otis forced Boyce out and assumed full
control of the *Times*. The paper, along with the city, began to grow,
in no small part due to the military-like efforts of the man who
insisted on being called "The General."

He had steel-blue eyes and a barrel chest and treated the
paper—some said the city itself—as his own personal kingdom. He
was rigid in bearing and practice. He often wore his uniform to

work in "The Fortress." Indeed, the *Times* building had its own armory—complete with rifles, ammunition, and a small cannon. If the upstart union movement ever wanted a war, Otis would be ready for them.

Kit had met him once, when she had been a guest at a dinner held at the California Club. Otis at that time had plainly stated he did not think women should be practicing law. His tune changed later when Kit defended Ed Hanratty, the policeman accused of murder. Otis was always a defender of the cops. His rival, William Randolph Hearst of the competing *Examiner*, wanted to see Hanratty swing. Seeking any chance to pound his competition, Otis began to champion Kit's cause.

Passing through the lobby, Kit was greeted with a "Hiya!" from one of the reporters, a man named Hughes.

"Hiya, Hughey," Kit said with a little salute. "Tom Phelps in?"

"I seen him upstairs," Hughes said. "Give him a big kiss for me, will ya?"

"You can kiss him yourself." Kit smiled and made for the stairs. She passed the telephone switching station, where three young women sat in front of a tangle of wires, linking telephone calls to and from the premises. Kit had read there were five telephones now for every one hundred people in Los Angeles. It seemed that General Otis, the master of this ship, had a good deal of them.

Kit found Tom Phelps smoking at his desk in the city room. It was a wide-open floor, flooded with light from the big windows overlooking Broadway. New electric ceiling fans whirred above them. General Otis had determined to bring all of the modern conveniences to his reporting staff. That was why each desk in the city room had its own typewriter.

And each desk its own cuspidor, along with crumpled papers, cigar and cigarette butts, broken pencils, and various discarded items of the reporters' trade.

"Well, Kit," Phelps said as she approached his desk. "To what do I owe this distinct pleasure?"

The former muckraker for Hearst's *Examiner* now seemed happy working for the *Times*. While Kit was wary of him—he had once made a play for her and had written some rather unflattering stories about her for the *Examiner*—she could not deny that he knew the city and which closets held the most skeletons.

"Money," Kit said.

The reporter's forehead wrinkled in confusion. He was about forty and beginning to lose his hair. "Money?"

"I figure you owe me a goodly sum," Kit said.

"I owe *you*? What sort of malarkey is this?"

"For all the stories I've given you. I pretty much have made your career. For that you can pay me in gold coins, or the other coin of your realm—information."

A wry smile swept to Phelps's lips. "We always end up paying the lawyers, don't we? All right, what is it you need?"

"The lowdown on the blackmailers in town. Anybody operating here you've heard about?"

"Blackmail? Sounds serious."

"It always is."

"You usually defend these people, don't you?"

"Only if I'm convinced they are not guilty."

"Then what do you want with a real blackmailer?"

"That's my business."

Tom Phelps cocked his head. "I have a feeling, Kit Shannon, that you have some information *I* might be interested in."

"Come now, Tom. How about I give you an exclusive if I find anything worth printing?"

"Like your wedding to Ted Fox?"

Kit folded her arms. "That's for the society page."

"I only have one question for you," Phelps said. "What's he got that I ain't?"

"The Lord."

Phelps shook his head. "Still preaching salvation, huh?"

"Only to those who need it, Tom. And there's no one who needs it more than a newspaperman."

Phelps chortled, then tossed his cigarette into the brass spittoon by his desk. " 'Tis the gift of gab you have, you Irish temptress. All right. Tell me about this blackmailer. We'll talk about my eternal soul another time."

"Is that a promise?"

"The blackmailer, Kit."

"I can only tell you that a man posing as a minister came to see my client. He gave her a song and dance, started asking some personal questions. Thinking him aboveboard, my client did not hesitate to respond."

Phelps laced his fingers behind his head in an attitude of complete indifference. "And your client's name was. . . ?"

"Sorry, Tom."

"Can't blame a guy for trying."

"He ended up stealing a photograph of my client's daughter."

"Which is the subject of the blackmail?"

"That's all I can tell you at the moment." Kit sat on the stool next to Phelps's desk. "I'd be very grateful if you could help me on this. Does the pattern sound at all familiar to you?"

For a moment Phelps was silent. "It's not blackmail," he finally said.

"It's not? Then what could it be?"

"A chaser."

"A what?"

"Picture chaser. Grief snatcher."

"I'm afraid I—"

"Look." Phelps reached for an edition of the *Times* that was sitting on his desk and showed it to Kit. On the front page was a portrait of a pretty girl, and next to it a headline: *WOMAN FOUND DEAD IN DYE WORKS.* Below that, in smaller type: *Horrible Culmination of a Prolonged Debauch.*

"You ever wonder," Phelps said, "how the pictures and drawings of dead girls, of grieving families, of victims of murder and mayhem, get into the papers so quick? It's a chaser. Usually a young cub reporter, their first job. They go out to the scene, get into the house where the family is exposing their grief, and when no one's looking, slip into bedrooms or cabinets so they can snatch a photograph or even a portrait painting and hotfoot it back to the office."

"That's awful," Kit said.

Phelps winked. "We always return the item."

"Then you think this fellow, whoever he was, works for a news-paper?"

"My guess."

"Maybe the *Times*?"

"Could be, if it's a murder we're talking about." With an eager look Phelps said, "Is it a good murder?"

"No, Tom, I'm afraid not."

"Drat." He leaned back in his chair. "If it isn't for a crime that's been committed, my guess is the guy works for that scandal rag."

"The *Gazette*?"

"Like I say, that's my guess. They like to uncover old stories, secrets, things that aren't on the stove. Dress it up with pictures. Circulation's pretty good, I hear."

Kit shook her head in disgust. "Thanks, Tom. I'll try there."

"Whoa," Phelps said. "What do you mean you'll try there? They're not a group of society ladies out sipping tea—they're a tough bunch. Starting with the publisher, Mahoney. An Irish thug if there ever was one. I hear he's got an even bigger thug for a per-sonal bodyguard. You start giving him the needle and there'll be trouble for sure."

Kit stood up. "Thanks for the warning. But if it concerns my client, I may have to make a little trouble of my own."

"I'm serious here!" Phelps said.

"So am I."

4

THE GAZETTE WAS HOUSED IN a dingy building off Tenth Street and Figueroa. The business district of Los Angeles was laid out in a grid. Tenth Street was the southernmost edge of the district, Figueroa the eastern edge.

The tabloid was, in other words, hanging off the corner of the business map. *Fitting*, Kit thought as she approached the two-story walk-up.

The building was of 1880s vintage, its wood exterior testimony to the impermanence of paint in this region of warm sun and dry winds. Shrouded in a thick layer of brown, the building seemed to be trying to cover up secrets, like a fast woman with too much rouge. At the same time, it almost seemed to be thrusting its painted jaw in the face of polite uptown society.

Kit was met within by a tight-lipped young woman with nails painted the most ostentatious red Kit had ever seen outside the walls of Pearl Morton's bawdy house. The woman was engaged in the act of filing those nails, approaching the task as if it were the single most important event in Southern California.

"Excuse me," Kit said.

The nail woman paused in her endeavors to scan Kit with a jaundiced glare. "No positions," she said.

"I am not here for a job."

"You got a story, then?"

"I would like to speak to the editor in chief, please." Kit looked to a door with frosted glass behind the desk.

"What may I say this is in reward to?"

"I beg your pardon?"

The woman huffed with irritation. "What may I say this is in reward to?"

"Do you mean in *regard* to?"

The woman slapped her hand on the desk. "I always get that wrong!"

"No matter," Kit said. "May I see him now?"

Gathering up what seemed like an armload of wounded pride, the young woman said, "The *Gazette* is looked over by Miss Jade Stringham."

"A woman?" Kit immediately thought she should not be so surprised. After all, she herself was practicing law, though one of only ten women in the entire state of California. And until Clara Dalton Price joined the county district attorney's office, the only woman trying cases in Los Angeles.

The nail woman almost snorted. "What's wrong with being an ambitious woman? Look at me."

Kit looked. The woman seemed to be in her early twenties.

"I'm going on the stage," the woman said. "And you will see the name Valerie Amman on the marquee of the Belasco someday."

"I shall look forward to it," Kit said.

"Oh? Do you frequent the theater?"

"On occasion. In fact, I am going tonight, escorted by my fiancé. I believe we are to see a magician."

Valerie Amman clapped her hands together and practically shrieked. "Oh, what fun! I was just telling my fella—Jay is his name—I want a little magic in my life, too, and when he kisses me I—"

The door opened and a woman of about fifty practically leapt into the room. "What's all the noise about?"

Valerie Amman got quiet very quickly and almost sank behind the desk.

Kit said, "I am here to see the editor on a matter of some importance. Would that be you?"

The woman folded her arms. She wore her hair extremely short and her dress had the least possible adornment. A plain white shirtwaist tapered to a dull brown skirt. Her high ankle shoes seemed very close to men's boots. "I am Jade Stringham," she said. "I'm the one who decides what's important around here."

"I would like to ask you a few questions, if I may," Kit said.

"You may not," Jade Stringham said. "I have an issue to get out. Talk to my girl here and set up an appointment. But mind, I'll want to know what your business is before I see you."

"Do you employ a man by the name of Rasmussen?"

A glint of annoyance hit Jade Stringham's face. Her eyes were gray and severe, like cold iron. "No," she said. "Now if you'll—"

"He'd be a picture chaser."

The exasperation in Stringham's face became a glare of fury. But Kit, studying the eyes as always, thought the anger was of a defensive nature.

"I told you I have no one here by that name," Jade Stringham said.

"That name may have been a ruse," Kit said. "Do your reporters ever use false names?"

"Just who are you, anyway?"

"My name is Kathleen Shannon."

"The lawyer?" Stringham suddenly seemed the slightest bit impressed. "Well, I know a little bit about you. Seen your picture in the papers, too. They don't do your red hair justice."

Kit nodded, feeling a bit uncomfortable at Stringham's perusal of her.

"You defended that woman—what was her name? The one who had caused you so much trouble?"

"Elinor Wynn," Kit said. Elinor, Ted's former fiancée, had been accused of murdering Heath Sloate. But Kit had proven it was self-defense, not hard to do with the smarmy Sloate as the dead body.

"Never could figure why you took her on," Stringham said.

"Because she was innocent," Kit said. "And because she sought forgiveness."

"You forgave her for all she did to you?"

"Forgiveness is a divine command."

"Yeah, I know about your Bible thumping, too. Excuse my language."

"May we talk in your office?"

Jade Stringham sighed. "All right, but only for a few minutes. Like I said, I got work to do."

Jade Stringham's office was spare, given almost entirely to paper of one sort or another. Stacks here and there practically fell off shelves. The walls were almost completely covered with newsprint and photographs hung on nails. Loud headlines from previous editions shouted DOCTOR'S LOVE NEST TURNS DEADLY and SHE THOUGHT SHE COULD TEMPT THE DEVIL.

"You like it?" Stringham said, motioning.

When Kit hesitated, the editor said, "Oh, I forgot. You're from the nice part of town. Respectable. A lawyer. You probably think you're slumming here."

"Not at all," Kit said. "Though I must confess your paper is not on my current list of reading material."

"Why should it be, class act like yourself?" Jade Stringham snatched a cedar box from her desk and opened it for Kit. "Cheroot?"

Kit looked at the thin cigars and almost reeled back from the smell. "No, thank you," she said.

"Mind if I do?" Without waiting for an answer, Jade Stringham snatched one with her right hand and held it aloft, almost as if to advertise her eccentricity. With her other hand she grabbed a wooden match from a holder and swept it across a strip of igniting paper. The effect was one of almost operatic exaggeration. After blowing a stream of smoke toward Kit, the editor said, "Not scandalized, I hope."

"This is your office, not mine."

Jade Stringham nodded. "I like you, Miss Shannon. You and I are cut from the same cloth. We're outrages in a man's world. We are pioneers, explorers, if you will. And when we get the franchise, watch out. The world will never be the same."

Out of the corner of her eye, Kit noticed a small, almost imperceptible interruption of light by the door.

"My concern today is not for women's suffrage," Kit said. "I am here on behalf of a client."

Puffing casually on the cheroot, Jade Stringham said, "What's that got to do with the *Gazette*?"

"I was hoping you could tell me. You say you have never heard of a Dr. Rasmussen?"

"Never."

"Do you employ reporters?"

" 'Course I do. This is a newspaper."

That was a generous term for it, but Kit let the comment pass. "Are you planning to run a story about someone who was in trouble with the law about twenty years ago?"

Squinting through the plumes of smoke, Jade Stringham regarded Kit for an extended moment. "I don't talk about my stories before they come out."

"I would like you to make an exception in this case."

"Now, why should I do that, Miss Shannon?"

"Because it just might be the right thing to do."

Jade Stringham huffed. "Your moralizing doesn't cut any ice around here."

"What does cut the ice? Money?"

"That's a little closer."

Kit cast a quick glance at the door. She was sure now the movement she saw was behind the keyhole.

"Let us suppose," Kit said, "that you were planning such a story and that the subject of the story would be facing great personal harm if the story should run. Might you reconsider your position?"

"Miss Shannon, we publish facts in the *Gazette*. Facts sometimes hurt, but that's the way it is. If I killed every story that was going to hit somebody hard, we'd be out of business."

"Maybe that wouldn't be such a bad thing," Kit said, instantly regretting it. But her Irish was rising, like a hot sun over County Cork.

It seemed as though Jade Stringham had the same heat inside her. She threw the cheroot onto the floor and crushed it with her foot. "Let me tell you something, Miss Shannon. The *Gazette* is going to be around long after you retire to raise little kiddies. You want to know why? Because people like it. They like what we print. Can't get enough of it. And in this country, that means we can exchange that for money. It's the American way."

"What about scruples?"

"Scruples don't put eggs on your plate."

"But advertisers do."

"How's that?"

"I wonder what your advertisers would say if enough people told them just what they thought of their support of this paper."

Jade Stringham folded her arms. "That almost sounds like a threat."

"Not at all," Kit said. "If I wanted to threaten you, I would bring up the law of libel. I would talk about seeking money damages for hurting the reputation of a respected citizen. And then you know what I'd do?"

The editor of the *Gazette* glared.

"I would ask you kindly, as a favor, not to run the story."

For a moment Kit wondered if Stringham might suddenly open a drawer in her desk, pull out a gun, and settle the matter in the style of the Old West. But just as quickly Stringham's visage softened, though in a very deliberate fashion.

"Like I said, Miss Shannon. I like you. And I'll be right up front, the way you are with me. We don't threaten. We have a lawyer, too, you know. Even if we did have some story about a client of yours, we'd do with it what we please. As long as we print the truth, we've got no cares. And Mr. Mahoney insists we always print the truth."

"Maybe I should speak with Mr. Mahoney himself."

"Others have tried to get tough with us, Miss Shannon. I wouldn't advise it."

"Thank you for the advice," Kit said. "Tell Dr. Rasmussen he can come out from behind that door now."

Stringham looked at her. And then she laughed. "Hank!"

The door opened. A tall fellow in a rather ill-fitting suit stepped into the office.

"Miss Shannon here knows about your preaching career," Stringham said. "How many times are you going to use that gag?"

Hank smiled. "It works wonders."

Jade Stringham shook her head. "Go on down to Schneider's and get your lunch. All that brain work must have given you an appetite."

As Hank moved toward the door, Kit said, "I'll take that photograph you stole."

"Already in the mail," Hank said. "We've done a likeness of the girl, and we always return what doesn't belong to us." His dull teeth mocked her.

5

HOUDINI.

The marquee over the Orpheum Theatre on Main Street held this one mysterious word.

"This is where you're taking me?" Kit said.

"I've heard he's amazing," Ted Fox said. "Almost as amazing as you."

Kit smiled and held his arm tightly. All through dinner with Ted, and then on their stroll in the cool evening down Main Street, Kit had been quiet, introspective. Not even the feel of Ted's arm, the closeness of him, could completely free her from thinking about the encounter with Stringham and the *Gazette*. Or keep her from the concern of knowing Celia Harcourt was pinning all her hopes on Kathleen Shannon, attorney-at-law.

But now she was out for the evening with the man she loved, and wherever he took her was all right with her.

With one hand Ted held the cane that helped him walk. He was able to make his way on his own quite well. It had been some time since the accident in the plane that caused the loss of his left leg. With the strength Christ gave him, Ted had vowed to fly again and to do whatever it took to rehabilitate himself.

There was a small crowd outside the Orpheum, well-dressed Angelenos milling about before show time. The electric lights of the marquee gave the sidewalk a festive glow. Just before reaching the doors, Kit and Ted were surprised by a young woman in ragged clothes stepping out from a darkened doorway.

"Flowers, mister?" She had an old bucket filled with an assortment. Her face was streaked with dust.

"I'll take the whole lot," Ted said. He fished in his pocket for money. As he did, Kit noticed the young woman looking up and down the street.

"Here you are," Ted said, handing the woman some coins. "Will that do?"

The woman's eyes widened in virtual wonder. "Thank you, sir. Bless you." And she hurried off down the street.

Ted handed the bouquet, of many colors and shapes, to Kit. "They seem to sum you up," he said. "Colorful, sweet, and unpredictable."

Kit smiled. "And haven't *you* picked up the blarney of late, Ted Fox."

"Here we are."

The theater was the grandest in the city—a high-ceilinged, ornate, three-tiered auditorium complete with a crystal chandelier donated by the railroad magnate Henry E. Huntington. The stage— which had seen the likes of Sarah Bernhardt and the Barrymores— was vast, covered with a huge burgundy velvet curtain. Perhaps this outing was a good thing, Kit thought as she and Ted took their seats. A small diversion from the troubles of the day might clear her mind.

They took their seats. Presently, a smiling man in a tuxedo walked to the center of the stage.

"Good evening, ladies and gentlemen," he said, "and welcome to the Orpheum Theatre, the finest theatrical establishment in the West. Shall we begin our festivities with a few of the old favorites? Come on along for a stroll in the memory grove!"

The lights dimmed, the curtains opened, and a large white screen lit up with words. The Orpheum boasted a state-of-the-art illumination projector for slides and silhouettes. The orchestra struck up the tune.

Kit followed along merrily, but it was Ted who sang with a certain out-of-tune gusto that was hard to resist.

> *I've had a secret in my heart, Sweet Marie;*
> *A tale I would impart, love to thee.*
> *Every daisy in the dell*
> *Knows my secret, knows it well,*
> *And yet I dare not tell*
> *Sweet Marie!*

That ditty of young love was followed by another, the crowd warming up as it went along.

> *I wandered today to the hill, Maggie,*
> *To watch the scene below;*
> *The creek and the creaking old mill, Maggie,*
> *As we used to long ago.*
> *The green grove is gone from the hill, Maggie,*
> *Where first the daisies sprung,*
> *The creaking old mill is still, Maggie,*
> *Since you and I were young.*

These were followed by "In the Good Old Summer Time" and "Meet Me in St. Louis," the popular song commemorating the 1904 World's Fair.

When the singing ended, the curtains were drawn. Then a tall, angular man in a baggy baseball uniform strode onto the stage. Los Angeles, like the rest of the country, was baseball crazy. The Angels of the Pacific Coast League was the local team. They were not yet on a par with the National or American League teams, but Angelenos were justly proud of their squad, now in first place.

The man in the uniform, who looked about as much like a baseball player as a stork, began to orate. Amazingly, uncharacteristic of his crane-like form, his voice was a rich, honey baritone.

> *The outlook wasn't brilliant for the Mudville nine that day;*
> *The score stood four to two, with but one inning left to play.*
> *And then when Cooney died at first, and Barrows did the same,*
> *A sickly silence fell upon the patrons of the game.*

Kit was immediately caught up in the poetic story, which she recognized as the tale of the mighty batsman named Casey, who came to the plate as the last chance to win the game for Mudville. The audience was rapt as the actor brought the narrative to life, leading up to the last, mighty swing by Casey that "shattered" the air!

> Oh, somewhere in this favored land the sun is shining bright;
> A band is playing somewhere, and somewhere hearts are light.
> And somewhere men are laughing, and somewhere children shout,
> But there is no joy in Mudville—mighty Casey has struck out.

Enthusiastic applause erupted for the actor who, according to the playbill, was Mr. De Wolf Hopper.

"Enjoying yourself?" Ted whispered.

Kit squeezed his hand in affirmation.

There followed, in rapid succession, a juggler (quite good), a dog act (a bit under-rehearsed), and a contortionist who finished his act by wrapping both of his legs behind his head.

"That's the way a lawyer treats the law," Ted whispered to Kit. She jabbed him with her elbow.

After a moment's pause, the gas lights on the sides of the theater began to dim. The orchestra struck up "Pomp and Circumstance" as the curtain slowly parted, revealing a solitary man in the middle of the stage, dressed in evening clothes. Almost immediately it was clear this was no ordinary man.

Of average height, he had a shock of curly black hair that seemed to be made of steel springs. His figure was perfect, and he was obviously strong as a bull. But what stood out above all were his eyes—the only word Kit could think of to describe them was *electric*. It was as if his eyes had been wired by Edison himself. They seemed to give off light.

This man stepped forward on the stage as the orchestra completed its introduction.

"Good evening, ladies and gentlemen," the man said. "I am Harry Houdini."

The audience offered him polite applause. As they did, he removed his coat and threw it into the orchestra pit. He then began to roll up his sleeves, revealing forearms that rippled with muscles.

"I can best any man in the house," Houdini said. "Oh yes. But not with mere fisticuffs. I speak of any man's attempts to constrain me. I am here to declare what no other man or woman can—that no chains can bind me. No locks can hold me. No force can keep me from the freedom to go where I please. The last to try was the entire New York City police department. They put me in their finest jail at two o'clock in the afternoon. At four o'clock I was having tea at the Plaza. Ladies and gentlemen, I give you myself."

He bowed, once again to slight applause.

"I have asked your own police department to be represented here tonight. Come forward, if you please."

Kit saw Detective Michael McGinty, whom she knew well, walk up on stage.

"And now," Houdini announced, "I will ask the representative of the Los Angeles police department to explain what he has brought with him."

McGinty took out a large pair of manacles from his coat pocket and held them up.

"These here are handcuffs," he said to the audience. "Finest we have. Special made. No man can get out of 'em. Only I have the key. See?" The detective held up a longish key in his fingers.

Houdini put his arms out. "Sir, in front of these witnesses, please place the handcuffs on me."

Kit watched as McGinty did as ordered. The cuffs certainly looked impressive, made of thick steel. McGinty closed them around Houdini's wrists.

Houdini showed his manacled wrists to the audience. With a nod of his head he motioned for an assistant to come out from the wings. A man in a brown suit entered with a Japanese folding screen and placed it in the center of the stage.

Houdini gazed once more at the crowd. "And now, ladies and gentlemen, I hope I will be with you shortly."

With that, Houdini stepped behind the screen as the orchestra began to play a haunting melody. Whatever else this man was, Kit thought, he certainly knew how to put on a show. It was something she had seen Earl Rogers do on a number of occasions, turning a courtroom into a theater. There was more than a little commonality between trial lawyers and show people.

The sound of hard breathing and grunts became audible from behind the screen. A bit of jangling, too. "These are magnificent cuffs!" Houdini's deep voice announced.

McGinty, standing in front of the screen, looked pleased. He nodded at the crowd as if to say, *You see? The Los Angeles police won't be trifled with!*

Thirty seconds ticked by. Forty. The orchestra continued to play. And Kit began to feel just a little uncomfortable for this man calling himself Houdini. What if he failed in his attempt? She knew the sort of scorn the elite of Los Angeles could lather on people. She did not want to see it happen right in front of her eyes.

Almost a minute gone, and still no resolution.

Then the voice rose, with a hint of sorrow: "I am afraid I must ask the police officer to step behind the screen."

For a moment, Mike McGinty looked perplexed. Houdini said, "Please!"

McGinty went behind the barrier.

A disaster in the making, Kit thought, and the next moment the screen fell forward, crashing onto the stage.

There stood Houdini, smiling, his arms in the air, free of the shackles, which were now firmly around the wrists of Detective Mike McGinty!

The theater erupted into applause. McGinty's face turned an instant shade of red as he looked as baffled as a rube at a carnival.

And the show was only beginning. Houdini went on to perform several feats of legerdemain, topped off by a grand finale that had Kit and Ted breathless. Houdini was lowered into a large milk container that had been filled with water. It spilled over the sides as he displaced it. The cap was securely fastened by two volunteers from the audience, and a screen was once more placed in front. For several agonizing minutes Kit, along with everyone else, wondered if the man had drowned.

But no! He emerged once again, dripping wet and smiling triumphantly.

And then he stood for his final bow. Silencing the enthusiastic response with his hands he said, "I thank you for your kind reception tonight. I wish only to add that what you have seen is a performance in the art of magic. It is not supernatural but the work of my own hands. I say this because as I have traveled this country and Europe, I have seen those who claim to have supernatural powers fleecing—and that is the only word that applies—hapless victims who pay these frauds to contact the dead for them."

Kit was keen with attention now. This was just what she had been writing about to the *Times*!

"And so I offer this challenge, as I do in every city where I perform: five thousand dollars cash to anyone claiming to be a medium if I cannot expose them as a fake. If you are such a one, you may contact me in care of this theater. I thank you."

As the orchestra struck up a tune, the great curtains closed. And the audience broke out in thunderous applause.

"Let's talk to him," Kit said.

"Who?" Ted asked.

"This Houdini fellow."

"Now?"

"I want to speak with him about his crusade against fraud."

"Kit—"

"Let's go backstage."

6

LOUISE HARCOURT WAS AS GIDDY as a schoolgirl. That's how Celia thought of her at this moment, showing off her wedding dress just in from the shop on Broadway. In the morning light, the dress reflected almost as brightly as Louise's face. The entire effect turned Celia's anxious heart into a quivering thing, a thing that might burst at the slightest provocation. She was determined to hide her fears from Louise, though, and forced a smile.

"Oh, Mother," Louise said, spinning around the room holding the dress to her. "It is more than I could have asked for."

Celia only nodded. Mrs. Norris, the city's best dressmaker, had indeed fashioned a masterpiece. The gown was white crepe de chine over white satin. The scalloped flounce skirt gathered at the waist, with an inset of puffing bordered with shirred bands. Frills of lace opened over an embroidered yoke set off with silver threads. Fans of lace with sprays of orange blossoms adorned the skirt all around. It was the most beautiful dress Celia had ever seen.

"I shall be the envy even of Alice Roosevelt!" Louise chimed.

"The president's daughter?"

"She's the talk of Washington society," Louise explained. "Haven't you kept up?"

Celia slowly shook her head.

"Oh yes," Louise said, admiring the dress again. "She's the Gibson girl all right."

Charles Dana Gibson was an illustrator whose portraits of beautiful, dignified young women had captured the imagination of America's youth. Celia knew that, of course, from all of the *Collier's* weekly magazines Louise kept in her room. But Celia could not see any way to improve upon Louise's golden hair, sparkling blue eyes, and the certain *something* that brought more life to any room Louise entered.

If this had been only two days ago, that spark would have caused Celia to cry for joy. As it was, it took all her strength not to weep for sorrow.

As if on cue, Truman came bounding into the sitting room, his contagious smile further illuminating the proceedings.

"Why, it is beautiful!" he said, opening his arms for Louise.

"Yes, Papa," Louise said. "Hasn't Mother done it again?"

Celia saw in Truman's eyes a quicksilver flash of sadness, even as he said, "Mother always does it, doesn't she?"

"John will love it," Louise said, holding the dress out admiringly. "He'll go absolutely bughouse!"

"Bughouse?" Truman said.

"Crazy," Louise explained.

Truman said, "Such talk."

"Now, Papa, I—" Louise stopped. "Where is my photograph?"

Celia spun around and felt that her look must have betrayed a thousand secrets. But before Louise could react Truman stepped forward and put his arm around her. "Your mother and I . . . that is, we wanted to do something very special. A surprise. Do us a favor and don't ask about it right now, will you?"

The girl seemed perplexed but covered it with an innocent smile. "Of course, Papa, if that's what you want."

"That's a good girl. Now, why don't you take the dress upstairs to your room, eh? And later, you and Mother can go out for some of that shopping you need to do."

Celia was relieved when Louise bounded up the stairs. She was not sure she could have hidden her feelings a moment longer. Truman immediately went to her and guided her gently to a chair.

"Tell me," he said.

Celia took a deep breath. "I saw Miss Shannon this morning. The man who came here, that Rasmussen, is a reporter for the *Gazette*."

"That gossip tabloid?"

"They know about me, about us, and they are planning to run the story."

Truman's face twisted with concern. "Did Miss Shannon say we had any recourse?"

"She said she was going to try to reason with them."

"Did you have the impression that she thought there was something she could accomplish?"

Celia looked at the floor, which seemed a dark abyss. "She said we should be prepared and . . ."

"Yes, dear?"

"Perhaps tell Louise." Celia desperately grabbed at Truman's lapels. "Oh, Truman! I cannot! She would hate me! And if the Whitneys found out . . ."

"Now, now," Truman said, bringing her close. Celia smelled the wool of his coat, felt it prickle her cheek. "I will take care of things if Miss Shannon cannot."

Celia pulled her head back. Truman's face had become hard and cold. "What are you thinking?"

"Never you mind. I will take care of it."

"But, Truman, you—"

"Hush, dear." He put his finger to Celia's lips.

7

GERALD MAHONEY LIVED ON LAUREL STREET in a fashionable residential district on the southern edge of the city. The houses here were of the grand Victorian style, set back from the street, fronted by well-kept lawns, trees, hedges, and gardens.

Kit pulled her carriage to a stop in front of the house bearing number 406 and regarded its grandiose presence. As with most residents of Los Angeles, Mahoney was listed in the city directory. That book was growing thicker each year as the population swelled. There were now over 200,000 registered Angelenos. The city was bursting at the seams.

Mahoney's house was the largest on the block—Kit thought it rather brazen. As she alighted from the carriage, Kit had the feeling that the house itself disapproved of her arrival—a single woman behind a horse, here to interrupt the ordinary business of the day.

Kit smoothed her skirt, set her hat more firmly on her head, and walked boldly through the iron gate. It creaked in surly protest. Kit proceeded up the walkway.

A gardener was hunched over, clipping rose bushes under a large bay window. He turned—no, whirled—at the sound of Kit's steps. He was an older man, rather thin, with bushy white eyebrows that tapered downward. He reminded her of the drawings of Ebenezer Scrooge she had seen in a copy of *A Christmas Carol.*

He said nothing. His stare was as welcoming as ragweed.

Kit nodded out of common courtesy.

"Keep away!" the man snarled.

"I beg your pardon?" Kit said.

"Keep away!" He held the rose clippers out at her, snapping them open and shut like the jaws of a ravenous animal.

"Sir," she said softly, "are those your roses?"

He did not take his eyes off her.

"It is rather early for roses, is it not?" Kit said. "How do you manage to—"

"Stay away, I said!"

Insane, Kit thought suddenly. Best to leave him to his delusions. She turned and continued up cold stone steps to the front door. She used the brass knocker—the head of a wild boar, tusks and all—to announce her presence.

And waited.

When a minute had passed she knocked again, more forcefully. She peeked behind her and saw that the gardener had stepped out a bit from his duties to stare at her again. He held his shears out in front of him, slightly open. He seemed as if he wanted to clip *her.*

Then she heard the clacking of a lock, and the big door opened. A man who filled the doorway stood there. He was nearly as wide across the chest as he was tall. His hair, black and shiny, was plastered to his head and parted in the middle, in the style of some waterfront bartender. His scowl was as menacing as any Kit had ever seen.

She stood up straight and said, "Am I addressing Mr. Mahoney?"

The man, who seemed to have lived forty hard years—every one of them etched in his features—said, "Who wants to know?" His voice was reedy, as if some fist had hold of his larynx.

"My name is Kathleen Shannon. I am a lawyer. I have some business to discuss with Mr. Mahoney."

The large man shook his head. "He don't wish to be disturbed."

Kit removed a sheet of paper from her inner suit-coat pocket and held it out for the man. "Please disturb him," she said.

The man snatched the paper and looked at it as if it were a

curiosity from a shop on Bouchet Street. His face crinkled around the eyes, a movement Kit took to indicate the permutations of thought. He seemed conflicted then, like a dog stuck between two masters. Kit got the impression this man did not make his living by the use of intellect.

"You wait," he said.

The door slammed.

Kit looked behind her in time to see the gardener slip back to his post under the window. She got the distinct feeling there were more eyes about, watching her. She had read the Brontë novels, and that sinister sensation that formed in the pit of her stomach when lost in those Gothic, fictional worlds was present now.

Father in heaven, you are my guide always, she prayed. *Give me wisdom to see what I need to see. Help me to help Celia Harcourt.*

The door swung open and the big man jerked a thumb the size of a small ham over his shoulder. Kit entered and followed the man through the ornate hallway—high-beamed and in dark tones—and noticed the fancy boots he wore. They were some sort of skin, not really in keeping with his plain suit. The lout opened a door and, once more, indicated with his thumb that Kit should go in.

A stout man with gray hair encircling a balding pate stood, back to her, at a fireplace. When the door closed behind Kit, the man turned around. He had a ruddy face, elfin in a way but of the sort found in fairy stories that scared the daylights out of children.

"I am Gerald Mahoney," he said. He made no move toward her. In his fist he held the paper that Kit surmised had been handed him by the lug with the big thumbs.

"Kathleen Shannon."

Mahoney held the paper up. Most of it was concealed, and crushed, within his fist. "What is the meaning of this?"

Kit stood as serenely as she could under his growl and glare. "The law of libel explained in layman's terms," Kit said. She had written it out the night before. "Did you have a chance to look at it?"

"What do you take me for, young woman, a schoolboy?" He had an Irish brogue mixed with American pugnacity.

"I am an attorney, sir, representing—"

"Ah, don't you be givin' me that!" Mahoney crumpled the paper violently and tossed it onto the fire. The ball ignited immediately. "You are a girl, is what you are. Barging into a man's home. Feeding him guff, tossing the law at him." He pointed his finger at her. "Let me tell you a thing or two."

"No, Mr. Mahoney." The words came out of Kit of their own accord, as fiery as the paper now burning in front of her.

Mahoney's mouth dropped open, his lower lip quivering. "What did you just say to me?"

"I am not here to receive a lecture, sir," Kit said. "I am here on a professional matter, involving one Celia Harcourt and your plans to smear her name in your so-called newspaper." She wished at first she hadn't said *so-called*. Then she didn't care. It was a scandal rag, nothing more. She spoke the truth and that was that. "I am here to ask you not to do it."

Mahoney placed his hands behind his back and scanned Kit from toe to head. "Stringham told me you were a spirited one. Why don't you sit down, then?"

Kit paused, then sat in a decorative wing chair facing the fireplace.

Mahoney remained standing. He plucked a pipe from the mantel and dipped it into a pouch, working the tobacco into the bowl with his thumb. "Shannon. Are you from the old country?"

"My father was," Kit said.

Mahoney lit his pipe and rested one elbow on the mantel. "What year found him in America?"

"1856," Kit said.

"Ah, eleven years before myself, as a lad of seventeen. But I'll venture a guess, miss, that he found what we Irish always find upon first stepping ashore here—scorn and indifference."

It was true. Her father had to fight for everything he ever got. Even as a man of God. "Times were hard, indeed," Kit said. "But Papa never let on to me."

"There you have it," Mahoney said, waving his pipe toward her. "That's our pluck, you see? Never show the world when your heart is breakin'. And never let the other fella break *you*. I can see you have the Irish in you."

Kit had been told as much, many times.

"And when it comes to fightin'," Mahoney continued, "sure, I did my share with my fists. I never backed down from a good donnybrook. But more of the fightin' comes from up here, miss." He tapped his head with the stem of his pipe. "And what I've got I've fought for, and I sure didn't build it by backin' away. Nor do I intend to start now."

He looked every bit as tough as Phelps had said, with a streak of stubbornness a mile wide. But Kit had been in fights herself, attempting to practice law in a man's world. And her stubbornness could match anyone's, she was sure. Aunt Freddy would have been the first to tell the world so.

Kit stood up. "Mr. Mahoney," she said patiently, "if I were to explain to you that a woman's life will be ruined by the story, would it make a difference to you?"

"No, Miss Shannon," Mahoney shot back immediately. "I am afraid not."

"May I inquire as to the reason?"

"No."

"Do you have some sort of grudge against the Harcourts?"

The question seemed to land on Mahoney, if not like a left hook, at least like a good jab to the jaw. But Kit watched him quickly recover, his face returning to an angry glower.

"Our interview is at an end," he said.

Kit did not make any move toward the door. "You have not responded to the possibility of a lawsuit."

Mahoney stiffened, his cheek muscles twitching. "I do not take threats lightly, Miss Shannon. If it's a fight that you're wantin', you can be sure I will accommodate you."

Kit returned Gerald Mahoney's stare. "I assure you, sir, that if there is to be a tussle, I will follow the words of Polonius."

Mahoney's forehead wrinkled. "How's that?"

" 'Beware of entrance to a quarrel, but, being in, bear it that the opposed may beware of thee.' "

"Axel!" Mahoney shouted.

A moment later the big man bolted into the study.

"Show Miss Shannon out," Mahoney ordered.

The man called Axel shambled toward Kit, a big grin on his face.

"If you touch me," Kit said, "I will have you hauled in for battery."

Axel stopped dead and looked to Gerald Mahoney for instruction.

"Easy, Axel," he said. "Just make sure she gets to the front door."

Kit turned slowly. The fire crackled in the fireplace, snapping at the room like an angry dog.

"Just one more thing," Mahoney said, stopping her. "If you ever step on my property again, I'll have *you* hauled in as a trespasser."

Axel gave her a warning glare as she proceeded out the door—but with a smile that told her he would love to see her again.

8

"I AM SO SORRY, MRS. HARCOURT," Kit said. She had come with the bad news personally, hoping to soften the blow. But Truman and Celia Harcourt were clearly taking it hard. She hoped Celia would not sense the burning anger Kit held inside her. Gerald Mahoney's intransigence still galled her.

"Then there's nothing to be done," Celia said in a barely audible voice.

Kit, scouring her mind for some angle she might have missed, could only suggest one thing. "There is always the injunction, but . . ."

"Go ahead, Miss Shannon," Truman Harcourt said. He sat on the arm of the chair his wife occupied, his hands holding hers.

"I am afraid it would not be granted," Kit said, "and even if it were, the newspapers would pick up the facts from the arguments in court. The story would come out anyway."

A sadness hovered over the room like a morning fog. Kit had never before felt so powerless. This couple had come to her for help, and there was nothing she could do for them.

"Perhaps now," Kit offered, "would be a good time to talk to your daughter and then to the Whitneys."

Celia's face said no.

"I know who the Whitneys are," said Kit. "My great-aunt Freddy knew them well. I'll help in any way I can."

"You've done what you could," Truman Harcourt said, standing. "We'll have to take it from here." His face had a sudden steely resolve.

"After the story runs," Kit said, "if you wish to file suit—"

"No," Truman interrupted. "That will be too late."

Something in his voice made Celia sit up stiffly. Kit noticed it.

"I'll see Miss Shannon to the door," Celia said, then escorted Kit out to the front porch. The afternoon was heavy with the threat of rain. That always gave the city a sense of urgency, of things moving too fast before the darkness on the way.

———

The smell of stale beer and sawdust assaulted Kit's nose as she entered Jakob Schneider's saloon on Main Street. The lighting from the kerosene lamps—apparently Schneider's landlord was too cheap to install the electric wiring most buildings had now—was muted by the amber globes. Here men could eat and drink in relative peace. Or so they thought.

Schneider's was the favorite watering hole and luncheon establishment of Los Angeles newspapermen, including, as Kit had picked up from her visit to the *Gazette* office, Hank the phony preacher.

The saloon had a bar top that ran the length of one wall, with a brass footrail below and three evenly spaced spittoons along the rail. A bar mirror almost as long as the counter gave the impression of doubling the size of the room. Round wooden tables, wooden chairs with wicker seats, and spindly coatracks made up most of the decorative scheme of Schneider's, with some booths off to the side.

Hung on a floor-to-ceiling post was a chalkboard, upon which was written:

> **Our Special Lunch for Today, 35¢**
> **Calf's Liver and Onions, Lettuce with Egg**
> **Glass of Anheuser-Busch Pale Lager**
> **Coffee**

There were three men at the bar, one of them smoking a cigar.

Kit felt several pairs of eyes—male eyes—rebuke her for her invasion. Women who were not barmaids, prostitutes, or drunks did not frequent such establishments. She only hoped no one would recognize her—an increasing problem due to her notoriety. Such was the price of her success, she conceded, but it was still something of a nuisance.

Kit quickly scanned the place, looking for her mark. Several male patrons looked right back. Kit ignored them and finally spotted a lone diner sitting in the far corner at a table, his back to her. Though not entirely sure it was him, Kit decided he was the only one who looked remotely like the man she'd seen in the *Gazette* office the day before. She strode past the other tables, ignoring the scowls, and stopped behind the man at the corner table.

"Excuse me," she said.

The man twisted around, chair legs scraping against the hardwood floor. "What the—?"

It was indeed Hank. "Am I disturbing your lunch?" Kit said, looking at a plate of sausage and sauerkraut next to a half-empty glass of beer.

"You!"

"I just have one question for you." Kit leaned over him like a nimbus cloud. "Where did you get that story?"

"What—"

"The Harcourt story, the one you blasphemed the name of God to get."

Hank's eyes widened. "Who said anything—"

Kit gave him no time to collect his thoughts. "You lied to a vulnerable woman by presenting yourself as a man of God. Do you know, sir, what the Good Book says about liars?"

The snatcher—for that is how Kit thought of him now, a snatcher of photographs, lives, and reputations—pulled the linen napkin from his collar and threw it down on the table. "I'll ask you to leave me alone," he said, his voice shaking.

" 'All liars shall have their part in the lake which burneth with fire and brimstone: which is the second death.' "

Hank swallowed, long and laboriously, his Adam's apple a

frightened thing. "What do you want from me?"

"Where you got the Harcourt story." Kit slid a chair out from Hank's table and sat.

"Now, I can't tell you that," Hank said, eyes darting.

"Oh, I think there are a great many things you could tell me, Hank."

"Look here—"

"Has anybody ever written about your past? Hmm?" She had no idea what his history consisted of, but the Rule of Human Probabilities told her it had to contain a few dancing skeletons. The Rule, taught to her by Earl Rogers, had given her insight into human character that she had used in her trials.

"Come on, now," Hank protested, "can't a man eat his lunch in peace?"

"You want to be left alone, is that it?"

"That's right."

"More than you ever did for people like the Harcourts," Kit pressed. She wanted him to crack just a little, in frustration or anger, like a witness on cross-examination who was hiding something. Emotion often led to revelation.

"That's business, miss," the reporter said.

"I will tell you my business, then: It is upholding the law and protecting my clients. When I see someone trying to take advantage of them, I take it quite seriously. If someone is party to an ill-conceived venture, I take it upon myself to be quite a nuisance."

Hank nodded. "I can believe that."

"So you can be sure that whoever was your source for this story had better watch out. And so should you, sir. I'll have the law down on both of you."

"Now, you just—"

"That is a promise." Kit stood up, paused another moment to hover over the man, then turned and walked out into the sunshine. She stopped just outside the door, looked across Main Street, and nodded at Corazón. The plan was in motion, and if Kit was any judge of character, Hank the reporter would be making a very important beeline soon. And Corazón would be close behind.

"This is Truman Harcourt."

"I was wondering when the father would call."

Truman gripped the telephone receiver as if strangling a cat. And if he could have, he would have held this Stringham woman's neck the very same way. He was old-fashioned and believed that women acting like men, in tone of voice and action, were a blight on society. He was not against women in the workplace—women like Miss Shannon carried off their chosen roles with dignity. But women like Jade Stringham, who threw off all notions of civility and womanliness in the name of progressivism, filled him with ire.

"See here," Truman said. "I am not going to tolerate this another moment. You will not run this story about my wife. If you do, there will be consequences."

A short pause over the crackling phone line. Then Stringham's voice shot back. "You had better not be threatening me, you louse."

Fire raced into Truman's head. "I am threatening you, oh yes! And your boss. I will not stand by while you victimize my wife and child!"

"She's not your child, now, is she?"

The words stung like hot needles in his flesh. Truman could almost see the malice in this woman's eyes, even though he himself had never met her.

Jade Stringham's strident voice came back again. "Your lady lawyer already tried the strong-arm routine. It won't work. Mr. Mahoney is not in the habit of backing down. He has instructed me to publish this story, and I assure you he won't change his mind before he leaves for the East on Friday."

The day after tomorrow. Truman couldn't let the man go without a confrontation.

"I will show you what works," Truman said, almost blinded by rage. He thrust the receiver down onto the switch hook so hard it almost snapped off.

He paused, breathing heavily, glad at least that he was in his private office and not at home. The episode would have upset Celia terribly, as if she wasn't upset enough.

The room seemed to close in around him, trapping him.

There is no other way, he thought. No other way for Celia, for Louise. For him. He opened the right-hand drawer of his desk, paused, then retrieved the Colt .45.

9

THE SIGN, IN GAUDY RED LETTERING over a black background, read: *Spiritualist, Medium, Clairvoyant: Séances, Palmistry, Fortunes. Inquire Within.*

Kit regarded it for a moment from the street. It might have been the header for a circus sideshow. Indeed, that is where activities such as these belonged, if anywhere. It was a free country, however, and in Los Angeles these frauds had been permitted to operate—a situation Kit had vowed to change in the near future.

On any given day, in the city's two main newspapers, one could find advertisements for spiritualists of all kinds. Every time she saw one of these ads, Kit felt the anger rising in her.

So it was with all her restraint that Kit took Corazón's arm and entered the establishment as calmly as possible. A little bell on the door tinkled.

The antechamber was dim, cloaked in black velvet and maroon wallpaper. A large eyeball—painted on black felt—hung on the back wall so it beheld all who entered.

Below the eye was another sign:

KAJAR!
The Greatest Living Astral Dead-Trance Medium!
He will tell you the outcome of your present distress!
He will guide you with certainty higher than human power!
He will tell you the truth—good or bad!

"Not one for modesty, is he?" Kit said.

Corazón smiled.

But another notice brought the anger back to Kit. It was in the form of a framed letter:

I desire to bear evidence to the genuineness of Kajar's work. God does give us an intuition whereby we may guide our lives. That Kajar possesses this guiding power to a marvelous degree is evident. The fact that his clients are his warmest and truest friends is alone a tribute to his sincerity and honest methods in dealing with all. He has rendered me immeasurable assistance.

—Rev. W. C. Jessup

"A minister!" Kit said. "I shall have to pay this man a visit."

Then, through a beaded curtain, a man in a turban and long, dark coat entered and bowed.

"I am Kajar," he said, in an accent as American as draw poker. Kajar? More likely Carl. He was not old—Kit guessed he was, like herself, in his middle twenties—and his skin was pasty, even in the dim light. Kit noticed the faint scent of gardenia in the room now. It had not been there before his entry.

"My name is Kathleen Shannon, and I am—"

She was silenced by the man's raised hand. He closed his eyes and put his fingers of his other hand to the bridge of his nose. "Do not tell me. You are here because you have lost a loved one, quite recently."

Kit hesitated. Aunt Freddy was only a few months gone, but he couldn't have known that. This was no doubt his standard introduction, and it would, in most cases, be right. That was why people came to mediums in the first place.

"Sir, I—"

"Tut!" The turbaned man waved his hand toward her with delicate censure. His hand reminded Kit of a butterfly. "I see a face . . . an older face . . . someone older . . . who loved you dearly. Who still loves you dearly. . . ."

"If I may—"

"Ah! And you have come to me for help!" Kajar opened his eyes and smiled through thin lips.

"Remarkable," Kit said dryly.

"That is why I am at your service," said Kajar. "I help the bereaved to communicate with their dear departed."

"I see. And what does this service cost one?"

A hard edge flashed into Kajar's eyes. "You are a woman who comes to the point."

"So I have been told."

"Then Kajar will not withhold the help you desire. Please, won't you come in? Who is your friend?" He whipped a glance at Corazón.

"Mr. Kajar," Kit said, "I—"

"Kajar, miss. Simply Kajar."

This was beginning to feel like a vaudeville act to Kit. She half expected dancing dogs to file out from the beaded curtain.

"Sir," Kit said, "I am not here for your services. I wish to ask you some questions."

The man's eyebrows shot downward into a scowl. "Kajar does not answer questions without an arrangement!"

Kit ignored him. "I want to know about Hank, the reporter who works for the *Gazette*."

Kajar's face lost all pretense of a mysterious, swami-like aspect. "Look, lady, I have a business to run here and—"

"I wouldn't call this a business," Kit said. "Businesses trade value for money. What you trade are false hopes and deceit."

"Hey, I got a right—"

"Hank, the reporter," Kit snapped.

The man's cheeks twitched. "I don't know any Hank the reporter. Now if you'll—"

"Are you familiar with the *Gazette*?"

Kajar's face froze for a moment. "Somewhat."

"But you are denying a reporter for that paper came to see you yesterday? Because that is what my assistant saw."

The man folded his arms, barely glancing at Corazón. "I deny it, and I will ask you to leave."

"I will not," Kit said. "I wish you to contact the dead."

Corazón let out a surprised yelp behind Kit. *Good*, Kit thought. The element of surprise might work on this Kajar fellow, as well.

"I beg your pardon," Kajar said. "After what you've just said, you now want to employ my services?"

"I want to test them," Kit said.

The man shook his head. "I am not interested."

"The *Times* might be," Kit said. "They might be very interested in a story about your refusal to take on a challenge. The city might be interested, too. It's amazing how quickly a reputation can be—"

"Enough! If you wish me to consult the spirits for you it will cost you one hundred dollars."

Again Corazón yelped.

"That seems rather stiff," Kit said. "Is that your going rate?"

"For you it is," he snarled at her.

"Done," Kit said. "And I will bring guests."

"Guests?"

"A Mr. Houdini."

Kajar's eyes narrowed.

"A magician," Kit continued. "I happened to catch his act and know he has a keen interest in spiritualists. I should like to invite him."

"Why not?" Kajar said confidently.

"And a reporter from the newspaper, a Mr. Phelps. It should be quite an interesting evening. Shall we say Saturday night?"

Kajar pulled himself up in a dismal show of pride. "What time will you be arriving?"

Kit smiled wryly. "Shouldn't *you* be telling *me*?"

———

With the help of his cane, Ted Fox stepped back slowly from the open door of the barn-hangar on the bluffs near Santa Monica. He looked in at the monoplane, carefully reconstructed now after its disastrous first flight.

"Looks good," Ted said.

Gus Willingham, wiping his greasy hands with a rag, snapped at him. " 'Course it's good. I worked on it."

"You're just amazing," Ted teased. Gus was truly a genius as a mechanic. His social skills were not as well oiled, but he could coax any engine into sweet music.

Ted had dubbed the plane, made of spruce and wire and linen wings, *The Kathleen*. Gus had grunted at that one, in what Ted took as the most sentimental gesture he'd ever get from Mr. Willingham.

"Still need to make a few adjustments," Gus said, "before you take her up."

"Soon," Ted said. "We can't just monkey around, we . . ." He stopped at Gus's faraway look.

Ted turned and saw a gas-powered automobile coming up the dirt road. As it approached, Ted immediately appreciated the fine design of the machine. Its engine was quieter than any he had ever been exposed to—no backfire to be heard, no chugging as if it were a man with a bad cough. Its combustion sound was smooth and rhythmic.

The auto pulled to a stop. It was trimmed with polished brass, offsetting its shiny black exterior. It had a cape-cart hood that was, in the sunshine, folded down. Behind the wheel sat a well-appointed autoist. He wore heavy leather gauntlets, swiveled amber goggles, an elegant brown duster, and a peaked riding cap.

The driver offered a quick smile. "Gentlemen!"

He bounded out of the car and, in one motion, removed his gauntlets. He tossed the gloves on the seat of the auto and whipped off his goggles. He had a thin black mustache, curious brown eyes, and a jovial expression. He was about Ted's height and build, though Ted judged him slightly older than he.

"Fine looking tin horse you got there, mister," Ted said.

"A Haynes," the stranger said. "Like it?"

"What's not to like?"

"The price, I'll fancy," Gus said. The mechanic spit and said, "Must've set you back at least a thousand."

"Three thousand," the man said. "And I'll wager another three to keep it up every year. But a man must have his passions, eh?" He craned his head, as if wishing to see inside the barn.

"What's your business?" Gus snapped.

Ted cuffed Gus on the shoulder, then said to the stranger, "Pardon my friend's manners. He was raised by coyotes." Ted put his hand out. "Ted Fox is my name."

"Duncan Chase." The man's handshake was strong. Gus did not offer to sample it.

"What my friend was asking," Ted said, "is what brings you out our way this fine morning?"

"The sun, the sea," Chase said, "and the air." He looked upward, knowingly.

Gus spat again. Ted hit him once more.

"You see, I did not come out this way by pure chance," Chase said. "I knew I would find you here. And I knew your name."

"I don't follow you," Ted said.

Duncan Chase started to unbutton his duster. "May I have a look at your wings?"

Ted began to feel unease now. Aviation had become, in just the last few months, an enterprise of energy and good old American competition. Air fever, as the newspapers called it, was spreading through bicycle shops, carriage factories, country farms, and city lots. Backyard aeronauts were cobbling together all sorts of wild contraptions, virtually all of them doomed to failure. Ted had even heard about a blacksmith in Jetmore, Kansas, who had used the town's main street to house a huge, overhead rotor contrivance he was calling a "helio-coptor." It never got off the ground.

But that did not mean there weren't successes. A man named Glenn Curtiss was reportedly right on the Wrights' tail with a biplane design. And it was not just America that had the bug for flying. In France, a man named Blériot was having some luck with a monoplane, the very design Ted and Gus were trying to perfect.

In this environment there had been some notable thefts—of design plans, materials, and patents. Ted had to be cautious. The farther he got off the ground, the greater the danger someone would try to steal what he was doing.

"Sir," Ted said, "you must excuse me if I give pause. May I ask how you came to know we were here?"

The lips under the thin mustache pursed. "Mr. Fox," Chase said, "you are not exactly a hermit in this town. Your experiments in aeronautics have been noted in the papers. You had, I believe, quite a serious setback, one that cost you a leg."

Who was this man who had done personal research on him? Ted turned and noticed that Gus had slipped away, back into the hangar.

"That's true, Mr. Chase," Ted said. "But I still don't know why you bothered to come out all this way."

"Common interest," the man said. "And, as a representative of a party who may desire to aid you in your venture, I have a proposition to make."

"I appreciate that. But right now we're not looking for partners. We'd just as soon go at it alone for the time being."

"That is, may I say, a rather narrow view. Are you aware of what is happening in the world, sir?"

"If you're referring to some of the others involved in the making of aeroplanes, I've got an idea."

"More than that," Duncan Chase said. "I'm not merely talking about individual inventors such as yourself, I'm talking about—"

Chase stopped as he glanced over Ted's shoulder. Gus had re-emerged and was holding a crowbar in his hands.

"You best be gettin' along now, mister," Gus said. "We ain't interested."

"Gus!" Ted turned all the way around to face him. "You put that thing down. Are you crazy?"

Without a word Gus dropped the crowbar, which surprised Ted. Usually when he gave an order, Gus found six arguments before complying. But now he obeyed without so much as a peep.

When Ted turned back to the man, he suddenly knew why. Duncan Chase was pointing a revolver at them.

"Now," Chase said, "let's have that look at your plane."

10

WHERE WAS TED?

Kit looked at the clock again—half past nine—and wondered whether to be appropriately angry or simply worried. Ted was not one to miss appointments, though sometimes his creative energies kept him focused more on his aeroplane than the time.

Maybe that was it. Ted and Gus had been working on the plane at a fever pitch, partly at Kit's urging. She was sure, as Ted was, that God was calling him to this enterprise. There was going to be something good to come out of it sometime.

She did not mind her extra time at the office tonight, however. She used it to further delve into the law of defamation, should that ever become a course to pursue on behalf of Celia Harcourt.

At nine-thirty-five she heard heavy footsteps coming up the stairs inside the building. They were irregular, starting and stopping. She sat still at her desk, listening, wondering if she should call the police.

Then, through the door, she heard the lilting strains of someone singing "My Wild Irish Rose."

Kit opened her office door. "Earl Rogers," she said reprovingly. "You're drunk."

The trial attorney bowed to her, his beige suit still looking perfectly pressed on him. "I saw your light, Miss Shannon," he said grandly. "If I don't watch it, you're going to outwork me." He leaned to the right but did not fall, only because a wall was conveniently located there.

Kit grabbed his arm. "You sotted fool," she said. "Come in here and dry out."

She helped Rogers into her office—no easy task. Rogers slumped in a chair. Kit poured him a glass of water from a carafe.

"You smell terrible," Kit said. She owed Earl Rogers her career, but she did not approve of his drinking. It was sure to ruin the finest legal mind she had ever known. She knew he had never gotten over the death of his father, a Christian minister, and that he always took his solace in alcohol.

"Don't you be mean to me now, Kathleen Shannon," Rogers slurred.

"When are you going to grow up?" Kit said.

"Now, Kit—"

"I mean it. You have Adela to think of." Adela Rogers was his ten-year-old daughter.

Rogers' face grew dark. "Please, Kit, not tonight."

She sat in the chair next to him, thinking of him as a lost brother. She put a hand on his arm. "Why must you drink so, Earl?"

His blue eyes were deep and distant. "God gives us troubles, and the devil gives us whiskey."

The comment saddened her. If only Earl Rogers could recover his childhood faith, what an asset he would be to the Kingdom's work. But as long as he thought of God as giving troubles and nothing more, the devil indeed would have him.

The one thing that seemed to cheer him was the law. Kit decided to converse with him on the subject to get his mind off his troubles. When he sobered up, she would once again speak to him of God.

"Earl," she said, "I have a client who is going to be the subject of a story in the *Gazette*."

Rogers' eyebrows shot upward. "A filthy rag!"

"Why has no one stopped them before?"

"The law of libel is a tenuous thread. If there is truth, it is an absolute defense."

"No matter how much damage is done?"

"Truth is truth, Kit," Rogers said, sitting up a little straighter in his chair.

"And the *Gazette* has never been sued for libel?"

"There was a case," Rogers said, "back in '02 or so. A man named Tanner. Lawrence Tanner, yes. He was an ophthalmologist. It was claimed in the *Gazette* that he blinded a man. He sued, but the paper was actually able to produce the blind man. The jury believed the blind man, though it was whispered—" Rogers leaned forward, almost slipping off his chair—"that Mahoney bought and paid for this witness."

"What became of the man Tanner?"

Rogers shrugged. "Don't know. All I know is the *Gazette* plays for keeps." His eyes looked sober. "Beware, Kit. Things always seem to get worse with them."

Kit shuddered, partly in anger. That any paper—even the *Examiner* or the *Times*—should hold such power over people was outrageous. If it took a lawsuit to stop them, as hard a prospect as that was, Kit thought maybe she would do it.

"But by gum," Earl said suddenly, "if you best them in court, it'll bring you greater glory than even I've enjoyed!"

"That's not the kind of glory I seek," Kit said.

"Still looking to please God, eh?"

"His glory. Always."

The phone on her desk jangled. "Excuse me, Earl."

She picked up and heard the anxious voice. "Oh, Miss Shannon, please come," Celia Harcourt cried. "Truman has been arrested! For murder!"

11

TRUMAN HARCOURT HAD WHITE GAUZE wrapped
around his head. He was dressed in a brown suit that had once been
pressed but was now unkempt. His eyes were glassy, almost as
though he'd been drinking. But Kit knew he was not a drinking
man.

How could he be a criminal? That was not like him either. But
here he was, in a cell in the county jail.

"Thank you for coming." Truman's voice was barely above a
whisper.

"Are you all right?" Kit noted that he staggered when he
approached the steel bars.

"My head. It feels like . . ." Truman closed his eyes, as if hit by
sharp pain. He put his hand on top of his head. "Like I got kicked
by a mule."

"Can you tell me what happened?"

His eyes, frosted over with confusion and doubt, froze momentarily as he gazed at the ground. "I don't know. My head. It's all a
muddle."

And it could be a major problem in Truman Harcourt's defense.
While Kit had learned, from Earl Rogers and some of his medical
friends, that head trauma could produce short-term loss of memory, she had also learned juries distrusted such accounts.

"The police say you were found incoherent at Mahoney's

house," Kit said. "Do you remember how you got there?"

Truman rubbed the bridge of his nose. "Yes, I think so. I remember leaving the house and walking to Laurel Street."

"What time was it?"

"I don't remember. It was getting dark."

"Go on."

"I got to the house, I remember that. There was a light on in the window."

"Let me stop you there for a moment. What was in your mind as you approached? I mean, what was your purpose in going to the house?"

Truman Harcourt thought a moment. "I was going to try to talk some sense into him."

Kit saw something else behind Truman's eyes. "Just talk?"

Truman looked at her as if he were a child caught stealing cookies. Good. Unless a client was completely open with her, she could not help him. Information withheld had a nasty habit of surfacing at just the wrong moment, usually in front of a jury.

"All right," Truman said. "I was going to try to force him not to run the story."

"Force him how?"

Hesitating, Truman looked at the floor of his cell and took a deep breath. "I brought a gun." Quickly he added, "But I was never going to use it, Miss Shannon. I would not shoot a man in cold blood. I was desperate, you see, for Celia. For Louise. That Stringham woman . . ." His voice trailed off in a cloud of anger.

"How does she figure into this?"

Truman's eyes flashed as he told her. "She is a cruel woman. I spoke to her by way of the telephone. She would not listen. She insulted me. She said Mahoney was not going to back down, and he was leaving town. Yes, it's all coming back to me, Miss Shannon. I felt I had to get to him before he left or there would be no hope of stopping the story."

"When did this telephone call take place?"

"I think it was in the afternoon sometime."

"How much time passed before you went to Mahoney's house?"

Truman rubbed his head. "I don't know."

"You must try to remember. Was it a matter of hours?"

"I think so. Yes."

That was not good. If he had shot Mahoney while in some sort of heat of passion or distress, there would be a mental defense to the charge of murder. But the passage of time worked against that.

"All right," she said. "Tell me about walking up to the house. You said you saw a light in the window. Which one?"

"The one that faces the street, on the left side of the house."

"The left side as you approach?"

"Yes, my left as I was walking up the path."

"What happened next?"

"I went into his house."

"You did not announce yourself?"

Truman shook his head. "I opened the door quietly and slipped in. I wanted to surprise him, not give him a chance to think."

"The door was unlocked?"

"Yes."

"What happened next?"

"I walked to the room where the light was coming from. It was the first room on the left, the library, I believe. Then somebody hit me from behind and that's the last I remember until the police found me wandering in the yard."

And in that time someone had used Truman's gun to shoot Gerald Mahoney—if Truman was telling the whole truth. People who were frightened, who had done something out of keeping with their character, often felt their best defense was to obscure the facts. Truman might be holding back essential information.

"Miss Shannon," Truman said. "Must I stay in here?"

"I will ask a judge to grant bail," Kit said. "But this is a murder charge. I have a feeling the district attorney is not going to look kindly upon the request."

12

THE FOLLOWING MORNING, Truman's arraignment was held in front of Judge Clement DePew. He was a rail-thin man of fifty or so who made up for his lack of stature with a glare that could lay out any aggressors. "The People of the State of California versus Truman Harcourt," he intoned in a deep voice. "The People are represented by Clara Dalton Price and the defendant by Kathleen Shannon. Miss Shannon, is your client ready to hear the charges against him?"

Kit stood at her counsel table. "Your honor, my client will waive a reading of the indictment, enter a plea of not guilty, and ask that this matter be set for trial. In addition, I would ask the court to release Mr. Harcourt on his own recognizance."

The judge looked at the prosecutor. "Mrs. Price, do you have a response?"

The woman at the prosecution table rose. What Kit knew about Clara Dalton Price was only what she had read in the newspapers when District Attorney John Davenport hired her.

She was the sister of U. S. Senator Samuel Dalton. At forty years of age she had come to the legal profession. That was a mere seven years ago, but in that time she had established herself as a woman of startling ambitions.

Clara Dalton had been the first woman admitted to the College of Law at the University of California in Hastings. Upon graduation she was immediately hired by the Southern Pacific Railroad as counsel for its San Francisco office. She left that job in 1902 to defend a man accused of murder. The accused was Roland Price, a wealthy lumber magnate. After his acquittal, Clara Dalton married him.

A year later Roland Price himself was murdered. The case was never solved, though Clara always suspected a wealthy Nob Hill business rival. Frustrated, Clara Dalton Price decided to spend the rest of her legal career prosecuting criminals. She did so with stunning results in San Francisco, earning the title "The Iron Lady."

The newspapers did not say so, but it had been whispered in town that Davenport's decision to hire Mrs. Price was motivated by one reason—to have someone in his office defeat Kit Shannon. Fearing that male jurors might be harboring some sympathy for a young woman lawyer, Davenport had simply decided to employ one himself.

"If Your Honor please," Mrs. Price said. Her voice was strong and sure, her face fiercely intelligent. She wore a high-necked dress suit with a large brimmed hat. The hat she kept on at all times. Kit always took hers off in court. "The defendant is accused of murder in the first degree, the cold-blooded killing of a respected citizen of this community. That being the case, he might not hesitate in the slightest to threaten witnesses. The People would therefore request that the defendant remain behind bars pending trial."

Kit did not even wait for the judge to return his gaze to her. "Your Honor, the prosecutor suggests that the victim, Mr. Mahoney, was a respected member of the community. With all due respect, we contend that he was not respected at all, and even so this should not be relevant to—"

"I object," Mrs. Price interrupted. "Mr. Mahoney is not the accused here. It is Truman Harcourt."

"All right, now," the judge said. "Let's not have a catfight in my courtroom." He seemed pleased with himself. The newspapermen in the gallery roared with laughter.

"You have anything else to say, Miss Shannon?" the judge said.

"Only that it is Truman Harcourt who is the respected citizen here," Kit said. "He is a man without a criminal past, a family man, a man of enterprise. He is not a threat to this community. He is anxious to go to trial to clear his name."

"The guilty may be just as anxious," Mrs. Price said, "if they think they can get away with it."

The comment burned into Kit. What right did Mrs. Price have to say that? "Your Honor," Kit began, but the judge cut her off with a pounding gavel.

"I am not going to tolerate this, I told you," the judge said. "Bail denied. You can try again at the preliminary hearing." And with that, DePew gaveled an adjournment.

Outside the courtroom Kit was stopped by Clara Dalton Price. "We have not formally met," Mrs. Price said. "But I have heard a great deal about you."

"A pleasure to make your acquaintance," Kit said formally. Aunt Freddy would have approved. She always wanted to "make a lady" out of her volatile niece.

"They tell me you're quite good in the courtroom," Mrs. Price said. "A protégée of none other than Earl Rogers."

"Mr. Rogers gave me my start in the law."

"And what was your motivation, if I might ask? As women, we both know the hurdles we are up against."

"That is true," Kit said. "Which is why the law must be a calling."

"That is what you believe?"

"I do."

"And who called you?"

Kit wondered how familiar she should be with Clara Dalton Price. There was something about her Kit did not quite trust. But what harm could come from sharing the truth about her faith?

"I believe my practice is the call of God," Kit said. "I would not have pursued this course if I thought otherwise."

The prosecutor studied Kit's face. "I can see, then, I shall have to be on my guard. Taking on the Almighty as well as you will be quite a challenge."

The way she said it made Kit feel Mrs. Price did not believe in the Almighty in the slightest. "The challenge for you will be the presumption of innocence," Kit said.

A coy smile came to Mrs. Price's face. "That is what I expect to hear from a defense lawyer," she said. "But I intend to win this case, Miss Shannon. You see, I have a calling, too."

Kit looked at the woman's stern face and set features. "And that is?"

"To win at all costs," Mrs. Price replied. "Every time I set foot in a courtroom."

———————

"There is no answer, ma'am," the operator said.

"Thank you." Kit replaced the earpiece and turned to Corazón. They were back in the office after the arraignment. "If we do not hear from Ted by the end of the day, we will contact police head-quarters."

Despite her worry, there was work to be done. "Corazón," Kit said, "go to the central library and ask to see all of the issues of the *Gazette* they have in their possession. Work from the most recent issue backward. Write down the names of every person who was the subject of their main stories."

Her assistant nodded eagerly. "I will do it."

"Then see if you can track down a man, a doctor, named Lawrence Tanner. The city directory from 1902 would be the place to start. He had an office. Find out where it was, and see if anyone down there remembers him."

"Sí. I am the excitement!"

Kit laughed. Corazón had taken to her role as assistant with a vigor that was inspiring. "I am going out to Mahoney's house. I want to have a look at the crime scene."

13

A LARGE CUMULUS CLOUD obscured direct sunlight as Kit arrived at Gerald Mahoney's Laurel Street home. No one seemed about. She had half expected to encounter a police officer or two. But the place was desolate.

Alighting from her carriage, Kit proceeded through the gate. She did not know precisely what she was going to do. The doors would be locked, no doubt, but perhaps she would be able to get a look at the crime scene through the window.

According to Truman's account, he had walked toward the library, the first room to the left. It was the room that could be seen through a large window. Below that window were the rose bushes Kit remembered seeing the last time she was here. She also remembered the crazy gardener.

Kit stepped off the walking path and proceeded toward the window. The grass beneath her feet seemed overgrown, as if it had not been cared for as it should. Closer to the window she could see that the rose bushes had been severely trimmed. There were only two or three small buds appearing amid the thorns.

Something slammed behind her.

Startled, she turned and saw that the gate had shut. But how? There was no other sign of life.

Kit's heart drummed a little faster now. She put a hand to her chest and breathed deeply. There was a sense of menace about this place.

She walked to the outer reaches of the rose bushes, which stood guard like thorned soldiers. She could not get to the windowpanes directly but had to look in from a distance of about three feet.

The inside was dark, and it was difficult to see clearly. She could see that the door to the room was open. The wall that ran from the door toward her did not, so far as she could tell, have anything on it or attached to it. That seemed odd for a library, but perhaps there was a reason. Maybe the police had removed some evidence.

If only she could get inside somehow.

She decided to slip around the side of the house to see if she might gain entry through a window. It would be a bit cumbersome in her walking dress, of course, but she had always enjoyed athletics. At St. Katherine's, the Boston orphanage where she spent several hard years, Kit was one of the fastest runners and could wrestle the bigger girls in a pinch. What was one little window?

A breeze blew down the side passage of Mahoney's house, slapping Kit with an unseasonable chill. In some distant place a cat screeched. For a moment Kit thought, *I should get out of here*, but she decided to press on. She had to, for Truman's sake.

There was a side window that was within her reach. It had a single sash frame, with two rows of square panes separated by a slender mullion. It was finely crafted, but was it secure? Kit pressed the bottom of the sash, feeling for some give . . .

"Ahhhh!"

The scream from behind her sent her heart scrambling to control its rhythm. Kit spun around and saw the crazy gardener but a few feet away.

"I told you to stay away from them roses!" His eyes were ablaze, and he held clipping shears up like a weapon. He took a threatening step forward.

"Stop!" Kit said as strongly as she could. And, as if she were talking to a rational person, she added, "Before you do something you'll regret."

"I'll show you!" He thrust at her with the shears, the points coming within inches of her face.

Now what? She was defenseless, alone. Where was a cop when you needed one? Wasn't this a crime scene?

Shick. The crazy man closed the shears and pulled them back.

He was going to thrust farther this time. Kit was sure. She saw it in his eyes.

In one quick, instinctive move, Kit grabbed her skirt and kicked the man with all her might. The point of her leather Oxford shoe landed with thudding assurance on his shin, hurting her toes but hurting the gardener more. He howled like a wounded animal.

Kit, still holding her skirt, ran.

She had gone a mere three strides toward the street when she felt her right leg go out from under her. She knew, even as she fell, that she had managed to step in a hole in the grass. Her momentum carried her forward in a bumpy roll.

Pain blazed through her right knee like the prod of a hot poker.

From the ground she looked back and saw the gardener, his face contorted with insane rage, limping toward her.

Kit tried to get to her feet but her knee collapsed under her weight.

The crazy man, holding the shears out, advanced.

"I'll fix you," he said. "I'll fix you for taking 'em!"

Looking around wildly, Kit saw a rake leaning against the side of the house. It had a thick wooden handle and iron teeth.

But it was ten feet away.

The gardener, seemingly confident of his prey, snapped the clippers a few times in his hands. The *shick shick* sound cut the air like some carnivorous beast.

Maybe he's just trying to scare me, Kit thought. But she was not going to rely on that. With one mighty effort she raised herself on her left leg.

The gardener was almost upon her, his eyes a lunatic whirl.

Ignoring the pain, Kit took two long strides and grabbed the rake. And from the corner of her eye saw the gardener lunge.

The room where Ted Fox sat was as spare as a pine coffin. The hard wooden chair he sat on was the only stick of furniture in the room. The paint was peeling from the walls and Ted noticed a few nail holes. It seemed as if the room had once been an office of some kind—one that was vacated in haste. An air of mystery hung over the hardwood floor and dusty corners.

The only illumination came from an electric light bulb hanging from a wire in the middle of the ceiling. Whatever this place was, it wasn't the Ritz.

But Ted waited patiently, as he had been promised an explanation.

More light flooded in when the door opened and a tall, fair-skinned man dressed in a dark wool suit entered.

"Mr. Fox," he said. His tone was clipped, formal. "I am Peter Garraty. I must apologize for the intrusion."

Ted folded his arms and did not stand. "Intrusion? That's what you call it? When a guy's taken by gunpoint? The D.A.'s going to call it kidnapping."

Garraty had a smattering of freckles on his forehead that bunched up when he raised his eyebrows. "I pray for your understanding in this matter, Mr. Fox, and when I am finished explaining, perhaps you will forgive me."

Ted regarded him closely. Garraty had light brown hair worn parted at the side in continental fashion. He was around forty years old and was obviously a man of means, as his cohort, Duncan Chase, was. Why he would have gone to such lengths to get Ted here was a puzzle, but perhaps one deserving of a hearing.

"First, tell me where Gus is," Ted said.

"Mr. Willingham is at this moment being hosted by Mr. Chase."

"Hosted?" There was still some anger in him from last night, when he and Gus had been treated like prisoners. They were given cots to sleep on in another room in the one-story building in the Wilcox area. Breakfast had been provided, in the form of coffee and egg sandwiches. But until Garraty had arrived, there had been no explanation of their plight. The only thing that kept Ted there that long was Chase's insistence that this was a matter of such gravity that he had to give his superior a hearing.

Now he was here, apparently. Peter Garraty leaned against a wall. "I work for the United States government, Mr. Fox."

"Oh, really? As what?"

"I am a spy."

The word came out like a striking musical chord. It hung in the air for a moment as Ted pondered it. "Do you mean like in the writings of Fenimore Cooper?"

"That is literature," Garraty said. "Quite entertaining. The real world is much more mundane."

"How do I know what you say is true?" Ted asked.

"I will gladly get you confirmation in due course," Garraty said. "I answer to General J. S. Hall, United States Army. He, of course, answers to the White House."

"That still doesn't tell me why we were brought here. Are we prisoners?"

"Not at all, Mr. Fox. Duncan Chase works for me, and I hope you will forgive his enthusiasm. His orders were to get you here. His means of persuasion were, perhaps, a bit overwrought."

"Mr. Garraty," Ted said, "since I am not a prisoner, I will give you five minutes to explain yourself, and then I'm walking out."

"Very well," Garraty said. He put his hands together in the manner of a schoolteacher about to begin the lesson. "Are you aware of what is going on in Europe at the moment?"

Ted shrugged. "Only what I read in the papers."

"There is, to put it mildly, a competition for arms."

"Weapons?"

"Precisely. Since 1871 or so, western Europe has experienced but one small war, between Russia and Turkey. Things have been in a state of rough equilibrium since then. Oh sure, the Russkies and the Japs are snapping at each other, but that's on the other side of the world. Europe is stable. And that is the time when countries seek to grow stronger, to emerge as the leading power when the inevitable conflict occurs."

Ted nodded. That much was pure history.

"Italy and Germany have grown by leaps," Garraty said. "Especially the Germans. Under Bismarck they became a world power. After Bismarck's fall in 1890, the situation became dangerously unstable."

"In what way?"

Garraty reached into his coat and pulled out a leather cigar case. He opened it and offered a cigar to Ted, who shook his head. As Garraty snipped the end of a cigar with a silver cutter, he continued. "The working of German diplomacy was left to fools. Inexperienced men who have not learned the fine art of avoiding insults."

Garraty pulled out a small cylindrical implement from his pocket. He held it with one hand, then pulled down on it with his thumb. A small flame flickered upward. Ted flinched.

"You like it?" Garraty used the flame to light his cigar. After issuing several starter puffs, he said, "It's called a flame lighter. Works with a small flint and some mixture of kerosene and oil. Latest thing back east."

"Could be dangerous in the wrong hands," Ted observed.

"Quite right, Mr. Fox. Just like advanced weapons. The army is most worried about the Huns. Back in '98, William II and his chief admiral, Alfred von Tirpitz, decided they wanted the German navy to surpass the Brits. It is almost there. In conventional weaponry, they have developed the first flamethrower, if you can imagine such a thing." He held the lighter up again. "Imagine this, only a thousand times more potent."

"But surely a country has the right to prepare defenses," Ted said.

Garraty motioned in the air with his cigar. "Of course. But the Huns have started to make claims. Just last week they asserted a right to Morocco, of all places."

"Morocco? Doesn't that belong to the French?"

Smiling, Garraty nodded. "Now you're catching on. It all comes down to land, eventually. And soon, the air."

Ted sat up. At last Garraty was getting around to the reason he was here—why Duncan Chase had forced him and Gus to show him the monoplane.

Garraty said, "The Huns intend to rule the skies, the same way the Brits have ruled the seas. I have been there. I've seen it. Our army, and Roosevelt himself, does not want to be at a disadvantage. We all have the feeling that someday, perhaps not for a long time, but someday there is going to be a European war in which we will have to take sides. We must be ready, Mr. Fox."

Ted nodded. "That makes sense. But where do I come in?"

"On behalf of the United States government, I would like to invite you and your associate to help lead the way into the air. We would like you to help us design and build aeroplanes."

"For the United States?"

"Yes," Garraty said. "Your country, to put it bluntly, needs you."

Ted thought about his request and all of the potential ramifications. The one thing that mattered, though, was that it was for the good of America.

"I'll give you time to think it over, of course," Garraty said. "I only have one condition to impose."

"And that is?"

"You must not tell a soul."

Ted frowned. "And why is that?"

Garraty, his face obscured in a cloud of smoke, said, "Because we will ask you to consider yourself a spy, Mr. Fox. Have you ever been to Germany?"

DETECTIVE MIKE McGINTY could not stop laughing.

"I am sorry if I don't find this at all funny, McGinty," Kit said. She was still shaking. They were standing on the walk in front of the Mahoney house. The crazy gardener was being led away in shackles by a uniformed policeman.

"If I hadn't happened along," McGinty chortled, "you would have plowed that poor man's face with that rake."

"Poor man? He was trying to kill me!"

McGinty shook his head, stifling his laughter. "That old coot is Dick Fitch. He's as harmless as a silkworm."

Kit was incredulous. "You didn't see what he was going to do to me."

"All I saw was you waving that weapon at him like you were a lion tamer and ol' Dick standing there like he didn't know whether to run or jump through a hoop."

"How do you know this man?"

"He's from the loony bin. Been in and out of our jails for years. Last five or so he's had himself steady work snipping flowers for people around these parts. He's crazy, but he loves his work."

"I am not a begonia," Kit said. "I was not about to let him clip me. The man is dangerous."

"He wouldn't hurt a fly."

"It's not flies I'm concerned with, it's my neck. Now, if you'll kindly open up the house, I want to have a look inside."

Kit made a move toward the front door but was stopped by McGinty's negative grunt. "Can't do that, Kit. It is the scene of the crime."

"Why else should I want to see it?" Still feeling a crashing brine of emotions, Kit was not yet temperate in her remarks. Besides, she thought McGinty owed her a little cooperation. She had always been straight with him.

"I wish I could, Kit, but . . ." He hesitated and looked as if something was on his mind, something he wanted to tell her.

"What is it, Mike?"

The detective shook his head. "The chief wants us to make cozy with the D.A. I have to follow orders."

"And that means denying me a chance to see the crime scene?"

"It's a house, not a public place. You got no right of access. If I let you in, Davenport's likely to bust a gut."

With an Irish bristle in her voice, Kit said, "Is Mr. Davenport so set on seeing me lose that he'll try to keep me from the facts?"

"You know I'd let you in if I could."

"I'm not so sure."

"Believe me. I got nothing to hide here."

"Then where is the inventory?"

McGinty blinked once. "What inventory?"

"Of the crime scene. Surely you have gathered the evidence and catalogued it." When McGinty did not immediately answer, Kit added, "You have the evidence, don't you?"

"Like I said, Kit, I got nothing to hide. We don't have any inventory."

This was a shocker. "Then who does?"

McGinty shrugged. "It's not important. The facts, as you put it, are all against Truman Harcourt. I wish it weren't so, Kit, but he's as guilty as the day is long."

"For the last time, Mike, will you let me take a quick walk through?"

McGinty shook his head. "My orders are to arrest anybody found inside."

"Arrest!"

"What Davenport didn't say—" McGinty looked around like a conspirator—"was that I couldn't tell you what we found. I like you, Kit, always have. Even when I haven't liked you, I've liked you."

"Thank you. I think."

"So here it is. We found a Colt .45 on the floor near Mahoney's body. It had four bullets in it. We found two bullets in Mahoney. There might have been a struggle, because we found broken glass on the floor. We also found your client outside the house. He was dazed."

"Somebody hit him, Mike."

"That's what you say. The D.A. thinks otherwise."

"What do *you* think?"

With a glint in his eye, McGinty said, "Now, I wouldn't want to be giving too much to the defense. That might get me in some trouble."

"More trouble than if the real killer walks around scot-free? Did you know Mahoney had a bodyguard?"

"It so happens we have already questioned Mr. Axel Bagby. He has an alibi."

"And that is?"

McGinty shook his head.

"All right, then," said Kit. "What makes you think that gun, the Colt, belonged to my client?"

McGinty folded his arms and looked like the proverbial cat who ate the canary.

"Well?" Kit said.

"Sorry to be the bearer of bad news, Kit, but Harcourt admitted the gun was his, down at the station. He told an officer he had brought it with him to the house."

"He said that?"

"Yep."

"What was his condition when he made the admission?"

"I think he had a headache," McGinty said, winking.

"It still doesn't mean he fired the gun," Kit said.

With a sigh, McGinty said, "I've already said more than I should. I'll just say one thing more. The D.A. has solid evidence your client did it. Something not even you will be able to get around. This is one case you should give up on."

"I don't give up on my clients," Kit said. "Let me in the house."

"Can't."

"Then get ready for cross-examination, Mike. I'll be preparing to rake you over the coals."

McGinty nodded. "You can bet I'll be ready. You're pretty good with a rake, as I've seen."

———

The knock on the door was like a thunderclap. Celia Harcourt heard herself yelp.

Another rap at the door. Celia, breathing labored, rose from her writing desk and answered.

The three people she had most dreaded seeing were standing on her front porch.

"Good day, Celia," Edwina Whitney said. She entered without being asked, followed by her husband, Allard. Behind them, looking haggard, was Louise's fiancé, John.

"Please come in," Celia said belatedly, in an effort to sound unconcerned. But she knew from their expressions she had cause for alarm. Edwina's sharp-nosed face was pinched in disdain.

When the Whitneys had settled in the sitting room and refused Celia's invitation to refreshment, Edwina spoke. "I believe you know why we are here, Celia."

Of course she did, but Celia could not bear to give it utterance. With all her might she held her emotions in check.

"Under the circumstances," Edwina Whitney continued, "we cannot possibly proceed with the wedding. I am sure you will agree."

No! Celia wanted to shout. *I do not agree! Nothing should stand in the way of the happiness of two young people!*

Forcing a light tone, Celia said, "But this is all a terrible mistake. Truman is not guilty of this horrible crime. He would never—"

"We all know about Truman's temper, my dear," Edwina said.

"But murder!" Celia said. "He is *not* guilty of such a thing. You must believe that."

Edwina's expression did not change. It was grim and unforgiving. "Guilty or innocent, that is beside the point. That he is now in jail is enough of a scandal. Surely you understand that. The Whitneys have never been near such a disgrace."

Desperation began to creep up Celia's body. She turned from Edwina's merciless gaze toward Allard Whitney. He was an austere, stiff-shouldered man, well manicured and dressed as befit a business success. He owned a carriage works, making stylish conveyances for the very wealthy.

"Allard," Celia said. "Please. This cannot be—"

"I am sorry," he said, sounding as if he would rather not be here. "Edwina is right. Under the circumstances, the wedding cannot go forward."

Something hard and dark, like death, took hold of Celia. All her hopes for her daughter's happiness were being dashed in front of her, like shattered crystal. The only possible hope was . . .

"John?" Celia said. "Surely you have a say in this?"

"John agrees with us," Edwina said.

Celia looked at the handsome young man who, only days before, had been glowing with anticipation. Now he was a shrunken version of himself, as if pressed down by a great weight.

"Is that true, John?" Celia said. She felt like a drowning woman, pleading for the last lifeline to be thrown to her.

John Whitney looked at Celia, his eyes deep set and mournful. "I wish I . . ." His voice would not—or could not—continue.

Celia's own words came out in halting bursts. "You can't. . . . Oh, please. Won't you—"

"Don't beg them, Mother."

Celia turned and saw Louise standing at the door, a look of defiance on her face.

"Louise," John said weakly, not moving from behind his mother and father.

"Get out," Louise said.

The two elder Whitneys elevated their noses. John looked at the floor.

"I said get out!" Louise screamed.

"Come, John," Edwina commanded. She began to leave the room like a queen.

To her horror, Celia found she could not move. She watched the people move around her, as if she were merely a painting hung on the wall. She saw John Whitney, head bowed, pause at the doorway of the sitting room and look at Louise.

Louise slapped him, the sound ricocheting off the walls.

"Well!" Edwina spouted. "We know what stock you come from!"

The insult, hurled at Louise, brought Celia back to life. The deep despair inside her gave way to blinding anger. In an instant she was eye to eye with Edwina. "Get out, you loathsome thing!"

No words came from Edwina Whitney's open mouth, but her eyes made a speech. *No one speaks to me that way!* they said.

"Yes, *you*!" Celia cried.

Allard Whitney opened the front door and fairly pushed his family out.

For a long moment silence surrounded mother and daughter, like the dead of night in the Mojave Desert. Then Celia opened her arms. "Oh, my baby," she said.

Louise fell into her mother's embrace and wept.

15

JOHN DAVENPORT, DISTRICT ATTORNEY for the county of Los Angeles, liked to take his afternoons off for tennis at the athletic club on Flower Street. This bit of inside information was why Kit Shannon did not try to find him at the offices of the D.A. first. Had she done so, it would have been easier for his staff to put her off.

As it was, Davenport had nowhere to run as she walked, favoring her tender knee, onto the tennis court where he sat, apparently between sets, wiping his face with a towel. His tennis whites were damp with perspiration and his forehead gleamed in the sun.

"Rough game?" Kit said.

"What are you doing here?" Davenport said.

"As it happens, I have come to see you."

"I am right in the middle of a match."

"And I am right in the middle of a case," Kit said, "which you are doing your best to hinder."

Davenport threw his towel on the ground and stood. "I am doing nothing of the kind."

"Then why have you ordered that I not be allowed into Mahoney's house?"

"That is a crime scene. We do not want anything altered."

"I will go with supervision. Put McGinty on it with me."

"No. I've seen enough tricks from you and Earl Rogers to last me a lifetime."

"Tricks!" Kit was beginning to feel heat, and not just from the afternoon sun. "Whatever is done to bring out the truth is far from a trick, Mr. Davenport. Your implication is that I would alter the evidence."

Davenport said nothing, but his look confirmed that was exactly what he was thinking. He casually spun his tennis racket in his right hand.

From across the court a man, also dressed in tennis togs, approached them. Kit recognized him as Judd Ashe, the deputy district attorney who had prosecuted Juan Chavez, Corazón's brother. Kit had proved Juan's innocence and Ashe, though ambitious, had accepted the truth. She wondered if Clara Dalton Price would be as forthcoming.

"Well, Kit Shannon," Ashe said amiably.

"Hello, Judd."

"Am I interrupting anything?"

"Miss Shannon was just leaving," Davenport said.

"I am going to get a court order," Kit said, "to grant me access to the house."

"On what grounds?" Davenport said.

"The interests of justice," Kit said.

Davenport sniffed. "You still have much to learn about the interests of justice around here. I am the People's representative, and you'll find the judges grant me great deference."

Kit knew that was true. Criminal defense lawyers were not looked upon with the same favor as the prosecutors. Most of the judges in Los Angeles seemed to regard them as constitutional nuisances—necessitated by law, perhaps, but the sooner they were out the courtroom doors, the better.

"I will see that scene," Kit said, though she did not know how she would do it without judicial approval.

"You try it," Davenport said, "and I will have you thrown in jail and prosecuted to the full extent of the law."

———————

A bouquet of red roses flew inside Kit's office door, with a hand attached.

"That better be Ted Fox," Kit said.

It was. His smile sparkled as if nothing had happened.

"Please accept these as a small token of my absence," Ted said. "And a pledge of my undying love and devotion."

Kit, still hot about her conversation with Davenport, took the flowers with a grateful smile. "If I didn't know better, I would swear you were trying to butter me up, Mr. Fox. But your charms will need to work a bit harder, sir. Where were you?"

Ted walked to Kit's window, overlooking Broadway. "You love me, don't you?" he said.

His voice sounded lilting, the familiar way he teased. "I don't know," Kit said, smelling the roses. "The man I love would not seek to allay my fears with mere roses. A nice dinner out would—"

She stopped as Ted turned from the window.

"I am in earnest, Kit. If you love me, you must not ask me where I was last night. I will not make up a lie, because I could never lie to you. I just want you to know that I had some dealings that must, for the time being, stay unknown to you. At the right time I'll tell you everything. Can you accept that?"

Trouble. That's what Kit thought. Ted had a past that had, at some points in his life, caught up with him.

After a long moment, Kit said, "I will accept whatever it is you tell me, Ted. But I don't ever want you to forget that I will help you whenever, and wherever, you need it."

He came to her and put his arm around her waist. "You do love me," he said. "And that is no blarney." He pulled her to him and kissed her softly.

Corazón Chavez chose that moment to enter the office with a squeal.

"It's all right, Corazón," Kit said. "My impetuous beau was just leaving."

"Leaving?" Ted said.

"To get ready for the dinner to which you are escorting me."

"All right," Ted said, "but I warn you. I'm feeling very charming tonight."

Kit fanned herself. "I shall try to resist."

"Resistance is pointless." Ted started for the door. "Surrender is advised." He bowed to Corazón, who was still standing silent and sheepish, and left.

"I am sorry, Miss Kit," Corazón said.

"Think nothing of it. What have you got there?"

Corazón handed Kit a paper with a list of names. "The ones from that *Gazette*."

"Good work," Kit said. There appeared to be somewhere around twenty names, two of which she recognized. "Unfortunately, this means more work than we've ever seen before."

"Is true?"

Kit nodded. "What we have here are twenty or more potential suspects, people with a motive to do Gerald Mahoney harm. The police are not interested. They have their suspect. We, on the other hand, must search for the needle in the haystack."

Corazón squinted in thought. "I have a needle, I think."

Kit looked at her quizzically.

"The doctor, Tanner," Corazón said.

"You found him?"

"At his old office," Corazón explained, "there was a woman, working for a man of, how you say, real estate. She did not want to talk to me, so I did what you say with the grease."

Kit closed her eyes and smiled. "You greased her palm?"

"With the dollars that you gave me. She wanted to talk then. We met outside on the street. And she told me the doctor he has changed his name."

"To what?"

"She did not wish to tell. Should I have used more of the grease?"

"Don't you worry," Kit said calmly. "Tell me what more this woman said about the doctor."

"After the trial that he is having against the *Gazette*, the doctor he is drinking more and more. He can no work. The people, they do not come to him."

"He was ruined," Kit said. "Even though the *Gazette* story may have been false, losing his libel case convinced everyone in town that the story was true."

"Sí. He went away."

"Did this woman know where he went?"

"She said he is going to go to San Francisco, but then she said he is not."

"I don't understand."

Corazón looked at her notes. "He changed his name, she says, and did not go away. She saw him once a year ago. He came to her office and he was having a beard. He was dressed in rags. He told her he is going to kill Mr. Mahoney."

Kit put her hand on Corazón's arm. "Is she sure that he said this?"

Corazón nodded. "She said she is scared and will not forget his eyes. His eyes are full of hate."

"Did he say anything else?"

"The woman said he began to cry. She asked him why. He said it is because this man took his daughter from him."

"Dr. Tanner has a daughter?"

"This is what the woman said. But she does not know if this is the truth. She is wanting to help him, but he said no—he only wants to have the money that he has left in a place in the wall."

"What does that mean?"

"He was hiding money in a secret place. He was leaving it there until he needed it."

"I wonder why he didn't take it when he left."

Corazón shook her head. "The woman says he is crazy. She did not believe he had this money. But then he showed her where the brick is loose, and inside there is the money."

"Did she say how much?"

"To her it looked like very much."

"And that is the last she saw of this man?"

"Sí."

"Does she have any idea where he might be?"

"She says no but thinks his daughter would know, if we can find her."

"Did you get the name of the daughter?"

"She did not say. Miss Kit, I am sorry."

"Don't be sorry. You've done well. You are getting to be very good at your job."

Corazón beamed.

"But I have a feeling," Kit said, "both of our jobs are going to be getting more dangerous. I was almost sheared by a crazy gardener." Kit told Corazón about the incident. "My leg is still aching from that. If you're going to be snooping, and I'm going to be asking tough questions, we're bound to run into some very unfriendly people. I wonder if you and I shouldn't prepare ourselves."

"How?" Corazón asked.

"I've got a wild idea."

"Oh good," Corazón said. "I like when you have those!"

16

A MAN NAMED H. IRVING HANCOCK had opened a studio in Los Angeles for the teaching of the ancient art of jiu-jitsu. His lecture on "The Physical Training for Women by Japanese Methods" was published in the Sunday edition of the *Examiner*, and it was from this that Kit got the idea she and Corazón might benefit from such training.

The physical strength of Japanese women, Mr. Hancock wrote, *dates back to remote antiquity. In feudal Japan, three thousand years ago, the men did the fighting, but the women, who were to raise the sons of the next generation, were required to understand all the principles of jiu-jitsu. Grown men and women practiced the rigorous system, and the women did not take refuge in their sex from any aspect of it.*

He promised that any woman who would undertake to train in his studio would, with practice, be able to conquer an opponent possessing greater size and strength.

Kit and Corazón found the studio. It was on the first floor of the YMCA building on Broadway. On the large carpeted floor a group of about ten women, dressed in loose gymnasium clothes and low-heeled shoes, sat and stretched. An older gentleman, small of stature, sat cross-legged and serene in front of the group.

"To the side now!" he commanded, and the women, as one,

raised their arms in the air and leaned side to side, as if on a listing ship.

Then the man, seeing Kit and Corazón, clapped his hands and said, "Rest!" Without pushing off with his hands he raised himself from the floor and walked forward.

"You are most welcome," he said. He was not quite so tall as Kit. His face seemed old, perhaps seventy, but there was a vigor underneath that gave the impression of vibrant youth. He wore what looked like a white robe, a black belt of cloth around it, and white pants. His feet were bare. "My name is Hancock. Are you here for instruction?"

"Yes," Kit said. "I am Kathleen Shannon, and this is my assistant, Corazón Chavez." She watched closely to see Hancock's reaction to Corazón. Mexicans were not welcomed in certain quarters, and if he showed the least hesitation toward Corazón, Kit was going to walk out.

But he extended his hand warmly to Corazón. "I am honored by your presence."

"Tell me, Mr. Hancock," Kit said. "Are the claims made in your ads true? Is it possible for us to use these techniques on those who are stronger than we are?"

Hancock smiled warmly. "The claims are true. But you must remember that the way of jiu-jitsu is peaceful above all. It may be used to incapacitate an aggressor but not to inflict needless punishment."

Hancock put his arm out and instructed Kit to place one of her hands on his forearm, and the other underneath his hand. She did so. Then he told her to put pressure on this hand, upward, and when she did his entire body bent over.

"I'm sorry!" Kit said, releasing him immediately.

"No," he replied. "You have just demonstrated for yourself the power of jiu-jitsu. Well done." He stood up straight again. "When would you like to begin?"

"Would tomorrow be too soon?" Kit said.

"Not at all," Hancock said. "Shall we say four-thirty?"

"We shall," Kit said.

"I look forward to it." Hancock bowed and returned to his class.

Outside the studio, Corazón clapped with glee. "This will be much fun!" she said.

Kit was about to agree when a large shadow passed over her. Turning, she saw a big man entering the building, heading for the wooden stairs that led upward. From the back she thought she recognized the giant frame of Axel Bagby, Gerald Mahoney's bodyguard.

When she looked down and saw the fancy skin boots, she knew she was right.

"Come on," Kit said to Corazón, leading her back inside the YMCA. As they proceeded up the wooden stairs, Kit could hear the thumping of feet and the sound of punching bags being pummeled in rhythmic cadence. The smell of sweat and canvas was pungent. Entering the smoke-filled gymnasium, Kit saw a flurry of pugilistic activities, not the least of which was a couple of warriors sparring in the large boxing ring.

"Jab, will ya!" an impatient, gravelly voice screamed.

"Work the body! Work the body!" a higher, scratchier voice shouted.

Corazón slipped her hand into Kit's arm. The pair stood for a moment, watching. Kit saw Bagby ducking through a door marked Changing Room.

And then, almost as if cued by a conductor, the various sounds of the gym stopped, save for a few snaps of a jumping rope in a far corner.

All eyes, it seemed, were suddenly trained on Kit and Corazón. And then the jump rope stopped, too.

A man whistled a leering tribute to the presence of women on the premises. This was followed by a symphony of similar whistles and a few shouts of male invitation.

The man with the voice like rocks, who wore a tight shirt over a muscled body, stormed over to Kit. His face looked like it had been folded and unfolded several times.

"What are you doing in my gym?" the man said.

Kit put her shoulders back. "Waiting to speak to a gentleman."

The man looked around, then back at Kit. "I don't see no gentlemen here." A few voices laughed in response.

"A pug, then," Kit said. "I believe that's what you call them."

More laughter. A voice said, "She's got you there, Al."

The man called Al stuck out his chin. "Unless you ain't noticed," he said, "this here is a boxing gym. We got men working here. And you and your servant there are disturbin' the peace."

"She is not a servant," Kit said sharply. "You will do well to remember that."

"Look here, lady, I got things to——"

"I am here to speak to someone, and I will not be leaving until I do."

Smoldering rage lit Al's eyes. "I say who comes and goes in my own place!"

"And I say this is a public facility owned and operated by the Young Men's Christian Association."

"Yeah," Al shot back. "Young men. I don't see no *W* in them letters."

"Sir, I am not here to debate matters of the alphabet. I am a lawyer and I wish to speak——"

"Lawyer!" Al bellowed a laugh.

"That's right, Al," a man in the crowd said. "I seen her in the paper!"

Al's eyes bobbed and weaved.

"I wish to speak to someone on a matter of law," Kit said.

"The only law here is layin' leather on skin. You got a problem with that, take it up with the central committee."

"I am not leaving until I speak with Mr. Axel Bagby," Kit said. She was aware somehow that the entire gym was thinking this exchange was like two pugilists in the center of a ring.

Al turned and shouted, "Beans!"

As if emerging from the dark wooden walls themselves, a large man with a bull chest and dressed in boxing togs strode forward.

"Beans," Al said to the man, "will you be so kind as to show these ladies out?"

Beans smiled. His front teeth were missing. "Sure, Cap'n," he said.

Kit's body tightened into a knot as a huge paw reached out and gripped her arm. Kit yanked it away. "Don't touch me," she said.

"I'm yer escort," Beans said in a nasal tone. "Come along."

He grabbed Kit again, this time harder. Without thinking about it, Kit jerked free and gripped the man's arm the way Mr. Hancock had just shown her. With one hard push, Kit had the large man on his knees, shouting in pain.

Al shouted, "Let him up! Let him up!" The look of horror in Al's eyes made Kit immediately relent.

Al knelt at Beans's side. "Tell me you're all right, champ!"

"It hurts," Beans said, sounding like a 250-pound baby.

Al stood and faced Kit. "Don't you realize this is Beans Lassiter, the heavyweight champion of the whole Pacific Coast?"

"Sir," Kit said, "I am sorry I did that, but you did not leave me any choice. What do you mean by having one of your thugs man-handle me?"

"Pugs," Al snapped.

"It hurts bad," Beans whined.

"What's all this?" a new voice interjected. Axel Bagby had arrived. When he saw Kit's face his eyes grew wide with surprise and anger.

"You!" Bagby said.

————————

The boy shouted at the top of his lungs. "Read about the killer society lady! Her dark secret exposed! Right here in the *Gazette*!"

Celia heard each word as if it were a shout in her ear, and each word was like a sword. She had just exited N. B. Blackstone's on Main Street. She wanted to bring Louise something extra special— an Oxford cheviot waist, a new lace collar—not so much to ease the pain, but rather to change the subject.

Now she forgot all about the package in her hands. She felt as if the entire city of Los Angeles were staring at her, mocking her in her pretensions to social acceptance. If a hole had opened up in the sidewalk right then, she would have jumped into it.

Louise. What if Louise hears?

A horse-drawn cab got her home in less than fifteen minutes. Celia burst through the door. "Louise!"

No answer.

Celia hurried through the hall to the rear of the house. "Louise?" Again, silence. A desperate fear took hold of her. Something was terribly wrong.

She flew up the stairs. The door to Louise's room was open. It was a mess inside. Bed table overturned, drawers withdrawn from the wooden chest, and clothes strewn about.

And then Celia saw it, on the floor, crumpled. Even in that condition she could see quite clearly the pen and ink rendering of her own face under the large, ugly letters that spelled *Gazette.*

Louise *had* seen it. And now she was gone.

17

"I GOT NOTHING TO HIDE— from you or nobody." Axel Bagby puffed out his considerable chest, as if daring someone to strike it.

"Then you won't mind answering a few questions," Kit said. They stood just outside the gym's door, in a little alcove that held photographs of various boxers. It smelled of old leather.

"You think I had something to do with Mr. Mahoney's killing?" Bagby said. "Or are you just trying to save your client's skin?"

"It is important for me to know why you weren't at the house," Kit said. "Protecting Mahoney was, after all, your job."

"Not at night. Mr. Mahoney keeps—kept—to himself at night. If he wanted to go somewheres, he could call me."

"So you claim you were not anywhere near Mahoney's house when he was killed?"

"That's what I'm saying, Toots."

Kit ignored the insult. "Can you prove this?"

Bagby squinted. "I don't have to prove nothing, now, do I?"

"You may have to do it in court."

"How's that?"

"I can force you to answer questions under oath, in a court of law. Of course, if that's what you would prefer . . ."

The large man drew back. "Ask me, then, if you think it'll do you any good."

"Can you tell me where you were on the evening of February 8?"

"Tuesday, was it?"

"Wednesday."

"Ah. I surely can. I was with my pal."

"Does your pal have a name?"

"Don't all pals?" Bagby was smiling as if this were sport.

"Would you like to give me his name?" Kit asked.

"I don't think my pal would like that."

"Mr. Bagby, eventually all this is going to become a matter of record. When I put you on the stand, I will ask you whether you refused to give me this man's name, and if you deny it, my colleague here, Miss Chavez, will contradict your story. Then the jurors will determine which of you is the more truthful, and the district attorney will take a look at a perjury charge." Kit paused for a breath. "All of which is to say, Mr. Bagby, that we can speed things up considerably if you'll cooperate with me, and there will be no need for your public humiliation."

A dark scowl swept across the man's face. "One of these days, Toots, you're gonna go too far."

"I'm waiting, Mr. Bagby."

"Sid Gates is his name, and a finer friend never existed. If you go botherin' him—"

"Me bother someone? Why ever would you get the impression I would do such a thing? Where does he live?"

Bagby folded his massive arms across his chest. "I've told you all I'm gonna."

Kit thought for a moment. "Gates," she said. "Your boots, the ones I saw you in today. Alligator skin, if I'm not mistaken."

Bagby looked as if struck by a stone. "And what of it?"

"There is a Gates Alligator Farm on Mission Road. I'm thinking there is a connection."

A giant sausage of a finger pointed at Kit's face. "Don't be making no trouble for me, unless you want trouble back."

"You have nothing to fear if you tell the truth," Kit said.

———————

The Gates Alligator Farm was a trolley ride and short walk into the eastern section of the city. A bit of an attraction for locals, it had a small, round pool surrounded by a wood and chicken-wire fence. Going down into the pool was a long slide. At certain times of the day the proprietor, dressed in the outfit of an African adventurer, would prod the gators through a chute that led upward to the slide's top. Viewers, who paid a nickel, could then watch as the spiky lizards slid down into the pool, thrashed their considerable tails, and, if lucky, snapped angrily at some wide-eyed spectator.

Kit and Corazón arrived just as the last alligator took his ride and splashed into its destination. Kit counted ten alligators around the edge of the pool, none looking pleased at being a public spectacle.

"I do not like them," Corazón observed to Kit. "They remind me of . . ."

"The district attorney?" Kit said.

Corazón laughed.

As the small crowd dispersed, heading for the refreshment stand, Kit walked around the perimeter of the fence. One of the alligators fixed its reptilian eyes on her, as if anticipating lunch.

The man in the safari clothes was tall and ropey. He held a bamboo pole that he used as a prod. He was closing the gate to the inner circle when Kit reached him.

"Mr. Sid Gates?" Kit said.

"That'd be me," he said.

"Are you acquainted with Mr. Axel Bagby?"

Gates thrust the bamboo pole into the soft ground, where it stuck. "Who wants to know?"

"My name is Kathleen Shannon, and this is my associate, Corazón Chavez. It is a matter of law."

"Law, eh? I got nothing to worry about on that score. I run a legitimate business here."

"No one said you didn't, Mr. Gates."

"Then what have I got—" Gates stopped, looking past Kit. "Hey, rummy!" he shouted.

Over by the slide chute a dirty-looking man was flailing away at something with a bamboo pole. He looked frightened.

Gates ran over and jerked the man away, then pushed him to the ground. "I told you never do that!" Gates screamed at the man. "You want to work here, you follow my rules."

The pathetic man on the ground, unshaven and wide-eyed, crawled backward, as if trying to escape an alligator or something worse. Maybe that something worse was Sid Gates.

For a final indignity, Gates took up the pole and whipped the man once across the legs. The man screamed and rolled on the ground. Gates raised the pole once more.

Kit stepped in front of him. "You've no cause to treat a man like that," she said.

The unfortunate fellow on the ground stared up in stark disbelief, then took the opportunity to scramble away.

Gates spat on the ground. "You telling me now how to run my own place?"

"Common decency, Mr. Gates," Kit said.

"You want decency, you better look somewhere else than a gator farm. Decency'll get you bit."

"Without a little human kindness, Mr. Gates, civilization will end up like that." Kit pointed to the alligator pool, where the giant lizards looked ready to snap at one another.

"Suppose you state your business, then leave me to mine?"

"Axel Bagby claims that he was with you night before last. Can you verify that?"

"Sure," Gates said.

"You didn't think about it," Kit said.

"Don't have to. If Axel says I was with him, I was."

"I would like you to verify it yourself, Mr. Gates. I would like you to think back and tell me where you and Mr. Bagby were on that night."

Gates rolled his eyes toward the sky. Behind him, in the pen, an alligator snapped at a bird that had landed on the fence. The bird quickly vacated the premises.

"Now, if I recall," Gates said, "me and Axel had a few drinks around six o'clock or so."

"Where?"

"I don't remember exactly. We go to lots of places."

"How long were you with him that evening?"

"Oh, hard to say. Early morning hours, I'd guess."

"Please don't guess, Mr. Gates."

"I won't, then. Axel and me were together from early evening until after midnight."

"But you can't tell me where you might have gone with him? Please think about it, as this is important."

"Now, let me give you a little piece of advice. You see them gators?" Gates looked into the pen. "They don't think. They snap. People can be like that, too. You go around pestering citizens with questions, and you just might get that pretty little head of yours in the jaws of something that won't be so friendly."

"Irish lawyers don't chew so easily," Kit said.

18

"YOU OUGHTA TELL THAT COWBOY what he can do with his spying!" Gus yelled over the spurt of the automobile engine.

"He's under the authority of the President of the United States!" Ted shot back. "You don't thumb your nose at that."

"Why not? This is America. We can do what we want. And what we want to do is make aeroplanes without anybody else tellin' us what to do."

The scent of orange groves and grape vineyards engulfed the afternoon air as Ted guided the Oldsmobile Runabout toward Pasadena. He was going to bring Kit and Corazón a basket of oranges from the farmers' market, and Gus had come along for the ride. Only Gus was not at all sunny. He was as sour as a persimmon, and he didn't keep his mood to himself.

Ted wanted to laugh at his friend's outburst, but part of him was growing angry with Gus Willingham. He was used to his friend's sourness, but usually it was benign. This, however, related to an important government venture.

"Are you saying you're not in this with me?" Ted shouted.

"That's what I'm saying."

"Not even for your own country?"

Gus folded his arms. "What if you end up in Germany?"

"Then I'll learn to eat bratwurst." Ted waited for Gus to at least smile. The mechanic kept his lips tight and angry. Ted said, "We are not at war. I'll be back in two shakes of a lamb's tail."

"That's two shakes we won't be working on the plane."

"You have to think of more than yourself, Mr. Willingham."

Gus grunted into the air.

But he had Ted doubting himself all of a sudden, and that was one thing he did not want. He knew his patriotic duty. He was a supporter of Roosevelt and his big-stick diplomacy, and he knew the world was not as safe as it could be.

And his growing knowledge of God's Word convinced him that a good Christian was a good citizen, and where a government's aims were good, then it was a Christian's duty to help.

There were threats abroad, and if his knowledge of aeroplanes would help in any effort to keep a lasting peace, he had to offer it to the United States government. Even if it meant temporary separation from Kit.

But he already had in mind what to do about that. A plan. And he was going to drop it on Kit Shannon that very night.

————

In the little town of Jewel, forty miles north of Los Angeles, a cold wind blew down from the San Gabriel mountains. No one on the main street seemed to take notice of the slight, solitary woman with the shawl wrapped around her head as she walked toward the edge of town.

Louise Harcourt did not care if anyone noticed. She was adrift in the world now, beyond hope. She did not want hope. She wanted to die.

But suicide was out of the question. She did not have enough courage.

A man on a horse loped by, kicking up bursts of dust. He wore the outfit of a working cowboy—his clothes and hat covered with the dirt and the grime of long, laborious days—but he did not seem as dirty on the outside as Louise felt on the inside. He rode right on past, without so much as a glance at her. She might have been a ghost.

How could her mother have kept the awful secret from her all these years? Now her mother's disgrace was her own. How could she ever face her friends again? They would talk about her behind her back. Forever.

And John. He had betrayed her, too. After she had pledged her heart and soul to him.

It was too much. Couldn't she die now? Couldn't God arrange that?

Gnarled oak trees squatted at the end of Main Street, looking like odious trolls from some dark fairy tale. There was a one-room schoolhouse and a white church on the other side of the street. Signs of hope that she found no hope in.

She heard hoofbeats and turned around.

The cowboy was coming back toward her. He stopped his horse.

"Evening," he said.

Louise did not want to speak to him. But years of training in the social graces compelled her to say, "Good evening."

"You look a little lost."

"No . . ." But she knew she was, though not in the way he meant.

"You need a hand?"

"No, sir."

"How about a place to stay? You need a room?"

Of course she would need some sort of lodging. She felt as if she were emerging from a bad dream. What had she expected to find here? A place that was not Los Angeles.

But a strange man offering a room to a young woman? Louise told herself to be careful.

"I know a place you could stay," the cowboy said. He got off his horse and took off his hat. "Name's Dan. I'll walk you over and you can decide for yourself."

It seemed reasonable, and Dan was polite. And it was starting to get even colder.

"All right," Louise said.

Dan walked her to a two-story building on the edge of town. It had a saloon at ground level, with swinging doors painted a garish red. Louise had expected to hear the strains of a piano playing ragtime, as that was how such places were portrayed in the dime novels. But there was no sound coming through the doors, though Louise imagined the men inside were up to the business of drinking.

Dan took Louise around the back and up some wooden stairs to a door at the top. The door was painted a sky blue with clouds and gold stars. Dan knocked on the door. A second or two later Louise heard a scuffling inside, but no one came to answer. Dan knocked again.

"Who is it?" a voice from inside snapped loudly. Though it sounded like a woman's voice, it also made Louise think of an angry animal roused from sleep.

"It's Dan Curtis."

"Danny!"

The sound of a latch, and then the door swung open like a jaw. Filling the doorway was a woman with the brightest colored hair Louise had ever seen—a burnt orange that might have been an amateur artist's idea of a forest fire. Her face was powdery white. Louise could not see the woman's eyes, as the woman squinted at the light of day. Her camisole was barely covered by a sheer robe. The scent of cheap perfume and stale cigars wafted out from the doorway.

"You have good news or money?" the woman said to the cowboy.

Dan laughed. "Maybe a little of both, Eve."

The woman called Eve looked at Louise from head to foot.

"I think this little girl's in trouble," Dan said.

19

"YOU ARE NOT YOURSELF TONIGHT," Ted said.

Kit looked at him, his face reflected in the moonlight. "Who am I, then?"

They were seated in the park along the banks of the Los Angeles River. The night was warm, the waters a gentle rush. This was a part of the city Kit had come to love. The water gave hope for the future. In this arid part of the state, water was essential, and the river here was a symbol of promise. There was some talk that the city fathers were looking for a way to import water from California's central valley, but for now the river was the heart-stream of the town.

"You are thinking about your trial," Ted said. "I know you. You don't do anything halfheartedly."

"Including loving you, I might add." She did love him, now more than ever. Ted had become a part of her. His faith had grown strong since he had embraced Christianity. His financial work for the Bible Institute was superb, and even his labor on the aeroplane seemed to have taken on a new vigor.

She saw the flowering of God's spirit in him as he studied the Bible and lived by its principles. If only other men in the city— indeed, the country—had the same devotion, there would be a new revival in the land.

Ted's smile faded slowly as he took Kit's hand. "I must go out of town for a while," he said.

Kit was surprised. He had not mentioned anything that would necessitate a trip. "Does this have something to do with the affairs you cannot speak about?"

"Yes."

"Answer me one thing." She squeezed his hand in return. "Are you in trouble of any sort?"

"No, Kit."

"Are there people involved whom you cannot mention?"

"Am I on the witness stand now?"

"I didn't mean to cross-examine you."

"You are forgiven. I leave tomorrow."

"Tomorrow! When will you return?"

"I don't know as yet, but I have it all figured out. Are you ready to hear how?"

Kit swallowed, seeing a playful excitement in his eyes but beyond that a deep seriousness. "I'm ready," Kit said, though she was not so sure.

"We get married," Ted said.

"Yes, of course—"

"Tonight."

"Tonight?"

"Right now. We'll hunt up a justice of the peace and exchange our vows."

A charge of electricity crackled through Kit's body. "But a church wedding, that's what we wanted."

"And we'll have it," Ted said. "When I get back. We'll have tonight together as man and wife. You have a big trial coming up and need to give it your full attention. By the time you're all done, I should be, too. I can return and we will repeat our vows in church, with all of our friends around."

Kit was starting to feel as giddy as Ted sounded. *Why wait?* she asked herself. She had almost lost Ted once before, and part of her was quietly afraid that it could happen again if he went away. Why not marry tonight?

"You look unsure," Ted said.

"I only—"

"Let me convince you." He took her in his arms then and kissed her. And the waters of her spirit churned with a rush of desire.

"Yes," she said. "Now."

————

The telescope Corazón Chavez used was the finest to be had in the city. Kit had told her to spare no expense in getting one that worked well, and she had found a scope at Davis & Sons, which specialized in all manner of eyewear and magnifications. Corazón knew this telescope would become an important weapon in the gathering of information. If she was to be an investigator, she was going to be the best.

Corazón watched the activity within the Gates Alligator Farm. Mostly it was quiet in the moonlight. She was seated in the one-horse carriage across Mission Street. In the silvery light she could see, in the circular pen, the dark, shadowy figures of deadly reptiles.

But alligator gazing was not her purpose. She focused her attention on the shack behind the slide, where she had seen Gates's assistant, the one Gates had whipped, disappear. Earlier, Gates himself had donned his odd hat and yelled something at the man, then took his own carriage away from the farm.

Presently, the man emerged from the shack and latched it shut, finally fitting a padlock on the latch. He dusted his hands and began to walk toward the street.

Corazón had positioned her carriage near a sturdy oak tree on the south side of the grounds. The man walked out along the north side and continued on in that direction. Corazón kept him in her telescopic sights, then followed behind in her carriage. She kept a good distance between them so as not to be seen or heard.

Finally, after about a mile or so, the man entered a door of some sort. Corazón snapped her horse to a faster gait and arrived to see it was a saloon. She could hear voices inside, men laughing. Most of the words were in Spanish. This was a Mexican section of town, one of the older parts of the city. Knowing that, Corazón did not feel afraid for what she was about to do.

She entered the smoke-filled room. A plain, unfinished bar ran along one wall, set upon two large wooden casks at either end. There were no fancy furnishings, just tables and chairs and spittoons on a plain hardwood floor.

And Corazón was the only woman in the place. There was a momentary lapse in virtually all conversation. Then she heard two men conversing behind her.

Mira. Una mujer muy hermosa.

Me gusto su pelo.

She ignored the leering comments about her beauty and hair as liquor talk. But she was ready to speak or move quickly should the situation warrant it. These were her people. She felt confident she could handle anything.

Looking to the back, she saw the man she had followed slump into a chair and rub his face with his hands. He looked tired and worn thin, his clothes loosely thrown over his frame.

Corazón did not hesitate in approaching.

The man was stunned at her presence. He squinted at her. "I know you?" His voice was scratchy.

"I saw you at the alligators," Corazón said.

The man's eyebrows raised. "That's right! You and that redhaired woman, the one who put the thumb to Sid Gates! Who is she? Who are you?"

"I may sit, yes?"

"Sit, yes. Order you a drink?"

"No, thank you."

"Mind if I?"

Corazón shook her head.

"Hey, *amigo,*" the man shouted toward the bar. "Whiskey." His face was unshaven and his eyes had a pinkness around brown irises. He seemed to be in his middle fifties, though it was hard to tell with fatigue hanging over him.

"Now," he said to Corazón, "who are you?"

"My name is Corazón Chavez. I work for Miss Kathleen Shannon, the lawyer."

"Lawyer?" His face became a scowling question mark. "What's that have to do with me?"

"Please, and your name?"

The man paused before answering. "Martin," he said. "Just Martin."

The bartender slammed a small glass in front of the man. "The bottle, too," Martin said.

"*Dinero,*" the bartender said firmly.

"They think I don't pay," Martin said, fishing in his pocket. He handed the bartender a silver coin. "I always pay my debts." Martin drank his whiskey in one gulp. "All right, what is it you want?"

Corazón cleared her throat. "You have worked for the man Gates how long?"

"You mind telling me why you're asking? I don't much like talking to strangers."

"It is having to do with Miss Shannon's client. His name it is Truman Harcourt, and he is accused of murder."

The light of familiarity shone in Martin's eyes. "Oh yeah. I read about that. But that's got nothing to do with me."

The bartender returned with the whiskey bottle and left it. Martin poured himself another shot.

"You know well the man Gates?" Corazón asked.

"He pays me to do what he won't do himself," Martin said. "What of it?"

"You think this man he tells the truth?"

Martin looked suspicious. And, Corazón thought, a little frightened. "I don't get paid to think."

"Gates says that on the night of the killing of Mahoney, he was with the man Axel Bagby. Do you know this to be true?"

Martin paused with the whiskey at his lips. "You trying to pin this on Bagby?"

"Pin?"

"Listen, little one, you don't know what you're getting into here. You better drop this item like the hot potato it is and move along."

"But—"

"You hear what I said?" He interrupted himself by drinking the shot and immediately pouring another. "What's done is done, and the devil has his due. Now leave me alone before you get me fired."

"Please, if you will—"

Martin pounded the table with his fist. "Get out!"

Corazón stood. She was aware that the entire place was as silent as a cave. Something was wrong here, very wrong, but she was not sure what. The place seemed to have an aura about it—of something bad. Evil.

"If your mind change," Corazón said, "come to Miss Shannon. She can help."

"Nobody can help," Martin said.

Corazón wanted to stay and seek more information, but her instincts told her this was not the time or place. She turned and headed for the door but was stopped by something enormous walking in. Before she knew it, a giant hand grabbed her arm. Hard.

"Well," said Axel Bagby. "What have we here?"

20

THE CARRIAGE CLIP-CLOPPED through the night streets of Los Angeles toward Kit's office. Ted held the reins with one hand and with his other arm embraced Kit. She was nearly delirious with this impetuous decision, but she did not fight it. She wanted delirium tonight. She wanted Ted tonight and forever.

They would stop at Kit's office to get a marriage license form, which would need to be presented to the justice of the peace. Then quick trips to their homes for overnight belongings. In two hours they would be able to present themselves to the justice of the peace in Boyle Heights, who advertised that he was always on call because "love never sleeps."

Ted had mentioned a quaint hotel he had seen on his recent jaunt into Pasadena. There they would spend the first night of their married life.

It was all like a schoolgirl dream, but every bit of it was as real as the life in Kit's veins.

She breathed in the night air. Its freshness filled her lungs. *Thank you, Lord. Thank you for giving Ted Fox to me.*

Ted pulled the carriage to a stop in front of 238 W. First Street. Kit moved to jump down, but Ted's arm pulled her back.

He kissed her. "Hurry," he said.

She did not have to be prompted. Up the stairs she ran, like a child playing tag, down the corridor toward her office. And suddenly stopped.

Celia Harcourt was sitting on the ground, slumped against Kit's door.

Fearing Celia was injured or had fainted, Kit knelt beside her. Celia's eyes were red. She seemed drained and hopeless.

"Miss Shannon, I don't know what to do!" Celia cried. "I am so desperate—I can't go on. I know you are just my lawyer, but I have nowhere else to turn."

"Tell me what's happened."

"Louise has run away," Celia said, her voice choked off by sobs. She then took a deep breath to try to calm herself. "She read the story in the *Gazette*. That and the loss of her fiancé has been too much for her. I blame myself."

"No," Kit said softly. "That will do no good."

"But it is my fault. Everything."

"How do you know Louise has run off?"

Celia wiped her eyes with the back of one hand. "Her room. She took some clothes. There is no sign of her." Moans poured out of Celia in mournful waves.

Kit embraced Celia. The woman was shaking with tears. "Don't you worry. We will find Louise." Kit said it without knowing how.

"Do you think we can?" Celia said.

"I will do everything possible," Kit said.

"You would do that for me?"

"Gladly. Do you have any idea where she might be?"

"I cannot think," Celia said. "She has school friends."

"We will start there," Kit said. "God will help us, Celia."

There was a long pause, then a sigh from Celia Harcourt. "I wish my faith were stronger."

"Do you have a church?" Kit asked.

"Yes," Celia said, "though I must confess I have not felt the presence of God there."

"Who is your minister?"

"Dr. Edward Lazarus."

Lazarus! The man who had debated against Kit over the accuracy of the Bible. She might have known. His brand of Christianity, if it could still be called that, was in the grip of progressive thinking, which was intent on rationalizing God's supernatural power right out of the faith.

"We have much to pray about," Kit said. "But first let us get you home."

Ted was still sitting in the carriage when Kit came down with Celia Harcourt. His face registered surprise but then almost immediate understanding. He nodded at Kit.

"Where to?"

"We must take Mrs. Harcourt home. I need to be with her."

———

Axel Bagby's grip on Corazón's arm felt like iron claws. She tried to pull away, but it was no use.

"I asked you what you're doin' here," Bagby said, glancing again toward the back where Martin sat. Corazón wished now she'd had her jiu-jitsu lessons so she might escape this brute.

"Let me to go," she said. Bagby grunted and pulled her toward Martin's table. She felt like a rag doll, helpless.

"You been talkin'?" Bagby said angrily as Martin looked down at his drink. Bagby slammed his other hand on the table, making the bottle of whiskey dance and teeter. It fell on the floor, shattering, sending the strong aroma of whiskey upward.

"I asked you a question, rummy," Bagby said. Corazón slapped at the huge hand still holding her arm. The hand did not budge.

Martin's eyes were huge with fear as he looked up. "I said nothing," he protested. "I tried to get rid of her."

Bagby did not seem convinced. "Listen, if I ever get wind that—"

Suddenly Bagby stopped and turned around, finally letting go of Corazón's arm. She put her hand on the place his fingers had been. Her arm throbbed.

A voice from the other side of Bagby said, "That is no way to treat a lady." Corazón could not see the man, as Bagby was directly between them. But she could almost feel the menace radiating from Bagby's back.

"Butt out," Bagby said, "while you've still got a face."

The saloon was as quiet as a church now, and Corazón stepped back toward the wall. As she did, she saw the face of the man who had so recklessly intervened on her behalf.

He was Mexican, around thirty, and dressed in a work shirt. He was not nearly Bagby's size, though his shoulders were broad and his arms revealed strong, muscular cords. His black hair was neatly combed, and in a suit of clothes, Corazón thought, he might have been a man from a prominent family.

But this was a barroom, not a drawing room. And Axel Bagby was no manservant.

The young man looked at Bagby steadily and unafraid. "Now, a gentleman would not adopt such a tone," he said. He spoke with only the slightest accent.

Bagby thrust out his chin. "Listen, Mex, I'm givin' you one last chance to save your hide, you hear? Just turn around and walk away, and I'll forget you ever stuck your nose in my business. Savvy?"

The man did not so much as flick an eyelash. And that's when Corazón knew there was going to be trouble. Bad trouble.

"No," she said, fearing that Bagby could end up killing the young man. "Please not to do this."

Bagby looked at her. "You shut up," he said.

"Enough," the young man said. Bagby turned back to the man. The next thing Corazón saw was a fist whipping through the air and landing, full force, on Bagby's jaw.

The big man stumbled backward, hit a chair, and crashed to the floor.

Everyone in the saloon seemed just as stunned as Corazón. That a blow from this young man could have felled the much bigger Bagby was a shock.

To Bagby, too. But only for a moment. He slowly got to his feet, shaking his head and feeling his jaw with one big hand. He formed a chilling half smile on his face, as if he was going to enjoy what he was about to do. He slipped off his coat.

The young man did not move. Corazón was certain this was going to be a brutal beating.

"Please to stop!" Corazón said. She looked at the young man with pleading eyes, hoping he would do the smart thing and get out of there. The young man returned her look, but his face was unconcerned. He nodded at her and smiled. She knew then he had no intention of running away.

No one in the place, not even the bartender, made any movement to stop the combatants. Indeed, it appeared to be a wonderful evening of sport to the patrons. Many of them were smiling.

"I tried to warn you," Bagby said, forming his huge hands into fists the size of small boulders.

The young man assumed a classic boxing stance. His left fist was out in jabbing position, while his right protected his chin. Corazón watched, fascinated. Bagby himself paused a split second, looking upon this man as some sort of curio from a shop on Olvera Street. Or a strange insect that was about to be crushed under his massive foot.

Bagby put up his own fists and wasted no time. A huge roundhouse right seemed to come up out of Bagby's feet and up through his shoulder. Corazón thought she heard the *whiff* as it traveled through the air.

The young man flicked his head backward. Bagby's blow missed his chin by an inch. Then the man shot out a left jab that rocked Bagby's head backward like a punching bag.

Bagby, stunned, shook his head. His eyes widened; his face turned red. He took on all the aspects of a raging animal. Teeth bared, and with a growl, he charged forward.

With a deft sidestep, the man made Bagby miss and landed another blow to Bagby's chin as the big man shot by. Bagby hit the floor with an unceremonious thud.

"*Arriba!*" someone shouted, and suddenly the crowd began echoing the cry of impending victory. "*Arriba! Arriba!*" It reminded Corazón of the bullfights in Mexico, which she had once seen as a little girl. She hated the sport, as she hated needless violence. But she could not deny the thrill that was shooting through her now.

Bagby blinked as he slowly clambered to his feet. Gone was the look of animal rage; it was replaced with a growing awareness that he was being bested at his own game. Yet he could not back down. That would be a fate worse than a beating.

Raising his fists again, Bagby slowly approached the young man as a cautious hunter might stalk a sleeping lion. He began to side-step in a half-circle. The young man merely waited. They watched each other, looking for an opening.

They stayed this way for what felt like minutes. The crowd was now chanting all sorts of cheers and encouragements. Corazón saw some money changing hands as bets were taken.

Finally, Bagby lunged forward with a punch. The man bobbed backward. The punch bounced easily off the man's shoulder. But this time Bagby added a left upper cut. Once more the man pulled backward and Bagby's fist hit nothing but air.

"Stand still, why don't you!" Bagby screamed.

"Apologize to the lady," the other man said.

Looking confused now, as if he could not believe this request, Bagby said, "Are you a crazy man?"

"Apologize."

"I'll kill you first." With that, Bagby reached down and picked up Martin's broken whiskey bottle by the neck. The jagged glass looked like shark's teeth. Bagby raised it to the level of the man's face.

"Stop!" Corazón shouted.

The young man's eyes grew cold now, narrowing in anger. *"Señorita,"* he called to Corazón. *"El sobretodo."*

Bagby's coat. He wanted her to throw him Bagby's own coat.

Corazón did not hesitate. She snatched the coat and tossed it to the man. He immediately wrapped it around his left hand like a huge glove.

Bagby gritted his teeth. Weapon held out, he stepped slowly toward the young man. For one long, agonizing moment everything seemed to stop—the cheering, the movements, the money chang-ing. The air was as still as a man's dying breath.

And then Bagby charged, thrusting forward with the bottle. The young man reached up, deflecting the broken bottle with his covered hand and landing a vicious right blow to Bagby's jaw. Bagby went down again, still holding the bottle. This time he did not get up.

The mysterious man stepped around the sprawled body of Axel Bagby and went to Corazón. "I will see you home now," he said.

21

IT WAS NEARLY MIDNIGHT when Kit finally returned to her home. She had managed to comfort Celia and help her to bed. Expecting darkness, Kit was surprised to find a light on in the study and Corazón waiting for her.

"Everything is all right?" Corazón said. She seemed exhausted but full of some sort of inner energy. It was that quality, the ability to stay active even when tired, that made Corazón such an effective assistant.

"What are you doing up?" Kit said.

Corazón put a hand to her forehead. "Oh, Miss Kit, I am having—how you say? Too much excitement."

"Tell me."

Kit listened as Corazón recounted her evening, starting with the surveillance of the Gates Alligator Farm. Kit got gooseflesh as the tale went on, right up to the point of rescue by the man named Raul Montoya. It was like a story from one of those women's magazines. The damsel in distress.

"And he brought me here," Corazón said. "I ask him to have coffee and wait for you, but he say no and is gone!" Corazón's face got a faraway look. "What am I to do?"

Kit patted her friend's shoulder. "There is nothing you need do. You did nothing wrong. You may perhaps be a witness for the police—"

"No," Corazón said suddenly. "Not that."

Puzzled, Kit said, "What were you speaking of?"

Corazón looked at her feet, shyly.

"I see," Kit said. "The man, Montoya. You would like to see him again?"

Like a little sister with a big secret, Corazón's face was beaming now. "He is so handsome!" she said. "And so brave! I have never had a man, how you say, *campeón*?"

"Champion?"

"Sí!"

"Then we shall have to find him," Kit said.

"Oh no!" Corazón said, her voice full of scandalized fear. "That is not done."

Kit well knew the conventions of courtship, especially among the traditional families of the region. A woman making such an arrangement would be considered less than acceptable.

"Pish," Kit said. "This is a new time in America. Women are allowed to take a little more initiative now. We will not be forward about it—we will be clever. But we certainly won't wait."

With a slow shake of the head, Corazón said, "I do not know. It is so different."

"Was he very handsome?" Kit said.

"Oh, very," said Corazón, her eyes beginning to dance. "And without fear. And without . . . Oh, Kit, you have put the hook into me like the fish, I think."

Kit laughed and embraced her friend. "I just wanted you to hear your own heart. And now that you have, let's talk a little business before bed, shall we?"

"Yes, Miss Kit."

Kit began to move slowly about the room, thinking as she went. "Celia Harcourt has reported that Louise is missing. She believes her daughter has run away from home."

"But why?"

"It seems the parents of her fiancé, John Whitney, instructed their son to break off the engagement because of Truman's arrest."

"This is true?" Corazón said with concern.

"And then the story in the *Gazette* was released about Celia's past. Celia had not told Louise about it. She never wanted Louise to find out. Both of these things must have hit Louise like a train. Celia tells me Louise is rather high-strung by nature, another reason she hid the truth from her. Now, if you were such a girl, what might you do?"

Corazón furrowed her brow for a long moment. "I would go to be with a friend maybe."

"Maybe," Kit said. "Or she might fear becoming an outcast in her social set over this. Just as John Whitney cast her aside. In that case, what would you do?"

"Go far away."

"That leaves endless possibilities. Celia said Louise did not have a lot of money with her. They gave their daughter an allowance, but Louise had no savings of her own. It seems to me that would limit how far she went. She also did not take many of her clothes with her. What does that tell you?"

"Where she is going she must try to find work."

"I will check the train station tomorrow to see if a girl matching her description bought a ticket. That is the place to start."

There was a long pause in the stillness of the room. Then Kit said, "Tomorrow evening is our scheduled meeting with that spiritualist. I want you with me for that."

"I am not having good feelings," Corazón said.

"Nor am I. But it must be done. We will allow him to go through his routine, but both Tom and Mr. Houdini will be there as well. If we can expose this one man, it may lead finally to a crackdown on such frauds in the city."

Corazón heaved a deep sigh. "It is not like when I was a little girl."

"No," Kit said. "As the city grows, so do the problems, so does wickedness. It has always been so." She grasped Corazón's hand. "But God has called us here, hasn't He?"

Corazón did not hesitate. "Sí," she said. "I am a little girl no more."

Ted Fox secured the final latch on the suitcase, ready for the train. That was everything he would need. Three days, four at most, in San Diego. Then he'd be back to support Kit at her trial.

"I still say you're crazy," Gus Willingham intoned. He did not lift a finger to help Ted pack.

"You're such a pal," Ted said. But he was a bit troubled just the same. Was this trip a crazy idea? What could a one-legged dabbler in aviation truly have to offer his government? Chase and Garraty seemed convinced that Ted was the right man at the right time.

"You don't even know these two fellas," Gus said. "How do you know they ain't just trying to steal our design?"

"Trust me," Ted said. "I'm being careful."

"Don't look like it to me."

"Do I look stupid or something?"

Gus nodded.

"Thank you, Mr. Willingham."

"Who says you got to give them the time of day?"

"Duty," Ted said. Duty was important to him, and he recognized that fact. As a boy he had thrilled at stories of the military told by his uncle Rufus, who had been with Robert E. Lee in the last years of the war. He would quote Lee's words often: "Duty, then, is the sublimest word in our language. . . . You cannot do more. You should never wish to do less."

And what did God want in all of this? Ted had been studying the Bible with Reverend Macauley at the Institute and had come to see the role of government in a whole new light. The apostle Paul taught that governments were instituted of God to do good. Also to prevent evil. And Peter taught that Christians were to be in submission to rulers, "for the punishment of evildoers, and for the praise of them that do well."

"Now," Ted said to his mechanic and friend, "you take care of the plane until I get back."

"I might just give it to some other flier." Gus folded his arms across his chest.

"I love you, too," said Ted. Then he added, "Keep an eye on Kit for me, will you? If anything happens you can send a wire to the Hotel Del Coronado."

"Ah, she can take care of herself."

"I have to go to the Institute and finish up some accounting. Want to come with me?"

"No, thank you. I got just as much religion as I need."

"Religion is not going to save that soul of yours, Gus. Religion is just grease."

Gus cocked his head, like a cat looking at a mysterious stranger. "What are you talking about?"

"Grease helps machines go," Ted said, "but it always gets dirty eventually. The engine of our souls doesn't need more grease. It needs to be completely cleaned. The dirt of sin, the grease of phony religion, has to go."

"You never used to talk like this."

"And you know what will happen when you're saved?"

"What?" Gus said with trepidation.

"You'll gain eternal life. And maybe a sense of humor."

Gus did not so much as crack a smile.

22

"ARE YOU READY TO CONSULT the dead?" Harry Houdini said.

"I am ready to expose a fraud," said Kit. "Tom Phelps, a reporter for the *Los Angeles Times*, will be joining us there."

"Capital," Houdini said. "Good publicity. Thank you for arranging this, Miss Shannon. We will do good work together."

Kit and Corazón had met him outside the Orpheum. There was an hour and a half to go before Houdini's next performance. Dressed in stylish evening clothes, Houdini put a smart bowler on his head and walked the ladies down the street.

Kajar, as the man called himself, was waiting at his establishment. He had arranged his séance room in the fashion Kit had read about in an article in *Harper's Monthly*. The room was dimly lit by an oriental lamp. In the middle was a round table topped with green felt, and six chairs were arranged in a circle around it. The smell of incense was faint, like a sigh of sandalwood.

In the center of the table was a small framed chalkboard, as a child might use in school, with a piece of white chalk resting on top.

"The spirits welcome you," Kajar said to the group of four—Kit, Corazón, Harry Houdini, and Tom Phelps. The medium sounded confident and unconcerned.

"I could use some spirits right about now," Tom Phelps said.

"Whiskey. This place gives me the creeps."

"Do not be alarmed," Kajar said. "The spirits here are benign, only wishing to help." He wore a turban, as before, and indicated with his skinny fingers that the party should sit down.

Houdini, Kit noticed, was already trying to get a peek under the table.

"You may look all you wish, Mr. Houdini," said Kajar. "But I assure you there is nothing to be found. My power to communicate with the spirits, and they with me, is housed up here." He pointed to his head.

"You got a ghost in that turban?" Phelps said.

"Please do not mock the spirits," Kajar said. "They are very sensitive."

Corazón had not said a word since entering, and Kit could feel tension rising from her assistant. Kit was a little bit unnerved, as well. The Bible clearly taught that mediums were an abomination and attempting to communicate with the dead a grievous sin. That she was here to expose Kajar as a fraud was of scant comfort. What if he indeed conjured up some power from the dark side? The devil had a long history of using men such as Kajar.

But Kit was firmly convinced the name of Jesus Christ was protection enough. Papa had taught her that. Sometimes that was the only protection he'd had as a circuit-riding preacher going into towns where the devil ruled the roost. Kit silently called on the name of Jesus now, as all were seated at the table.

Kit sat directly across from the medium, with Corazón on her immediate left and Tom Phelps on the right. Next to Phelps, at Kajar's left hand, was Harry Houdini. The magician's eyes were fixed on Kajar, like an owl's on a nocturnal rodent.

"Tonight there is a spirit who wishes to communicate with one of you," Kajar said in a theatrical tone. *Ham actor*, Kit thought. If her friend John Barrymore were here, he would no doubt have left the room. "We must let the cards decide," Kajar added.

With that, the medium reached into his coat pocket and pulled out a set of five cards. Not playing cards, but pasteboards with strange markings on them, multi-colored and Asian in effect. These he shuffled and placed on the table, face down, in a row.

"The All Seeing Eye will decide," Kajar said. "Only the spirits know who will be the chosen one."

"I'll bet," Phelps muttered.

"Please," the medium said in rebuke. "Your skepticism is noted by the spirits. You are a reporter, are you not?"

"That's right."

"Do you seek the truth?"

"General Otis insists on it."

"Then leave your mocking behind or suffer the consequences!"

Silence like a tomb overtook the chamber, though Tom Phelps looked ready to shout some choice obscenity. Kit kicked him under the table. The reporter winced but held his tongue.

Kajar nodded at Kit. "Please, since you have orchestrated tonight's session, be the first to reach out and touch one of the cards. Only one."

Kit glanced at Houdini. He was closely watching every move. He nodded at her to go ahead.

Kit touched a card just to the right of center. Kajar slid that card toward her. "Please do not look at it."

Then Kajar had each of the other three select a card, which he slid in front of them. There remained one card in front of Kajar himself.

"I shall begin," he said. He flipped his card over, revealing a stallion snorting fire from its nostrils. "The card of truth," he said, "that rides throughout the land."

Oh, brother, Kit thought.

Kajar nodded to Houdini, who turned his card over. It showed an Indian fakir in front of a rope that rose to the sky. "The conjurer," Kajar said. "One who must be watched."

Houdini grunted.

Next was Tom Phelps. Kit thought she saw his fingers shaking just a bit as he turned his card to reveal a cat with illuminated eyes. "The curious one," Kajar said. "His curiosity shall be satisfied."

"Ladies," Kajar said, turning first to Corazón. Her eyes were wide and she was breathing quickly. Kit put her hand on her arm.

She wanted to say to Corazón that this was just part of the man's ruse and soon all would be well. God would not be mocked.

Corazón turned over her card. And gasped. A snake, coiled with deadly fangs, seemed to hiss at its bearer.

"The sign of the snake," Kajar said. "Who knows where it will strike?"

Corazón's arm tensed under Kit's hand. Kit almost stood up to call off this charade. Scaring people in the name of his illegitimate trade was over the line of decency. But they had come this far, and Kit knew Corazón well enough to know she would be embarrassed if Kit retreated on account of her.

Now, finally, it was Kit's turn. The card she turned over had only one large eye on it—a dark, brooding orb that seemed to possess forbidden knowledge.

"The All Seeing Eye," Kajar intoned. "You have been chosen."

Chosen by God, bub, thought Kit. But her bravado was definitely being tested here. This man, though a fraud, was certainly adept at setting up a mood.

"Just what does this mean?" Kit inquired.

"You have a loved one, a dear departed one, who wishes to speak to you," Kajar said. "Do you know of whom I speak?"

Suddenly, as if a cold hand gripped her heart, Kit felt a desperation of both longing and fear. She had not expected this. To be called chosen, to be the mark. Her longing came from her desire. Aunt Freddy was not yet a year passed away. And what of her beloved father?

Yes, she thought in a fleeting instant, *if I could speak to Papa or Mama or Aunt Freddy, I would. But this is not of God! Why isn't Mr. Houdini saying anything?*

"Do not be frightened," Kajar said. "And please, all join hands."

Reluctantly, Kit clasped Tom Phelps's hand and Corazón's hand. They would have to play along if they had any hope of catching this man at his tricks. Houdini had counseled patience. Patient she would be.

With the circle completed, Kajar closed his eyes and began to breathe deeply. His chest rose and fell in a rhythmic manner. *Like a blacksmith's bellows*, Kit thought. *Full of hot air.*

Kajar did this for a full minute. And then, in a loud whisper, he announced, "The spirit is here!"

Kit's arms tingled. She heard nothing but the breathing of Corazón beside her and perhaps the pounding of her own heart.

Snap.

The sound so startled Kit she jumped in her chair.

Snap. Snap.

Where was it coming from? The air! The sound was in the room, around them.

"The spirit wishes to speak," Kajar said in a faraway voice. And then, to the room itself, he said, "Come, O spirit, come! We invite you into our presence! We would ask your name!"

Kit felt Corazón's hand squeezing hers harder and harder. Kit tried to give back reassurance with her own grip. She had been very clear with Corazón that they were not here for participation but for exposure. Sitting through the séance was merely part of the process. She had prayed about this decision thoroughly and explained to Corazón that God would use them for a greater good—saving innocents from being taken in by the likes of Kajar the Medium.

For a long moment there was silence, and then Kajar opened his eyes and looked at Kit.

"Do you know someone named Frederica?" he said.

Icy needles ran up the back of Kit's spine. The others at the table looked at her. "Yes," she said.

"She was your—" Kajar closed his eyes, as if listening to someone speaking to him in a whispering voice—"great-aunt?"

It can't be. It just can't. Had this man somehow managed to summon a ghost from the grave, like Saul and the witch of Endor? Kit's mind reasoned quickly. She was not an unknown woman in the city. She'd been in the newspapers. It would have been very easy for Kajar to get information about her and her aunt Freddy.

But Kit had been selected at random in the choosing of cards, she reminded herself. What was this about the All Seeing Eye?

"She wishes to communicate with you," Kajar rasped. "She has something that is very important to her, and she wants you to know it."

Was there going to be a voice?

Kajar reached down to the floor and brought up what looked like a black Chinese hat. He placed this over the framed blackboard.

"You will know now that Kajar speaks the truth about the world of spirit!" the medium said.

In the ensuing moments, the only sound Kit heard was a soft scratching, like chalk on a board!

Everyone in the room, it seemed, tensed at the same moment. All save Kajar.

Then the scratching stopped.

"Ah," Kajar said. He then lifted the hat from the table.

Corazón gasped. Tom Phelps said, "What the . . ."

Houdini scowled.

What had been a blank slate was now covered with a written message. Kajar lifted the slate so Kit could read what it said.

Kit put her hand to her mouth. She felt faint. It was Aunt Freddy's handwriting.

———————

The lights were burning long in the office of the district attorney. John Davenport paced in front of the dark windows, his tie loosened, his hands making weird patterns in the air.

To Clara Dalton Price he looked like a man on the edge of some fever of the nerves. She admired his legal mind but was somewhat distrustful of his agitations. She was a woman who had, by force of will, learned to keep her emotions in check to better carry out her professional duties. Davenport, on the other hand, seemed to often work himself into a frazzle.

And nothing frazzled him more than Kit Shannon.

"She is not to be trifled with," Davenport said for the fourth time that evening. Price was here to discuss the strategy for the preliminary hearing in the Truman Harcourt case.

"No, sir," Price said quietly, for there was nothing to add. Davenport, it seemed, was talking to himself as much as to her.

"I mean, she's a protégée of Earl Rogers, and you know what he'd do," Davenport raged on. "He would do anything to win, including bribing witnesses."

"Has that ever been proven?" Price asked.

"Of course it hasn't been proven! If it had been, I would have personally seen to it that Rogers was ridden out of town on a rail. It's just a matter of catching him, that's all. And when I do . . ." His voice trailed off into insinuations of revenge.

Price thought a moment, allowing her calculating mind to do its work. "There are certainly many ways to skin a mule," she said.

Davenport stopped, turned. "How's that?"

"I was just thinking," Price said. "If this Shannon woman is like Rogers, perhaps a trap may be set."

Davenport's eyes narrowed with interest. He looked at Price with some sort of new appreciation. At least she thought he did. "Do tell," the D.A. said.

"I will need a chance to observe her in court, of course," Price said. "But I will put her to the test. A little prodding might get under her skin, and with the case we have against Harcourt, that may turn her to desperation. Desperate attorneys often make grave mistakes."

For a moment Davenport considered her statement, then slowly shook his head. "There's one thing about Kit Shannon: She's a Christian and acts like it. There has never been a hint of unethical conduct on her part."

"Everyone has a chink in the armor," Price said. "I have seen many Christians fall in my day, to demon rum or money. Or ambition. Shannon strikes me as very ambitious. What is it that the Book says? Pride goeth before destruction?"

Davenport said, "When I hired you, I didn't think I was also getting a theologian."

Price smiled. "My theology is victory," she said. "That is what I worship. I am not going to let Kit Shannon get in the way."

And then, for the first time that evening, John Davenport heaved a sigh of relief. "Mrs. Price, how about you and I have a little drink?"

23

"BUT HOW?" KIT INQUIRED of Harry Houdini. They had convened at a café around the corner from the spiritualist's establishment. It was a working-class place, in which Houdini's white tie looked decidedly out of place. The smell of cabbage and corned beef, a familiar one to Kit, wafted out from the kitchen.

"It will take me some time to figure this out," Houdini said. "He is quite good."

"But still a fraud," Kit said, almost to convince herself. Her heart was still pounding from the shock of seeing Aunt Freddy's handwriting there.

"Looked pretty legit to me," Tom Phelps said.

"There is an explanation for everything," Houdini said.

Tom Phelps put his elbows on the table. "So you say, Mr. Houdini. But you haven't told us how he did it yet."

"Don't rush to conclusions," said the magician. "That is what these fellows desire. He was ready for us."

Kit's mind—trained in the rational art of the law, steeped in the truths of Scripture—was staggering like a punch-drunk fighter. "But the handwriting! Aunt Freddy's. And the message. About Uncle Jasper's monument. That information was not in any of the newspaper obituaries."

Phelps nodded. "Yes, the writing on the slate, that had me spooked."

Corazón, silent as a church mouse, was still wide-eyed.

"If you will suspend judgment," Houdini said to the reporter, "and hold off on your story until another session is arranged, I would be most appreciative."

"I don't know," Phelps said, stroking his chin. "This is a good story."

"Please, Tom," Kit said. "You don't want to run this unless you're convinced beyond a shadow of a doubt."

"That's the lawyer talking," Phelps said. "But you were the one to issue the challenge. Looks to me like Kajar met it."

"No," Kit said firmly. "I cannot believe this was real. The Word of God says—"

"Hang the Word of God," Phelps said. "Maybe there's more to this world than meets the eye. Who is to say there's no spirit world?"

"I, for one," said Houdini. "This man is a fraud."

"Then prove it," said Phelps. "I heard a snapping noise and I didn't see anyone else in that room."

Houdini frowned a bit. "Yes, I was looking for a confederate the entire time. The man, as I say, is good. Give me a day or two to mull this over," he added. "And we will gather one more time. Meanwhile, Miss Shannon, your task is to think of any way this fellow might have gathered information about your departed aunt. There has to be an explanation."

———

Kit and Corazón attended church on Sunday, but Kit's mind did not stop wandering. She could not help feeling clouds of spiritual darkness were gathering and that her concerns were all wrapped up together somehow.

First, there was her concern for Celia Harcourt. So much had happened to her in so little time: Truman's arrest, her story coming to light, and Louise's disappearance. How much could this poor woman take before snapping like a dry twig? It was as if the devil had decided, for his own perverted reasons, to unloose his demons at her. Kit was determined to intervene.

Then there was the whole experience with Kajar. The bizarre séance had thrown Kit. What if this man was truly in league with the powers of darkness? Then perhaps it would not be Celia Harcourt the devil was after but Kit herself.

Finally, Ted's absence was already a heavy weight on her spirit. She could not help but feel there was more to his "business" than even he would allow. A portent of things to come made a nest in her soul.

Kit kept trying to concentrate on the service. Rev. Macauley's text this morning was the fourth chapter of Genesis, the account of Cain.

"We see here," the minister said, "that the heart that ignores its own sinfulness will never cease to be a fugitive and a vagabond in the earth. Cain took his restless heart and dwelt in the land of Nod, on the east of Eden. And here did he build a city."

City, Kit thought. *Los Angeles is a city on the rise, but does it beat with the cadence of Cain's own heart?*

"Cain undertook building a city to divert his thoughts from the consideration of his own misery," Macauley said, "and to drown the clamors of a guilty conscience with the noise of axes and hammers."

What noise is there in my own heart? O Lord, make my soul still before you that I might hear your voice.

"In this mighty city of ours, I see the raising of many buildings. I see great industry and accomplishment, the flowering of art and the creation of means. Yet I do not see the Spirit of God moving in the hearts of the people. God's holy spirit and man's sin cannot live together peacefully; they may both be in the same heart, but they cannot both reign there, nor can they both be quiet there. Instead there will be a perpetual warring in the soul, and in society."

O Lord, help me fight false religion!

When the sermon ended, Kit felt physically and emotionally exhausted—and convinced that a warfare of the spirit was real in this city and in her life. It was as if someone or some group had in their mind but one thing: her destruction. But who? And where?

Or was she merely too taxed by worry to think clearly?

As she exited the church with Corazón, another cause for concern reared up on the sidewalk just outside the building. A group of three men and two women were busy passing out leaflets to the church members. One of the men she recognized immediately.

"Benjamin Stillwater," Kit said aloud.

He was dressed in a sleek black suit with a red ruffle tie fixed with a pearl tiepin. He appeared to be enjoying his work.

"Good day, Miss Shannon," he said with a theatrical bow.

Kit ignored the greeting. Stillwater was a fraud, a self-described clairvoyant who had tried to bilk Aunt Freddy of her estate—and almost succeeded.

"What is going on here?" Kit demanded.

"You are a lawyer, are you not?" Stillwater's mocking tone made Kit feel like practicing her jiu-jitsu on him.

Stillwater handed Kit one of the flyers. "This is the freedom of the press at work."

Kit quickly read the first part.

ATTENTION!

The free practice of religion is being challenged from within your very ranks! Kathleen Shannon, attorney-at-law, is seeking to destroy the work of legitimate practitioners of the spiritual arts. If she is a representative of your brand of Christianity, then we humbly ask you to repent.

"You have the gall to do this on the Lord's Day?" she said. "In front of a church?"

"I am entitled to express my own opinion," Stillwater said.

"And I am entitled to read to you the Word of God. Do you know the book of Ezekiel?"

"Of course."

"Do you believe it?"

"The Bible is a book of aphorisms."

"It is the very Word of God." Kit flipped through the pages of her father's Bible and found the verse in chapter thirteen of Ezekiel. "'Thus saith the Lord God; Woe unto the foolish prophets, that follow their own spirit, and have seen nothing.'"

"You assume I am false," Stillwater said.

Kit held her anger in check. "It is my duty to invite you to repent, sir. Turn your life around before it is too late."

"Why, thank you for thinking of me." He bowed mockingly, then continued on to pass out his leaflets.

Fire raced into Kit's cheeks and she felt herself squeezing the paper so hard her fingertips began to hurt. She read on.

> *For as long as man has been aware of the heavens, he has found many paths to search them. From the oriental mystics to the monks in their abbeys, from the prophets to the stargazers, from holy men to holy mediums, there is a long tradition in various religious practices.*
>
> *In America, we are free to do as we please in matters of religion, so long as we do not harm our neighbor. But Kathleen Shannon, and all that she represents, is the very opposite of Americanism.*
>
> *We demand that she cease and desist in her campaign against the forces of tolerance.*
>
> *We also commend to you the practice of new spiritual methods. Dr. Benjamin Stillwater, a known clairvoyant and distinguished seer, shall be happy to assist you.*
>
> *36 Main Street, Office 11*
> *Tel. Main 4377*

Kit crumpled the paper violently. She wanted to throw it in Stillwater's placid face. The only thing that stopped her was the pastor arriving at her side.

———

"How are you getting along?" Kit asked Truman Harcourt. She was still stinging over Stillwater, so talking to her client in jail was actually a relief.

"As well as I can, I suppose," Truman Harcourt said. "It's Celia I'm worried about. She's so broken up about Louise. Is there any chance we'll find her?"

"Of course there is," Kit said. "May I ask how Louise felt about this John Whitney?"

"She was in love with him," Truman said. "I've never seen a girl so smitten. Louise has always been . . . How shall I say this . . . emotional? She tends to take things very hard. That's what worries her mother and me. That she'll do something terrible."

"Do you think she might try to harm herself?"

Truman Harcourt's hesitation was answer enough.

"I want to get Whitney involved in this," Kit said.

"His parents control him." Truman shook his head. "If only he would stand on his own two feet."

"Let me try to convince him. I am a lawyer, after all."

A slight smile came to Truman's mouth. But it faded quickly. "I feel so powerless. Can't you get me out of here?"

"I'll try for bail again tomorrow," Kit said, "at the preliminary hearing."

"What are my chances?"

"One never knows. It all depends on the judge and whether he's got his finger to the wind."

Truman looked at her with confusion.

"Judges are human," Kit said. "You get the spectrum. Some are conscientious, some are more concerned with their reputations than with upholding the law. We shall pray that the judge we are assigned is one of the good ones."

"Pray," Truman said. "Will you say a prayer for Louise, Miss Shannon?"

Kit reached through the bars and took Truman's hand in her own.

ON MONDAY MORNING Clara Dalton Price opened the preliminary hearing under the watchful eye of the assigned judge, Hyram Quinn. He was a young judge, a dapper man with dark hair and intelligent brown eyes. He favored the muttonchop sideburns that had largely fallen out of fashion a decade ago. But he wore them with authority.

And he was one of the more eligible bachelors in the city of Los Angeles.

The rumor, whispered in some of the back rooms of the finest homes in the city, was that Judge Quinn had a wandering eye. And further, that it had lately landed on the fierce deputy D.A. who had charged into L.A., the widow Clara Dalton Price.

Kit had almost laughed when she heard of the assignment. Kit had not fared well with judges in Los Angeles. Most had been hostile to the idea of a woman trial lawyer. Now, of all things, here was a judge whose personal life with *another* woman lawyer might be an obstacle! When would she get a fair-minded jurist on one of her cases?

But there was a possible good side to this. Kit would monitor the situation closely. If the judge seemed to be favoring Mrs. Price, it could well be an issue on a writ seeking to overturn the bind-over.

Mike McGinty was the first witness for the prosecution.

"Detective," Price began with her witness, "you were called to the scene of a murder on the evening of February 8, were you not?"

"Objection," Kit said. "That is assuming a fact not in evidence, Your Honor. It is the burden of the prosecution to establish the *corpus delicti* before a murder may be presumed."

Quinn looked a bit perturbed. "I suppose Miss Shannon has a point," he said.

Suppose? Kit could almost feel flames jump into her eyes. His patronizing was a clear signal as to what he thought of her. But this was just a prelim, and no jury was present. She did not have to worry about what impression she was making. She just had to worry about the judge. Kit took a deep breath and sat down.

"Very well," Price said to McGinty. "You were called to the scene where police found a lifeless body lying on the floor in a pool of blood, were you not?"

A man in the gallery laughed. Kit did not find Price's baiting amusing. It was unprofessional but very effective. Judge Quinn tried to hide a smile behind his hand.

"Yes," McGinty answered. "I got a call from one of our beat cops, and he said a man had been shot and gave me the address."

"And that address turned out to be the home of Mr. Gerald Mahoney?"

"It did."

"And the body turned out to be Gerald Mahoney's?"

"It was so identified to me."

"By whom?"

"By Mr. Mahoney's neighbor, Norbert Strong."

That was the first Kit had heard about a witness named Strong. She wondered if this Strong had seen anything else and made a mental note to talk to him. One of the benefits of a preliminary hearing was learning what evidence and witnesses the district attorney had. The D.A., of course, would attempt to keep the evidence to a minimum at the prelim. Only enough to get the defendant bound over for trial.

"What was the condition of the body, Detective McGinty?"

"I saw that Mr. Mahoney had been shot dead."

"I object," Kit said, "on the grounds of competence. The witness is not a doctor and does not know the cause of death."

Judge Quinn said, "Wouldn't bullet holes do the trick?"

"Your Honor," Kit said, trying hard to mask her exasperation. "We have no idea about the condition of the body when Detective McGinty found him. It will be up to a medical witness to establish that fact. Therefore, the detective cannot conclude that the victim was shot to death. He can testify about what he saw, but his medical opinions are not relevant."

Clara Dalton Price looked at Kit with the eyes of a coiled snake. Kit looked right back at her. She was not going to let the prosecutor take liberties with the law, even if the judge was sweet on her. Kit would make sure everything was properly on the record.

"Better stick to the facts," Judge Quinn said to the witness, almost apologetically.

"Fine," Price snapped. "Tell us what you saw, Detective."

McGinty, who seemed slightly amused at the whole episode, continued. "I saw Mahoney, flat on his back. There was an ugly splotch on his chest. My guess, not my medical opinion, is that this was a bullet hole. There was a Colt .45 lying on the floor near the body. There was blood on the floor."

"And did you at some point talk to the defendant, Mr. Harcourt?"

"Yes."

"What were the circumstances of that conversation?"

"The officer on the scene told me he—"

"Objection," Kit said. "Hearsay."

"Overruled."

"You may answer," Price said.

McGinty sniffed toward Kit, then said, "He told me he caught Harcourt stumbling around in the yard. He brought him in the house and made him wait until I got there."

"And when you spoke to Mr. Harcourt, what did he tell you?"

"He said he came to the house but couldn't remember what happened once he got inside. And then he identified the gun as his own."

"He admitted to you that the Colt .45 was his gun?"

"Yes, ma'am."

"Thank you," Price said. "No more questions."

Kit wasted no time. Earl Rogers had taught her to get right to the point at a preliminary hearing, try to get admissions from the witnesses that they would not be able to take back when a trial began.

"Detective," she said, "isn't it true that on February nine you and I met at the Mahoney house?"

McGinty shifted a little in the witness chair. "I remember."

"And is it not also true that I asked you to allow me to view the scene of the crime, and you did not allow it?"

"Yes, but I was told—" he stopped himself.

"You were told what, Detective? Were you told by the office of the district attorney not to let me in?"

Clara Dalton Price objected.

"Sustained," said the judge.

Kit faced the bench. "On what grounds?"

"This is a preliminary hearing," Judge Quinn said sharply. "We are not here to badger witnesses. You will confine your cross-examination to what the detective saw or heard when he found the body. That is all."

Kit's angry sigh, she was sure, could be heard all the way out into the lobby.

"All right, then," she said to McGinty. "I want you to describe for the court the condition of the room when you entered it." If they were going to keep her out of the house, she would force them to put a description on the record.

McGinty shrugged. "It was the large sitting room just to the left of the entryway."

"The room with a window facing the front lawn, is that correct?"

"Right."

"Go on."

"Well, first thing I saw was the body, of course, lying just about in the middle of the room. And the blood. And I saw the gun lying right there, too."

"Where was the gun in relation to the body, Detective?"

"Oh, I'd say about four feet away."

Kit walked to her counsel table and took up a blank sheet of paper and pencil. "I would like you to sketch the position of the body and the location of the gun, please."

"Is this really necessary, Miss Shannon?" Judge Quinn looked tired.

"It is part of the cross-examination you have allowed me, yes," Kit said. She was trying hard not to sound impudent but was not having much success.

"Go on," Quinn instructed McGinty.

It took several minutes for McGinty to sketch the scene. When he was finished Kit took it from him. She studied it for a long moment.

Presently she said, "I believe you told me about some broken glass in this room, isn't that right?"

McGinty scowled. "That's right."

"And you said it was a sign there had been a struggle."

"I guess so."

"You guess so?"

"That's what a detective does, makes educated guesses."

"What sort of glass does your education tell you was broken?" Kit said, to the amusement of the reporters in the first row.

McGinty hesitated and looked toward Clara Dalton Price. Kit turned quickly and thought she saw the last vestige of a knowing look from the prosecutor to the witness. When she faced McGinty again he was fiddling with his coat buttons.

"Well?" Kit said.

"I don't have a guess on that, Miss Shannon. It might have been anything."

Kit was furious. McGinty was never shy about guessing when it suited his purposes. Right now it was his purpose to please the prosecutor and keep Kit from getting any more information about the case than was absolutely necessary.

"Was anything else out of order in the room?" Kit asked.

"Not that I could tell."

"And yet you say there was a struggle?"

"Maybe the defendant cleaned things up."

"But your testimony is that Mr. Harcourt was found outside, stumbling around, as you put it."

McGinty nodded, his face concentrating on Kit. "Yeah?"

"Not the attitude of someone who is going to clean up anything, is it?"

"I wouldn't know."

"You wouldn't guess?"

More laughter from the men of the press. Quinn gaveled for order. McGinty folded his arms.

"What was the décor like?" Kit asked, still trying to get a picture of the room.

McGinty shrugged. "It looked like the room of a man very well-off financially, though the place could have used a little cleaning."

"I beg your pardon?"

"Well, there was an empty spot where a portrait had once hung, and you could see the walls were a little dusty around it."

"What portrait are you referring to?"

"A portrait of Mr. Mahoney. It was out being touched up."

"How do you know this?"

"His assistant, Axel Bagby, told me."

Kit nodded. "You questioned Mr. Bagby?"

"Yep."

"Did you ask Mr. Bagby what might have been broken in the struggle?"

Clara Dalton Price stood up. "We have gone well over the subject of direct examination, Your Honor. Miss Shannon is now merely fishing for evidence."

"Sustained," Judge Quinn said. "This is not a trial, Miss Shannon."

No, Kit wanted to say, *this is a theatrical farce.* Instead, she said to McGinty, "Detective, you took no inventory of the crime scene, isn't that true?"

McGinty looked as if he'd expected the question. "We took a look around, but we didn't see the need."

That was what she expected him to say. Kit went to her counsel table and took a sheet of paper from her briefcase.

"Detective McGinty, you remember testifying under oath in the murder trial of officer Ed Hanratty?"

McGinty's eyes narrowed. "Sure I do."

"And do you remember giving this answer to District Attorney Davenport: 'I write down a description of the scene as I find it, all the items that are in a location, that sort of thing. First rule of detective work is to get a full picture of the crime scene before anything is moved.'"

The witness said nothing, but his cheeks began to look rosy.

"Why didn't you do that in this case, Detective?"

With a sudden defiance, McGinty said, "We had the defendant admit it was his gun. We had the defendant. So we didn't need to."

What was he hiding? Or was it someone else who was hiding the evidence? Kit had no idea and no way to find out now. "I have no further questions," she said.

And Clara Dalton Price had no further witnesses. Judge Quinn ruled from the bench that Truman Harcourt would be bound over for trial. It was as if he and Mrs. Price had rehearsed the whole thing. Maybe they had.

"Your Honor," Kit said. "I ask that you set bail for my client. He is an honored member of the community and—"

"Denied," Quinn said. "This is a premeditated murder. Is there any reason the trial cannot start next week?"

Clara Dalton Price said, "No, Your Honor."

"I wish more time to prepare my case," Kit said. Though a week between a preliminary hearing and trial was not uncommon, judges usually allowed more time when murder was the charge.

"Fine," Judge Quinn said. "I'll give you two weeks." He pounded his gavel and left the bench.

Kit turned to Truman just as the deputy sheriff was approaching him. "I'm sorry."

"Find Louise," Truman said pleadingly. Kit felt tears behind her eyes—half in sorrow for the Harcourts, half in anger at the judge. Then, with gritted teeth, she gathered her briefcase and strode out of the courtroom.

Outside the courthouse, Kit encountered McGinty standing on the steps, smoking his ever-present cigar.

"Kit," he said with a sharp nod. "You kinda made me look bad in there."

In no mood for idle chatter, Kit looked him dead in the eye. "This is a murder trial, Mike. And you didn't follow your normal procedure. I want to know why."

"Now, Kit, you know I'd help you out if I could."

"Is that so? Have you charged that crazy gardener with assault?"

McGinty put up his hand. "He won't bother you. He's cooling his heels in a lockup."

"Ever thought he might be the one who shot Mahoney?"

"Not with Harcourt's confession in our hands."

"That's not very careful police work. Maybe this man Fitch is the one who attacked Truman. Maybe he got the gun and shot Mahoney."

"And maybe the moon is made of green cheese," McGinty said.

25

JOHN WHITNEY HELD A BRANDY in one hand and a newspaper in the other. He nearly dropped them both when he saw Kit standing there.

"What is this?" His face was sallow and his eyes looked tired, almost lifeless.

"John Whitney?"

"How did you get in here?"

They were in the parlor of The Palmer Club, the most exclusive men's club in the city. Kit, who had once done a legal service for the head of membership, was able to gain admittance based on that past deed. *"If you ever need a favor . . ."*

Today she did.

"Who are you?" Whitney said.

"Kathleen Shannon, attorney."

He considered her for a moment, then gestured to the chair opposite him.

"I am the lawyer representing Truman Harcourt."

"Oh," Whitney said, seeming to drop back into ambivalence. "I have nothing to say on that matter."

"I am not here on that matter. I am here concerning Louise."

John Whitney's eyes widened with concern. "Have you heard—" He stopped himself and looked down.

"I suspect she is in a bad way," Kit said. "And you ought to do something about it."

"What can I do?" he said, shaking his head slowly.

"You can be a man."

When John looked at her, it was with a disconcerted longing. Kit saw in his eyes a small ray of hope that he might be reclaimed from the awful condition he had succumbed to. But then a quick intransigence slipped into his face.

"What right do you have to talk to me that way?" he said.

"Are you going to sit here and squabble about right? Or are you going to try to find Louise?"

"What good would it do? The decision has been made not to seek her."

"Who made it, John? Was it you? Or was it your parents?"

A flash of anger passed over him, like a fast-moving cloud. "Leave them out of this."

"Isn't that the root of all this?" Kit said. "You are not deciding things for yourself. You have broken a girl's heart. That is not to be taken lightly."

There was real torment now in John Whitney's face. He had slowly crumpled the newspaper he held with his left hand. "I love Louise," he said quietly. "But there was going to be trouble; we both knew it."

"What do you mean?" Kit watched him intently, as she would a witness.

"He told us there would be trouble," Whitney said, his face taking on a faraway look of remembrance. "He said there would be trouble unless the past was cleared up."

"Who said this? Who are you talking about?"

"Mother said we should go," Whitney said, still staring into memory's space. "Louise thought it would be fun. But he was right, wasn't he, after all?"

There was in his words a palpable clue, Kit was sure. "John, look at me."

He did, with vacant eyes.

Kit said, "Tell me who it was who—"

"What is this?" The booming voice belonged to a well-dressed man who looked none too pleased.

John Whitney immediately stood up. "Father."

"Who is this woman?" the elder Whitney demanded. "What's she doing in here?"

Kit stood up. "My name is Kathleen Shannon. I represent Truman Harcourt."

John Whitney's father registered a glare of disapproval. "In that case, I forbid you to speak to my son."

Kit bristled and paused only a moment before answering, "You may not forbid any such thing, sir."

The look on the man's face was no different than if some street urchin had set his trousers on fire. His mouth opened and closed in a silent spasm of shock.

Finally, Mr. Whitney set his jaw. "Then I forbid my son to speak to *you*. And don't think I will forget this, young woman. You have made an enemy of me, and I will not let this lie."

Kit looked at the two men and her disgust was matched only by her sense of loss. She had come here hoping to reclaim a little dignity from John Whitney, for Louise's sake. Now she saw him only as a lost cause.

She saw that John Whitney was easily cowed by his father. There would be no more talking here. Kit walked out without another word, but her mind was now churning.

Who told John and Louise there would be trouble?

The Hotel Del Coronado, where Ted met with Duncan Chase and Peter Garraty, was already a San Diego landmark. Opened in 1889, it was the largest resort hotel in the world—at least, that's what its own advertisements said.

Built out of redwood in the Queen Anne style, the Hotel Del Coronado boasted 399 rooms over seven and a half acres of peninsula between the Pacific Ocean and San Diego Bay. It had electric lighting throughout, a ten-thousand square foot dining hall, and an interior court of lush tropical plants and flowers. Jenny Lind and

Mark Twain had stayed here, as had Thomas Alva Edison. It had the feel of history in the making, which seemed perfect to Ted. History, at least according to Garraty, was hanging in the balance.

"The Huns," Garraty said as the three of them dined in the great hall to the pleasant strains of a live orchestra, "are determined to dominate Europe. We know they are intent on mastering the air. We've seen photographs of a three-wing design."

"A tri-plane?" Ted said.

"Precisely," said Garraty.

"Stable," Ted remarked. "Very stable. But for every wing there is a loss of maneuverability."

"Yes, we know that. That's why the monoplane, if it is practical, will be of great benefit to us. But we are concerned with, as you say, stability. We have not been able to figure out a way to deal with the stress on the wing struts."

Ted nodded. "You hit it. That's what Gus and I have been working on for the last few months."

"Is that ill-tempered gentleman back in Los Angeles?"

Ted smiled. "Oh, Gus is all right. He just cares more about machines than he does people."

"Not a bad choice in some circumstances," Garraty said with a smile. His accent sounded vaguely British all of a sudden.

"Where are you from, Mr. Garraty?" Ted said.

There was a momentary pause, as if Peter Garraty had not expected the inquiry. "Originally?"

"Yes. Where were you born?"

"Berlin."

Ted paused with a piece of prime rib hanging on the end of his fork.

"Yes," Garraty explained. "My father was in the diplomatic corps out of the London office. I grew up in Germany, until my twelfth year. You see, I am rather an expert on the Teutonic race."

"Yes, I gathered that," Ted said. "How about you, Mr. Chase?"

"Pittsburgh," Chase said. "Born and raised."

"My mother's family was from Pittsburgh," Ted said. "Ever run across a family by the name of Norton?"

Chase thought a moment, then shook his head.

"From the west side?" Ted added.

Chase opened his mouth to answer, but it was Garraty who spoke. "Tell me, Mr. Fox, are you familiar with the philosophy of Friedrich Nietzsche?"

"Can't say that I am."

"His works have yet to see translation into English. He is a German philosopher."

"Not my usual reading, I must say," Ted remarked. Though he enjoyed reading good literature, he preferred the science of aeronautics to philosophy when it came to books.

Garraty nodded. "This Nietzsche wrote with the power of the poet. He has caught on with a good deal of the German aristocracy, appealing to the Teutonic blood. You see, Nietzsche preached that God is dead and man is to replace Him."

Ted shook his head. "He sounds like a crazy man."

"Indeed," said Garraty. "He died in an asylum. But that is much beside the point. His ideas live on and are inspiring the German intellectuals. This sort of inspiration may lead to war. It always has in the past."

"That well may be," Ted said. "As I study the Scriptures, it seems to me that the moment mankind turns its back on God, evil acts are not far behind. A country that comes to believe God is dead— well, one can imagine what a disaster that would be."

"Precisely. And while ideas move slowly, they move inexorably. We must make our preparations now. Help us, Mr. Fox, to develop air power for the United States of America."

Ted Fox smiled. "So long as I can go back to Los Angeles within a month."

Garraty frowned. "The reason?"

"I want to get married."

The government man nodded with understanding. "Ah, women. War and women do not mix. But seeing as how we are not engaged in official combat, I do not see that I can stop you."

"That's good to know. I'd hate to think the United States government was against marriage."

Ted's two dinner companions chuckled. Then Garraty leaned over. "Dinner conversation is pleasant. But let me advise you not to speak with anyone else while you are here. It is no secret that spies on the other side have been about."

"You can count upon my discretion," Ted said.

"I knew I could," Garraty replied.

Part Two

26

THE COURTROOM, AS ALWAYS, was filled to overflowing. Kit had resigned herself to being a show whenever she had a trial. There was no avoiding the ever-curious press or the crowds of Angelenos for whom a Kit Shannon trial was a ticket to free entertainment. Even the society page had taken to describing Kit's wardrobe whenever she appeared in court.

Today she wore a custom suit, tan khaki, with a coat that featured two rows of white buttons on the front. The sleeves were thin, not puffy. The skirt was pleated and the hem—here is where the dressmaker, Mrs. Norris, objected but Kit had insisted—ended at the ankle line.

That meant her feet could be seen, Mrs. Norris said. That wasn't done! A proper woman should seem to glide, her hem barely above the ground. But Kit had to move and turn in court, and she was not going to get tangled up in fabric.

Somewhat surprising for Kit was the presence of Allard and Edwina Whitney. Were they here to see the final nails put in the Harcourts' social coffin? Perhaps Mr. Whitney wanted the satisfaction of seeing her lose this high-profile case.

Certainly Clara Dalton Price was going to try to make that happen. She spoke to Kit just before Judge Quinn entered. "Your many admirers are here, I see."

"I'm used to it," Kit said. "You will have to get used to it as well."

"I wish you luck, Miss Shannon, but only as a sporting gesture, you understand."

Kit nodded curtly. "I don't think of a murder trial as sport, Mrs. Price."

"As for me, I am enjoying myself immensely. We are making history, you know. Two women lawyers on opposite sides of a murder trial. That's never been done before."

"Let justice be done, then," said Kit.

"Oh, it shall," Clara Dalton Price said. And that was when Judge Quinn entered.

Kit took a quick look at the crowd. She saw several familiar faces, but the one she wanted to see most—Ted Fox—was not there. He had been in San Diego over two weeks now. An eternity! At least he had written letters.

She wanted him here, as always when she tried a case. He was a rock for her, a comfort. But she could not control the timing of the trial, and so it was not to be.

She turned to Truman Harcourt and Corazón Chavez, seated at the counsel table with her, and smiled. Time to concentrate on the trial.

The first order of business was picking a jury, and right away Kit noticed something Earl Rogers had told her to watch for—prosecutors who loved to paint themselves as keepers of the flame of justice. Mrs. Price was adept at this.

"Would you pledge to do your duty to justice if you are a juror in this case?" she said to the men seated in the jury box. All of them nodded. What else would they do? Kit had never seen a juror yet who stood up and admitted he was not interested in justice! But Mrs. Price was getting them used to nodding in her favor.

"And if the People of the State of California present evidence, beyond a reasonable doubt, of the defendant's guilt, will you vote for guilt?"

Again the looks of agreement. Clara Dalton Price asked a few more general questions, then said to the judge, "The People accept this panel as composed."

It was a dramatic gesture. Mrs. Price had not exercised a single challenge. Kit knew this was intended to paint Kit in a bad light should she excuse any jurors herself. It was also to reflect how confident Mrs. Price was in her case. Any set of jurors would do is what she was signaling to the jurors.

Kit wasted no time charging into Mrs. Price's own field. "The prosecutor has used the term justice many times here this morning," Kit said to the men, who looked back with steely eyes and down-turned mouths. "Do any of you believe that justice is the sole province of the prosecution?"

None of the panel admitted to this.

"Do any of you not believe that justice means that the innocent shall be freed immediately?"

"Objection," Clara Dalton Price said.

Kit did not let the judge rule. "Your Honor, I am only asking these gentlemen the same list of questions Mrs. Price employed, only from the other side. Is that not permissible?"

With an uncomfortable look, Judge Quinn said, "Overruled."

Kit asked the question again, and no one disagreed that the innocent should be freed.

"And further, do you all believe that the prosecutor bears a burden, the burden of proof beyond a reasonable doubt? Do you all accept that?"

They did.

"And will you make a pledge that if this burden is not met on every single element of the crime charged, that you will return a verdict of not guilty?"

No one protested.

"Then the defense accepts this jury as composed," Kit said. Two could dance to that tune.

After the jury was sworn in, Judge Quinn looked at Clara Dalton Price. "Call your first witness."

"The prosecution calls Dr. Raymond Smith."

The smallish man, whom Kit had tangled with before, came forward and was sworn.

"You are the coroner for the city and county of Los Angeles?" Clara Dalton Price asked.

"I am."

"And how long have you served in that capacity?"

"Seven years."

"On or about February 9, did you have occasion to perform an autopsy?"

Kit was amazed and a little awed by the military precision of Mrs. Price's questioning. She was assured and fast, giving the jury the impression she had the utmost confidence in her case. Kit would have to be keen on every word.

"I did," the witness answered.

"Was this autopsy performed on the body of Gerald Mahoney?"

"It was identified that way to me."

"Please tell the jury what your findings were."

Dr. Smith adjusted his glasses. "The victim died of internal bleeding caused by two bullets to the stomach and left lung. He also had an abrasion on the back of his head, probably caused by his hitting the floor."

Kit scribbled a quick note.

"And was there anything else about the body or wounds that you took note of?"

"Only that the bullets were fired from a .45 caliber pistol at very close range."

"Thank you. Your witness."

Kit paused a moment. Truman Harcourt looked concerned, but there was nothing she could say to him at the moment.

"Dr. Smith," she began. "Is it your testimony that Gerald Mahoney was shot at close range, causing death, and that he then fell backward to the floor, causing the head trauma?"

"That's what it looks like to me."

"You're not sure?"

"Well, anything's possible."

Kit turned slightly so the jury could see her look of consternation. "What other possibilities are there?"

"Objection," Clara Price said. "This calls for speculation on the part of the witness."

"Your Honor," said Kit, "this witness has just as much as admitted he is speculating about the scenario he just gave. I would like him to explore other scenarios."

Judge Quinn looked not at Kit but at Clara Dalton Price. Then he said, "Sustain the objection. Dr. Smith has given his medical opinion. We need not go off on a wild-goose chase."

Kit could hardly believe it. The judge might just as well have told the jury he thought Kit's case was built on nothing but smoke and mirrors—like Houdini's magic show! This was outrageous, but she dared not lose her composure. Keeping a poker face when the inevitable setbacks occurred was part and parcel of the trial lawyer's art.

"Tell me, Dr. Smith, were you able, by examining the body, to determine what time Mr. Mahoney died?"

The coroner scowled. Kit knew this aspect of medical science was rather new and not common for a standard autopsy. But it was about time it was. Time of death would be a critical factor—perhaps not in this case, but certainly in the future.

"That was not part of my charge," the coroner said.

"Do you have a guess as to the time of death?"

"Objection."

"Sustained."

Naturally, Kit thought. But at least the jury might be getting a message here. The prosecutor and judge both seemed anxious to protect this witness.

"So let me understand this," Kit said. "You believe Mr. Mahoney was shot to death, though you don't know what time, and suffered head trauma when he hit the floor?"

"That's what I'm saying."

"So your claim is that the .45 caliber bullets hit with such force that Mr. Mahoney fell backward?"

Dr. Smith stroked his chin, regarding Kit with suspicion. "Could happen."

Kit saw a small opening and was determined to push it open. "Let us be clear for the jury. Your testimony is that it is possible for such bullets, from the revolver that is the alleged murder weapon, to be enough to send a man of Gerald Mahoney's size backward?"

Now the coroner looked uneasy. Kit knew he was not a ballistics expert. She had cross-examined him on that subject in the murder trial of Ed Hanratty, and he did not fare well.

"You ever take two bullets to the chest?" Smith challenged, drawing a few delighted murmurs from the gallery.

"Your Honor," Kit said, "I move to strike that last answer as non-responsive and would ask the court to direct the witness to answer yes or no."

Instead of ruling on the matter, the judge turned to the witness. "Dr. Smith, you are a medical man, isn't that true?"

"Yes, sir," the witness said.

Kit stood by, smoldering. It was unusual and intrusive for a judge to ask questions of the witness. But he had the legal power to do so and she could say nothing about it.

"And as a medical man," the judge said, "your opinion is that Mr. Mahoney could have fallen backward because of the gunshots, right?"

"Right."

"Then this subject is closed," Judge Quinn said to Kit. "Leave it up to the jury."

"I have no further questions of this witness at this time," Kit said. "But I want him subject to recall."

"Anything further from the prosecutor?" Judge Quinn asked.

"No, Your Honor," said Clara Dalton Price. "We are quite satisfied."

The judge adjourned the trial for the day and Kit conferred with Corazón. "Clara Price is a very good lawyer," Kit said. "She and Davenport are trying this neatly. And they've covered their bases outside. I can't believe there are no witnesses for us. No neighbors, no passersby, nothing."

"Is crazy, no?" said Corazón.

"Is crazy, yes," Kit said. Then a thought clicked in her head. *Crazy. Yes!*

27

LOS ANGELES COUNTY HAD a special lockup for what were referred to as *dills*, short for *daffydills*—police slang for nut cases who could not always be dealt with through the judicial system. A lot of drunks ended up in the dill tanks for a night. Others, who may have caused a public scene due to some sort of mental condition or other, would likewise be housed here until they could be shuffled off on some relative or, in the worst instances, were let loose like some dog no one wanted anymore.

There were times, Kit Shannon knew, when some of the worst dills were taken outside the city limits by big-fisted men and given a "lesson." What they hoped would be learned was this: Stay out of Los Angeles.

So when Kit found herself in front of a large orderly at the front desk of the dill tank, she wondered if he might be one of the strong-armers. His initial tone suggested just that.

"Who sent you?" he said. He looked as if he'd come from the same litter as Axel Bagby. He had only a thin layer of flax-colored hair on the sides of his head.

"I am a lawyer," Kit said. "I wish to speak to Dick Fitch."

The big man's eyebrows, which seemed to be crafted from porcupine needles, narrowed downward. "You that lady lawyer who's always in the paper?"

Kit said, "Yes. Kathleen Shannon."

In an instant his face became friendly and welcoming, like a mastiff puppy. He stuck out his hand and Kit's got lost in it. He pumped her hand like he was trying to get water out of a well. "Now, this is a real pleasure, oh yes," the orderly said. "You are a real famous person, and I have never met a real famous person, except once"—he was still shaking her hand—"and that was back in Missouri when Buffalo Bill his own self came into town with his show, and I got to hold his horse for him."

Kit's hand was throbbing when she withdrew it. "Thank you, Mr. . . ."

"Longstreet, like the poet, only there's a *street* instead of a *fellow*." And he laughed.

"Yes, Mr. Longstreet. A pleasure to meet you. Now, I wonder if I may see Mr. Fitch."

"Oh, now, I don't know about that." The big, friendly face turned sad, as if he wanted to help Kit but could not.

"It's all right," Kit said. "I won't cause a disturbance. I merely want to ask a few questions relating to a case of murder."

"I read about that," Longstreet said. "I read the papers, you know. Just because I work here doesn't mean I'm slow."

"Certainly not," Kit said.

"But I'm not supposed to. I mean, I can't."

Kit knew he was holding something back, and she had a vague feeling about what it was. "You were about to say you're not supposed to allow me to talk to this man. Who gave you those orders?"

"Aw, now I'm gonna get myself into trouble."

"No, Mr. Longstreet," Kit said with all the assurance she could muster. "Don't think that at all. I am not here to get you or anyone into trouble. But I have a duty under the law to seek the truth for my client."

Longstreet scratched his nearly bald pate. "They said I wasn't to tell anybody."

"Who said?"

"If I told you, then I'd be saying." Longstreet looked genuinely tortured.

Kit thought a moment. Her quick judgment of him was that

there was a helpful citizen hiding within the loose white garb of the dill tank orderly. "What if I were to ask you a series of questions?" Kit asked. "You could just shake your head or nod, and that wouldn't be saying, now, would it?"

Longstreet thought about this, then smiled broadly. "You're smart, that's what the papers say. Okay, Miss Shannon. You ask."

"Fine," Kit said. "Someone has told you not to allow me or anyone else to speak to Mr. Fitch?"

Longstreet nodded.

"Is this person a policeman?"

A shake of the head.

"A lawyer?"

Nod.

"A prosecutor?"

Nod.

"A woman?"

Longstreet's eyes grew in amazement, as if Kit Shannon had uncovered some deep, dark secret only he knew.

"Don't worry," Kit said. "I know who it is." Apparently Clara Dalton Price was not jesting when she said she would do anything to win.

"Am I going to get in trouble, Miss Shannon?"

"No. I will not say a word. If anyone is going to get into trouble around here, it will be Mrs. Price."

Longstreet's face was suddenly aghast. "No foolin'?"

"You have nothing to fear, Mr. Longstreet."

"You're a good egg," he said.

"Then I must be up to fifteen cents a dozen."

A huge, toothy grin raced across Longstreet's face, and then he reared his head back and howled with laughter. "Oh, that's a good 'un!" His huge body rippled with mirth. "Come on," he said. "Let's go see Mr. Fitch."

Kit followed Longstreet through a barred door into a corridor of eight cells. The smell of sweat and dirt assailed her. Loud snores came from one of the cells where a large mound of humanity was curled up on a cot. Another man, gaunt and staring, sat quietly on the floor of his cell.

Longstreet stopped at the last cell on the left. Kit recognized Dick Fitch. And he recognized her.

"You!" he cried, pointing at her.

"Now, Dick, none of that," Longstreet said. "Miss Shannon wants to talk to you, is all."

"She did it!" Dick Fitch said to Longstreet as if the large man were his mother. "She did it, don't you see? Took 'em. Took 'em all! I know it 'cause I have her feet!"

There was such a look of purpose in his eyes that Kit was sure he was speaking what was, for him, the truth. Delusional, yes, but real in his mind.

"Why don't you give the lady a chance?" Longstreet said in a gentle, comforting voice. Remarkably, that had an effect on Fitch. He calmed down somewhat, though his eyes did not lose their suspicions.

"She still took 'em," Fitch said quietly. "I know."

Kit stepped up to the bars of the cell. "Mr. Fitch, what is it you suppose I've taken?"

"You know," Fitch said. "I have your feet!"

Kit looked down at his shoes. What was he talking about?

"Dick," said Longstreet, "why don't you tell me, tell old Longstreet, what it is this lady took from you?"

"The San Juans! My San Juans!"

Longstreet shook his head.

"The roses, you fool!" Fitch said. "My prize San Juan roses! I grew 'em special, took care of 'em. She took 'em! She took 'em all!"

Kit remembered the first time she'd encountered Dick Fitch. He had warned her to *stay away*. And later, when he'd tried to snip her with his shears like some ugly branch, he said she had taken something. He must have meant his roses.

"Mr. Fitch," Kit said. "I assure you I did not take your prize roses."

"I have your feet!" Fitch said. "I can prove it!"

Before Kit could pose another question, Fitch looked at her even more accusingly. "You seen who killed him, too. You were there. I seen you."

"What do you mean?" Kit saw that look in his eyes again.

Fitch looked at Longstreet. "Call the police!"

"There'll be no talk of police, Dick," said Longstreet. He turned to Kit. "I don't think Dick is going to be much help to you right now."

Kit nodded. That much was clear. But what was also clear was that hidden inside the head of Dick Fitch was something crucial. Something about the killing. And she could not get to it.

28

THE NIGHT WAS GOING TO BE a long one for Kit. With her hair braided and her nightgown flowing, she paced her room, unable to find sleep. A single lamp cast thin wisps of light. Aunt Freddy's grandfather clock on the floor below tolled midnight.

And Kit had the oddest sensation that Ted was in trouble.

She went to the window, looking out over the dark and sleeping city below, and whispered a prayer for Ted's safety, wherever he might be. Part of her resisted the notion, reasoning that all of the troubling aspects of Truman Harcourt's murder trial, the still-missing Louise, and the fraudulent medium were too much a part of her mind for there to be peace about Ted.

And she was still thinking about Dick Fitch and his curious statements. Her feet? Was that just the ravings of a lunatic? Or was there something to it?

Finally, she opened her father's Bible, her most beloved possession in the world. It had stayed with her since Papa's death, had been through every trial of her life. Now she looked to it for comfort.

The Psalms were always good for spiritual balm, and that is where she turned, skimming her father's notes as she did. He had marked up his Bible as D. L. Moody had once suggested to him. Red ink for references to Christ's blood and redemption. A cross in the margin for texts that prefigured Christ. There were several places where he'd placed a star in the margin. One of them was near the eleventh verse of Psalm 85: *"Truth shall spring out of the earth; and righteousness shall look down from heaven."*

A pounding from downstairs brought her out of contemplation. Someone was at the front door.

Bad news.

Kit threw a robe around her and took up a lamp downstairs. When she got there, Angelita, Corazón's mother and Kit's house-keeper, was already present in her own robe, wondering what to do.

"I will answer it," Kit said. The older woman nodded, looking a bit frightened. Kit opened the door. The small light illumined the face of a disheveled John Whitney. He was dressed in evening clothes, but his tie was askew and his coat was wrinkled.

"I want to see you!" he cried out. His voice was thick and he swayed slightly.

"Come in, then," Kit said.

Whitney took one step, then stumbled backward, landing with a grunt on his behind.

"Angelita! Come help me."

The two women got Whitney to his feet. He was groggy, his eyes heavy lidded. Kit could smell the liquor on his breath and clothes.

Suddenly he growled like an animal and with a jerk threw Angelita off his right arm. The woman fell into a sitting position on the porch.

"That's enough!" Kit said. She took Whitney's left wrist and with practiced jiu-jitsu technique bent his arm behind his back.

Whitney cried out.

"Hush!" Kit ordered. "Disgraceful."

She controlled Whitney into the sitting room and put him in a chair. She flicked on the new Edison electric light. Whitney's face was pallid and his eyes red rimmed.

"Coming here at all hours," Kit said, feeling like a big sister. "What has possessed you?"

A sort of snorting sound came from Whitney, as if his body were fighting against itself.

Kit looked at Angelita. "Would you mind brewing a pot of coffee?"

Angelita nodded and went off toward the kitchen. Kit leaned over the scion of one of the city's wealthy families and loosened his tie lest he choke himself.

"What would your parents think of you now?" Kit scolded.

The question brought a bit of life into Whitney's face. "To the devil with them," he stammered. Then his eyes suddenly brimmed with tears, and he put his head in his hands. "I'm done for."

Kit felt like slapping the whiskey out of him. Instead, she removed his handkerchief from his coat pocket. She opened a carafe of water on the desk by the arched window and soaked the linen. She wiped Whitney's face with it. He did not protest.

"Now," she said, "just what is the purpose of your visit at this hour?"

Whitney breathed in and out a few times. "I don't know where else to turn. I was downtown getting drunk tonight."

"I gathered that."

"I know where she is," he said.

"Louise?"

The sotted man nodded heavily. "I hired a detective. My parents don't know."

"Where is she, John?"

He looked at the floor as he spoke. "Dead."

Kit's body clenched all over.

Then John Whitney added, "As good as."

"John! Tell me what you know!"

"She's dead! She's living . . ."

"What are you saying?"

His eyes became feral, menacing. "She's selling herself to men and the devil."

The news stung Kit's ears. If that were true—and Kit immediately knew it was very likely—then it was indeed a living death. She had known a number of prostitutes, due to her criminal practice. Most lived in a dark world that seemed just outside, and forever beyond, the light. This news would hit Celia and Truman Harcourt harder than if Louise had actually died.

"John," Kit said. "You must tell me everything you know. Quickly."

He rubbed his temples. "She's out in Jewel, at a bawdy house. The detective brought back her description. He didn't let on who he was, so they don't know it was me who sent him. Oh, what have I done?" His tears began to flow again.

Kit thought a moment, but the answer was clear. Jewel was about a two-hour ride north along the mission road. They would have to go there. Now.

"Angelita," Kit called. The woman appeared at the door in the wisp of a moment. "Ask Juan to prepare the coach. We must travel tonight."

"No," John Whitney said. "I never want to see her again."

Now Kit did slap him. It happened without her even thinking about it. "No more talk like that," she said. "You have it in your power to save a young woman's life."

"Too late."

"It is not too late!"

"But my parents . . ."

Kit almost slapped him again, but modesty prevailed. "You are a man," she said. "Act like it."

"You don't understand," he said. "They control . . ." His voice trailed off.

"The money?" Kit said. "That's what you're afraid of? Well, you have a choice, John Whitney. You can live like a sponge, soaking up what Mama and Papa throw at you, or you can stand on your own two feet and do what is right."

He looked at her, with fear or awe. Kit did not know which. But she reached down, grabbed his lapels, and pulled him up.

29

JUAN GUIDED THE HORSES expertly along the dark road with the twin beacon lamps lighting the way. As the night air sobered up John Whitney, he began to apologize for his intrusion. That's when Kit knew there was a chance for him. Somewhere inside him he had a sense of decency. That could be the door to his restoration.

"But the thought is so horrible," he said to Kit. "That Louise should . . ."

"John," Kit said, "you must get it into your head that what is in the past cannot be changed. What we do now is the only important thing."

He shook his head slowly. "I am only human," he said. "How can I ever forget?"

"Are you a Christian, John?"

He looked at her. She could see from the interior lamp that his eyes were wide open and questioning. "I attend church with my parents."

"That is not what I asked you."

Whitney put his hands up in a questioning manner.

"Church attendance is not what makes a Christian," Kit said. "You must have an encounter with the living Christ. You must pledge your heart and mind, your entire life, to Him. You must come to Him with repentance and stand with Him in new life."

The clop of the horses' hooves and the squeaking of the coach's chassis were the only sounds for a long moment. "I don't understand," he said finally. "I have learned the principles of the religion. I am a good person—" He stopped, then added, "At least I used to be."

"No, John. It is not a matter of being good or principles or religion. All of that comes after."

"After what?"

"Your redemption."

The young man sighed but said with interest, "I have heard that preached, but I must confess I have not given it much thought."

Kit smiled with a warm memory. "My father had a joke. He liked to use it when he preached about sin. It seems a man walked into a pawnshop one day with a pig. The owner gave the man two dollars for the pig. My father would pause and say, 'That, my friends, was a ham hock.'"

At first, John Whitney was passive, but then a smile broke out on his face. And then a laugh. Kit noted it was a pleasant sort of laugh, good-natured.

"Then my father would say that we are like that pig, and the devil owns the pawnshop. We are bound to sin, and we will remain so unless someone comes to redeem us, to buy us out of bondage. That is what Christ did on the cross. It cost Him his life. That redemption costs us our lives, too. Not a life of church attendance, but a life of repentance and reliance upon God."

Even as she said the words, she could hear her father's voice preaching them. They had lodged in her memory and had come, as if Papa were sitting in the coach with them, at just the right time.

"But I have been reckless," John Whitney said. "And mean-spirited. And my heart is hardened toward everything."

"Hardened hearts are the very thing the Lord loves to change. But first you must be willing. Are you willing, John?"

He looked at her. "What of Louise?"

"The decision will be hers, as well. And you can help her, John. You can be the one who saves her life."

———————

Kit knocked insistently on the door. The red lantern that hung above the stairs was low in wick but still gave a salacious glow.

There was a rattling of locks and the door swung open. A woman with wildfire hair held a candle to the outside world. "We're closed," she barked.

Kit walked through the door, pulling John Whitney in with her.

"Hey!" the woman backed up.

"Louise Harcourt," Kit said. "I want to see her."

The woman faced her. She was ample in both bust and hips, and she looked like she could wrestle a young bull. "You cannot come barging in—"

"Madam," Kit said, "I am the attorney for the Harcourt family. I wish to speak to Louise. You may tell her Kathleen Shannon is here, along with John Whitney."

Squinting in the dim light, the woman with the flaming hair and outlandish silk robe said, "I don't take orders too good, and I have a gun. I don't care whose lawyer you are."

Kit was about to answer when John Whitney stepped between them. "I am Louise's fiancé."

The woman looked at him with interest. "So you're the one," she said. "I ought to shoot you just on principle. The way you treated her."

"Please. I am here to ask her for forgiveness."

"Now, that's not a word I hear around here too often," the woman said. "They call me Lady Eve, and if you get on my bad side, you stay there. Right now you're straddling the fence. Come on to the parlor, then, and wait."

Lady Eve led them down the stairway, her candle casting an eerie glow in the shadows. At the bottom of the stairs was a large room with two couches and several overstuffed wing chairs. A too-sweet smell, mixed with the dusky scent of stale smoke, filled the room. A burgundy curtain marked the doorway to another chamber. Lady Eve lit a lamp with her candle.

"I'll be back with your answer," she said. She ascended the stairs with, Kit noted, a substantial swaying of her caboose.

As they waited, John Whitney drummed his fingers on a table. He looked terrified.

"Remember what I told you," Kit said. "All things may be done through the strength of Christ."

Whitney breathed deeply and nodded.

"John, I want you to know something. You are doing the right thing. It is the response of a man of character."

"Do you really think so?"

"I do."

"My parents won't think so."

"The Book says to honor your parents, but you must honor God more. That's what you're doing."

A light in the corridor grew as it came toward them. And then Louise Harcourt appeared in the room. She wore a silk kimono similar to the one worn by Lady Eve, emerald green with a red hibiscus pattern. Her face was tired, not just from lack of sleep but something more. Kit thought it looked like a fatigue of the spirit.

John Whitney stood and faced her. He seemed like a man coming face-to-face with a ghost. He was half frozen with a sort of fright. Or despondency.

"Go away, John," Louise said quietly. "You shouldn't have come."

"Louise," he said. "I had to see you."

"Why?" Louise said harshly. "To see what a ruin I have become? You may be assured of that."

"No, no. I want you to come back. With me. And Miss Shannon."

Louise looked at Kit. "Is this your doing?"

"It is time to come home," Kit said.

"There is no going back, not now," said Louise. "Please go away and forget all about me."

"Your mother and father are sick with worry," Kit said.

"Then let them recover on their own."

Louise put her head down. Kit did not speak. It was up to John Whitney now. He would have to be the one to convince the girl otherwise. Kit prayed silently, asking for a miracle of grace.

John suddenly stood tall and walked to Louise, taking her hands in his. "My dear, I have been a blind man and a weakling. I have had many days to think about what I have done to you and to myself. It is not a picture I care to look at anymore. I am asking you to forgive me, and I am asking you to come home. Let me spend the rest of my life making amends to you. With the help of God."

Louise looked at him with eyes suddenly soft, the look of a drowning woman who is suddenly thrown a line from the bow of ship. "I have never heard you speak of God before," she said.

"Miss Shannon can explain it all in the coach," he said. "Please return. Say that you will."

The hope that brightened Louise's face quickly gave way to despair. She pulled her hands away from him. "No." She backed away several paces. "It is too late." Her eyes became wide with revulsion. "Go away!"

Louise ran from the room.

Lady Eve, who had been observing from the vantage point of her lantern, said to Kit, "Why don't you go home now and forget all about this."

"I'm not leaving," John Whitney said, "unless she leaves with me."

The look of astonishment on Lady Eve's face must have mirrored Kit's own.

"Miss Shannon," Whitney said, "you go on back. I'm going to stay here in town." To Lady Eve he said, "Is there a hotel around here?"

"Just a mite down the street," the madam said. "But I don't see—"

"I will be back in the morning. And I will keep coming back until Louise listens to me." He turned to Kit. "Don't worry. I believe God is on my side in this."

30

THE NEXT MORNING, Clara Dalton Price called Jade Stringham to the witness stand.

Kit, tired from her late-night ride to Jewel and back, blinked at Jade Stringham's appearance. Today the editor of the *Gazette* wore a blue wool walking suit with delicate lace over an embroidered cotton blouse. Lovely cord insertions ran down the front of the blouse and along the cuffs. Stringham looked entirely feminine, far from the image she projected the first time Kit met her. That Jade Stringham would have sent several of the male jurors muttering in disapproval. The witness today was the model of womanly propriety.

Yes, Kit thought, *Mrs. Price will stop at nothing to win this case.*

"Miss Stringham, you are the editor of the weekly newspaper, the *Gazette*?" Clara Price began.

"Yes, I am," Jade Stringham said pleasantly. She might have been the hostess at a tea party.

"How long have you been so employed?"

"About five years now."

"How did you happen to get into the newspaper business?"

"I grew up in a newspaper family," Jade Stringham said. "I guess you could say printers' ink runs in my blood."

Kit noticed a couple of the male jurors smiling. The thought of a woman in the newspaper game must have seemed like a pleasant one to them. Quaint, like a little girl trying on her daddy's shoes.

Clara Dalton Price, who was, as usual, wearing a wide-brimmed hat, paced slowly in front of the witness box. "What is your mission as the editor of the *Gazette*?"

"To always print the truth. Mr. Mahoney would not have had it any other way."

"Although some of your stories are what critics might call, shall we say, salacious?"

It was a clever question. By bringing up the issue of the paper's true purpose—which in Kit's mind was scandalous gossip—Clara Dalton Price was taking the sting out of anything Kit might try to show with her own questions.

"Some may try to put it like that," said Jade Stringham. "But it was important to Mr. Mahoney that people be portrayed as who they are, not who they pretend to be. Business cannot be done if we are deceived by those with whom we are engaged. Mr. Mahoney believed that honesty was the best policy."

Oh, how well rehearsed she was! But Kit did not allow her face to show any emotion.

"Has the *Gazette* ever been sued for libel?" Mrs. Price said.

"Only once during my tenure as editor."

"And what was the outcome of that case?"

"The judgment was in our favor. No libel." Jade Stringham glanced over at Kit and smiled.

"Turning your attention to the events in early February," Mrs. Price said. "Were you preparing to run a story about the wife of the defendant, Celia Harcourt?"

"We were."

"And what was the gist of that story?"

"Well, we had come into some information about Mrs. Harcourt concerning her past. It had to do with a case of homicide some twenty years ago in the east. Mrs. Harcourt was known as Celia Normandeau then, and she was accused of killing her lover, the father of her child."

Clara Price paused for a moment to let the effect sink in with the jury. The gentlemen seemed to lean forward as one. There was nothing like an illegitimate-child story to pique male curiosity.

"How did you know this story to be true, Miss Stringham?"

"I had my reporter on the story check his facts twice. We were actually sitting on the story, but then confirmation of its truth came to me."

"How did it come to you?"

"It came from Miss Shannon."

As gasps filled the courtroom, Jade Stringham pointed at Kit. Kit's cheeks began to heat up as she tried to keep a poker face. Kit wrote a note on a piece of paper in front of her. The note said, *Ignore.*

"Please explain to the jury what you mean," Clara Dalton Price said.

Jade Stringham looked at the jury. "Miss Shannon came to my office with a plea that the story not be run. She did not claim the story was untrue. She said she was representing a client who didn't want it to run. When I told her we only print the truth, she threatened me with a libel suit."

Kit felt the smoldering behind her eyes and prayed she could keep the fires low. She would get her chance at the witness. It was always best to approach cross-examination with calm collectedness. Only on occasion should fury be unleashed. This was not such an occasion. Jade Stringham was making a favorable impression on the jurors.

"Was that all the confirmation you received regarding the story's truth?" Clara Price asked.

"No. The defendant also threatened me."

Again, murmurs rose from the assembled crowd. Kit could see the reporters out of the corner of her eye, scribbling away.

"Please explain," said Price.

"Objection," Kit said. "Hearsay."

"Your Honor," Clara Price said immediately, "the hearsay rule does not apply to the statements of a defendant."

"The objection is overruled," said Judge Quinn.

Coolly, like a practiced professional, Jade Stringham answered. "I received a telephone communication from the defendant. He said if I ran the story, there would be consequences. When I asked him if that was a threat, he said, 'Oh yes.' He said it was a threat against me and my boss, Mr. Mahoney. And then—I'll never forget it—he said, 'I'll show you.' And he cut off the line."

Clara Dalton Price looked at the jurors. " 'I'll show you.' That's what he said?"

"He most certainly did, in a very threatening tone."

The prosecutor nodded, smiled, and looked at Kit. "Your witness."

Kit took a deep breath, then stood up. Jade Stringham's eyes grew steely, awaiting anything Kit could throw at her.

"Miss Stringham," Kit said softly, "did anyone else hear this alleged conversation with Truman Harcourt?"

"Over the telephone, you mean?"

"Yes."

"Not that I am aware of."

"And no one was in the room with you listening at the time?"

"No."

"And being on the telephone, you were not face-to-face with Mr. Harcourt, were you?"

Jade smiled. "Of course not."

"So you could not see his mannerisms."

"I could see them in my mind."

"What was in your mind is not evidence, Miss Stringham. Please answer the question."

"No, I could not see his mannerisms. Not that I needed to. I could hear him."

"So we simply have to take your word as to what was said and how it was said, do we not?"

Jade Stringham remained unflappable. "I am under oath, Miss Shannon. I take that quite seriously."

"I see," Kit said. "Then you will of course answer truthfully the following question. Isn't it true, Miss Stringham, that you goaded Truman Harcourt in your conversation on the telephone?"

"Goad? I don't understand."

"Isn't it true that you called him a louse?"

"I do not use such language," she said with just the right amount of indignation.

Kit was undeterred. "Then you are asserting you never use the word *louse* when speaking to anyone?"

"That is what I am saying, yes."

"So when Truman Harcourt, a man seeking to protect his wife and daughter from your newspaper"—Kit said *newspaper* as if it were another word for *disease*—"called you at your office, obviously upset, you are denying that you called him a louse, is that correct?"

"That's correct."

Something went off in Kit's mind, a feeling that there was a vein of fact here, buried, waiting to be mined. She wondered if this was the sort of instinct Earl Rogers had told her was the mark of the great trial lawyer. He himself had that instinct in abundance. He would sense when something was not quite right or when there was an untapped source of evidence somewhere. Usually, with dogged persistence, he'd find it.

Kit made a mental note to think about this later. For now, she still had Jade Stringham on the stand, and the witness was still unmarked in front of the jury.

"Miss Stringham, you testified that I came to your office and made a plea that you not run the story."

"That is true."

"Do you recall my asking you if you employed a man named Rasmussen?"

Kit watched Jade Stringham carefully, looking for a crack in her veneer.

"Rasmussen?" the witness said. "I don't recall that."

"You are denying knowing such a name?"

Clara Dalton Price's voice shot, "Objection! Miss Stringham is not on trial here. I fail to see how this line of questioning is relevant."

"It is relevant to credibility," Kit said.

The judge stroked his chin. "Are you prepared to impeach this witness with evidence, Miss Shannon? Or are you on a fishing expedition?"

Kit did not appreciate the sarcasm, which resulted in some guffaws. Jurors trusted judges, and if a judge indicated displeasure with an attorney, the jurors would consider that a bad mark for the lawyer.

"I am in the search for truth, Your Honor," Kit said. Let him deny that!

He did. "I will sustain the objection, subject to an offer of proof from Miss Shannon. Unless she can show the court a basis for these questions, I will not allow them."

Very tidy, very neat. The judge and Clara Dalton Price made quite a team. But until Kit could come up with something for the judge, there was nothing she could do to interrupt their dance.

"You did bring up the legal difficulties of the *Gazette*," Kit said to Jade Stringham. "A libel case, correct?"

"Which we won," Stringham said.

"That was the case involving an oculist, a Dr. Tanner, wasn't it?"

Jade Stringham, for the first time, looked surprised. "Yes," she said. "As a matter of fact, that was his name."

"Your paper alleged that Dr. Tanner had blinded a patient when he operated under the influence of alcohol."

"Those were the facts."

"It ruined his career, didn't it?"

After a moment's hesitation, Jade Stringham said, "I do not know what became of Dr. Tanner."

"Do you care what became of Dr. Tanner?"

"Objection."

"Sustained."

Kit did not hesitate. "Isn't it true that you do not care in the least what happens to your victims?"

"Objection!"

The judge growled, "Miss Shannon, that will be enough. I have sustained the objection."

"Then I have only a few more questions," Kit said. "What was your relationship with the deceased, Gerald Mahoney?"

"He was my employer," Jade Stringham said.

"Nothing more?"

Now the full hardness of the witness rushed into her face. "What are you implying?"

"I am not implying. I am asking a question."

"The answer is Mr. Mahoney was my employer, and a fine one. Nothing else. He did not deserve to die. He did not deserve to be murdered at the hands of that man over there!" Jade's finger once more pointed at Truman Harcourt.

"I demand that this response be stricken from the record," Kit said. "And the jury admonished to give it no weight."

"Denied," said Judge Quinn, with what seemed an unusual amount of good cheer.

Furious, Kit bore in on the witness. "Have you ever been to Gerald Mahoney's house?"

"Of course," Jade Stringham said defiantly.

"How many times?"

"Numerous. He often had meetings there."

"Was anyone else present at these meetings?"

"Sometimes."

"Who?"

"Axel Bagby. My own assistant, Valerie Amman. Sometimes we met alone."

"And where did you generally meet?"

"In the study."

"The room where he was murdered?"

"Yes."

"You can, then, describe the room, can you not?"

After a moment's hesitation, Stringham said, "I think so."

"There was something hanging on the wall just inside the door, to the right as one would enter the room. Can you tell us what that was?"

The witness thought a long time, her eyes cast downward as someone trying to remember. "A portrait," she said finally. "Yes, that was it."

"Portrait of whom?"

"Gerald Mahoney," Jade Stringham answered. "It was quite a nice portrait."

"Any idea what became of it?"

Jade Stringham said, "I believe it was out being repaired."

"By whom?"

The witness shook her head. "I did not inquire. That was not my job."

And that was the end. Kit had reached a cul-de-sac in the questioning of the editor. So far as she could tell, no ground had been gained. But there was something in Kit, a feeling she'd had before in other trials. It was the feeling that something was askew. Not quite right. And she knew she had better find out what it was, and soon.

31

TED WAS TIRED AFTER a long morning with Garraty and Chase. But great progress had been made. Garraty seemed most pleased.

Sitting on a wicker chair on the sand, looking out at the Pacific, Ted listened to the voices of children as they frolicked in the waves. Both young and old enjoyed the water. Would he soon be taking his own son or daughter to the beach? With Kit holding the lunch basket and he the umbrella? He smiled at the prospect, then removed a writing tablet from his satchel and began to compose a letter.

> *My dearest Kit,*
>
> *It will not be long before I am back with you! If all goes well, I should be able to fill you in on my adventures here in San Diego, which is a bit of paradise. Until then, know that I am thinking of you and not failing to lift up daily prayers for you.*
>
> *The San Diego paper carried an account of your trial so far. You have made a name for yourself down here as well! I don't know what I shall have to do to keep such a famous wife interested in the mundane matters of marriage. Maybe I should arrange to be arrested again so that you may defend me. Remember the first time? You did a pretty good job on your first case!*

Ted thought a moment about his own trial for murder and how

Kit had taken over for Earl Rogers and won a sensational victory by exposing the plot to frame him. Good thing, too, as his neck had almost been inside the noose.

> *Think of what you can do now with all your hard-won expe-rience, eh? I only have one suggestion for you. Be sure to enfold me in your arms and kiss me passionately at every opportunity.*
>
> *Do we have a deal?*
>
> *I have been praying and thinking a great deal about our life together. What would God have me do? My work at the Institute will continue, of course, for I believe in our work. Taking the Word of God to the world is a noble enterprise.*
>
> *God wants me to fly—I know that, too. Great things are going to happen for this country in the air. I will tell you more when I return.*
>
> *Are you thinking of me? When you do. . . ?*

Ted stopped writing, suddenly aware of another man sitting in the chair beside him.

"Good day," the man said, nodding. He was a trim, well-dressed man of about forty.

Ted nodded in return.

"Marvelous weather, eh?" the man said. He had a hint of an accent, though Ted could not place it.

"Truly," Ted answered.

"Reminds me why I live in this country."

"Are you from these parts?"

"Not these. I am from parts east. Name's Hill."

"Fox is my name."

"Pleased to meet you, sir. I've seen you about."

A surprise. Ted had not seen Hill before. At least, so far as he knew. "Have you?"

"Oh yes," the stranger said. "Few things escape these eyes."

Those eyes scanned the beach for a moment.

"What brings you to the Hotel Del?" Hill asked.

"Business," Ted said, not wanting to give anything more away. "I'm from Los Angeles."

"What sort of business are you in?"

"I have, as they say, a few irons in the fire."

"Quite the new man, eh?"

Ted shrugged. "In the city I am the financial officer of the Los Angeles Bible Institute."

"Is that so?" Hill said. "To what purpose?"

"The publication, distribution, and teaching of the Word of God."

"Well, now, that's grand. I'm a man of the Good Book myself."

"Then we have much in common."

"More than you know, perhaps."

Ted wondered what the man meant. Was he a preacher?

"Tell me," Hill said. "Do you know your Bible sufficiently well to know the Revelation of John?"

"I am still a student," Ted said. "I find much in that book remains a mystery."

"I am thinking of a particular passage. If I am not mistaken, it is found in chapter twenty-one. The twenty-sixth or twenty-seventh verse. Something like, 'And there shall in no wise enter into it any thing that defileth, neither whatsoever worketh abomination, or maketh a lie.' "

It certainly sounded like Revelation. "You are a preacher, I think."

"No, but perhaps a prophet. Tell me, Mr. Fox, have you ever made a lie? Practiced deception?"

The man's voice had suddenly changed, from sunny conversation to cold accusation.

"I am not sure what you mean, sir."

"Not sure?" Hill's eyes remained fixed on Ted.

"I think," Ted said, "I should be getting back." He started to get up.

"Remain seated."

The suddenness of the remark froze Ted.

"If you look behind you," Hill said, "you will see two men. Both of them are armed. They are with me. We are going to take you with us."

Ted looked back toward the hotel. Two suited men, unsmiling, stared his way.

"I would advise you," Hill said, "not to resist."

———————

"We have made no headway," Kit said to Corazón as they sat in Kit's office. The late afternoon sun streamed in through the window, casting a silhouette of the lettering—*Kathleen Shannon, Attorney-at-Law*—on the hardwood floor.

"I think the woman Stringham is not telling the truth," Corazón said.

"But does the jury think so? I am not sure. Clara Dalton Price has prepared her well." Kit delicately chewed on her thumbnail, hearing in the distance of her memory the voice of her great-aunt Freddy, who would have been scandalized at such a gesture. "We have no favorable witnesses. Without someone to contradict what Mrs. Price is presenting, we are left only to cast reasonable doubt upon her case."

"That is the law, yes?"

"Yes, the law. But I've learned that juries are not so moved by that. They actually want the defense lawyer to prove innocence. Unless a case is so weak that it is obviously without merit, that is what they secretly demand. But this case has merit. The D.A. has seen to that."

The telephone jangled its signal, and Kit picked it up. Celia Harcourt was on the other end. Her voice was tired, frazzled. "I had to call you, Miss Shannon. I cannot concentrate on anything unless I know. What are Truman's chances?"

It was the desperate, understandable plea of a woman whose life was diminishing before her eyes. "It is only the first full day, Celia," Kit said comfortingly. "There is a long way to go yet."

"I am sick with worry over it. And Truman, sitting in jail. And what of Louise? What of my daughter?"

What should she say? That she had found Louise living in a bordello? That John Whitney was trying now to bring her back? No, it was too much for this moment. "Celia, please try to hold on to hope. I am with my assistant now, and we are working on Truman's behalf. Pray for us."

"I have prayed and prayed," Celia said. "And things keep getting worse."

"Do not give up," Kit said. "Ever."

But upon hanging up the telephone, Kit did not feel hopeful in the slightest. "We need a witness," she repeated. "Let's think!"

Corazón Chavez sighed. "I am of the wish that the man Fitch could say something."

"His testimony would be worthless," Kit said. "If he knows something, even if favorable to our side, it would be a simple matter for Mrs. Price to show he is a raving lunatic. But I still wonder what he meant by his comment about my feet."

"Sí, I have wondered. Is he meaning shoes?"

"Shoes! Very good. I hadn't thought of that. Let's say he means he has my shoes. How could that be?"

"He looked at your shoes maybe?"

"All right, looked at them. I did give him a kick. Perhaps I made an impression on his mind as well as his leg."

Corazón's eyes were knitted in thought. A minute went by. Two.

"Impression," Corazón said finally. "That is like this?" She pressed her thumb into her palm.

"Yes. And it leaves a mark in the shape of . . ."

A flash of light went off in Kit's mind.

32

IT WAS NEARLY SUNDOWN when Kit and Corazón reached the Mahoney house. Kit lit the lantern she'd brought with her and led Corazón into the yard. No one else seemed to be around. Good. She did not need any more gardeners popping out at her or policemen trying to chase her off the place.

Kit went toward the big window where she had first seen Dick Fitch, the window into the room where the murder had taken place. Large curtains had been drawn so as to obscure any view. Yet there was a tiny crack, and Kit attempted to look inside. She could barely make out a portion of the room. But it appeared to have been emptied.

Below the window were the rose bushes Fitch cared about so much. All of the roses had been clipped off. Thin, thorny arms stuck up in haphazard fashion, like wounded soldiers on a battlefield.

Dropping to her knees, Kit held the lantern out in front of her. And saw what she had come to find.

"Look there," she said to Corazón. Her assistant knelt next to her and gasped at the footprints in the soft dirt.

"I am no expert," Kit said, "but it looks as if these are rather old. Under the rose bushes, they could be protected from the weather for a time."

"I think so," Corazón agreed.

"And protected further if Fitch wanted to keep them here." Kit looked at the footprints again. "Small feet. Rounded toes. Broad heels."

"I have seen these many times," Corazón said. "The shoes of a worker."

"Or a person without much money."

"Sí."

"And what is missing?"

Corazón shook her head.

"The flowers," Kit said. "That is what Dick Fitch thinks, that I came to take his flowers. And he thinks these are my footprints. His evidence against me."

"He is a crazy man."

"Maybe not so crazy as we thought."

Again, Corazón shook her head in confusion. Kit smiled and took her arm. "Fitch did see someone stealing his flowers. But it wasn't me."

"Then who?"

Kit was already up. "Come on!" She took Corazón's arm and fairly whisked her back to the carriage. Without a word she headed toward Main Street and the Orpheum Theatre. Within ten minutes they were outside the theatre, where the name *Houdini* still appeared on the marquee.

"A magic show?" Corazón said.

"Indeed," Kit said. "I am going to try and pull a witness out of a hat."

Corazón followed Kit onto the sidewalk as Kit started slowly up the street. With evening falling and the new electric streetlights on Main coming on, the district began to take on the activities of leisure. Just what Kit had anticipated.

She spotted a man in an evening coat and silk topper, escorting a woman in a grand evening gown. An instinct told Kit to keep watching them. And then it happened. From out of the alley the flower girl appeared.

Ted had bought flowers from this same girl when they had come to Houdini's performance. Kit paused, watching as the girl offered flowers to the gentleman. He seemed pleased and produced a coin from his waistcoat. In return, he was handed a beautiful red rose.

The transaction completed, the flower girl slipped quietly back into the shadows of the alley.

"Come along," Kit said to Corazón.

The flower girl was squatting by her bucket of flowers against the large brick wall of a building.

"Miss?" Kit said.

The girl spun around in fear, like a deer at the sudden appearance of a hunter.

"Don't be alarmed," Kit said. "I only wish—"

"Flowers?" the girl said hopefully. "Would you like to buy some flowers?"

"What if I bought your entire lot?" Kit said.

Wonder bloomed on the face of the girl. "Are you in earnest?"

"Quite," Kit said. "Would five dollars be enough?"

The girl's mouth dropped open. And then a huge smile. She was pretty, though unkempt. Kit wondered why she was out on the street like this, where her kin were. Perhaps she'd be able to help her later, but first Kit needed help of her own.

As the girl began to bundle the flowers together, Kit said, "May I ask you a question?"

"Surely, ma'am," said the girl, who kept busy with her task.

Kit spoke softly, sensing the girl's vulnerability. "First, may I know your name?"

There was a slight hesitation, then the girl said, "Sarah, ma'am."

"A fine, biblical name," Kit said. "Sarah, I am Kathleen Shannon, a lawyer. I represent a man who is in terrible trouble. He is being accused of murder."

At the word, the girl's face changed. And she stopped her bundling. Her body tensed.

"Murder?" Sarah said tentatively.

"Yes. I do not believe he is guilty. The man who was killed was named Mahoney. He lived in a large house on Laurel Street. Perhaps you have seen the place. It has a great garden of flowers. Roses, and—"

Suddenly, Sarah bolted upright and began running down the alley.

"Let's go!" Kit said to Corazón. Grabbing the front of her skirt in both hands, Kit pulled the garment upward and began to give chase. But it was clear the gamine was swifter and capable of a quick escape.

There was nothing else to do. This girl was perhaps the key to her entire defense. If she witnessed the murder she would be invaluable. Kit had to keep after her.

The girl disappeared up ahead, turning out of the alley on Third Street. There would be no catching her now. Kit heard Corazón behind her, bravely trying to keep up.

Then Kit heard a scream.

———————

Was that a scream?

A distant part of Harry Houdini's mind asked the question. But it was overtaken by the stronger part, the more immediate concern of his cogitations. He'd been unable to think of much else than what he called *the puzzle.*

He sat in his dressing room at the Orpheum Theatre, alone, dressed only in a pair of trousers. His bare feet were up on the makeup table, his fingers entwined in his wiry hair.

Kajar. That's whom he kept thinking about. The man was very good. During the séance Houdini had cased the salon several times, subtly, when Kajar was busy with the others. There was no way he could have secreted a device to make noise from above the table. And Houdini had made sure to have his right leg against Kajar's left, so as to feel any furtive movements.

He had felt none. Yet the "spirit" had made snapping noises.

Then there was the matter of the handwriting on the slate. That was a good one, all right. How did he do it?

How would I do it? Houdini wondered.

He began to loosen up for the show. Each night, about half an hour before going on stage, Houdini would move every joint and every muscle, warming up his body for the routines to come. People did not know that most of his escapes and stunts were acts of pure physical prowess. That was why others had not been able to duplicate his successes. He was, in addition to being a master with keys, locks, and sleight of hand, nearly perfect in his musculature. And he intended to keep it that way.

With his right foot, he began to pick up odd items from the table—a skeleton key, a linen napkin, a jar of cold cream. When he was on his tour in Europe, he used his legs to reach through prison bars and, with his toes, insert keys into locks and escape.

Now, with his big toe and second toe holding the lip of the cold cream jar, he paused to admire his skill. And it was then that the jar slipped.

Houdini bent his foot down sharply, attempting to regain his grip. It didn't take, and the jar fell. It cracked on the hard surface, and cold cream splattered about.

And Houdini, eyes wide, shouted, "Eureka!"

———————

The girl called Sarah was struggling in the arms of a policeman. In the dimness Kit could see the thick blue uniform and the police badge prominently displayed.

And then, getting closer, she saw who it was.

"Officer Hanratty," Kit said. The same Ed Hanratty Kit had saved from a false murder charge last spring.

The big cop looked up from his capture and smiled. "Why, Miss Shannon, as I live and breathe. What brings you out this fine evening?"

"Her." Kit nodded at Sarah, whose eyes were big and frightened.

"This one?" Hanratty said. "I've been after her for a month now. She's a tricky one, she is."

"What's she done?"

"Theft. Selling on the street without a proper license."

"No, please!" Sarah cried out. "I can't. I can't go to jail!"

"Quiet there, miss," said the cop.

"Ed," Kit said. "If I promise to take responsibility, would you release this one into my custody?"

The cop wrinkled his brow. "Why, Miss Shannon, I would move heaven and earth and a good deal of Los Angeles for you. If you say you'll take responsibility, you can."

He released his hold on the girl and looked at her like a stern uncle. "You remember this, young lady. Miss Shannon is the one who got you out of trouble. You listen to her. And don't let me catch you peddling flowers again on my beat."

With his nightstick, Ed Hanratty touched his cap. "Good night, then, Miss Shannon. Call on my family sometime."

"I shall, Ed," Kit said.

As Hanratty whistled in the other direction, the flower girl turned to Kit with an odd look of fear and gratitude.

33

THE TINY RESTAURANT run by Mrs. Lea Olson was famous for its rice-and-beef casserole. Kit ate lunch here often. It was the tomato sauce that did it, a delicious concoction that included cloves, peppercorns, parsley, onions, and a hint of something mysteriously delightful. Mrs. Olson never let on what it was. No matter. It was comforting food, warm and friendly.

It was here that Kit brought Sarah and ordered her to eat.

The girl looked as if she needed nourishment. She was much too thin—a spindle, Aunt Freddy would have said. Mrs. Olson herself served the steaming casserole, with a nod to Kit and Corazón.

Sarah went at it hungrily. They could wait to talk. The fear Kit had seen in Sarah's eyes was real. The girl needed some time for calm to overtake the fright.

As she shoved the last morsel into her mouth and dabbed at the dish with a chunk of bread, Sarah looked at Kit and Corazón sheepishly. "Thank you," she said.

"Think nothing of it," said Kit. "I want you to know you're among friends."

"It's been so long."

"Since what?"

"I've been among friends." Sarah looked at her plate.

"I want you to know," Kit said, "that you have nothing to fear here. What you say to me will remain in the strictest confidence. Do you know what that means?"

"I think so."

"It means what we say to each other is a secret. I am not going to tell anyone what you say to me."

Relief freshened the girl's look. "It's also been a long time since I trusted people," Sarah said.

"You can trust Miss Kit," Corazón said. "I mean, Miss Shannon."

"All right," said the girl. "What is it you want to know?"

Kit said, "When I mentioned the murder, you ran. Why?"

The girl opened her mouth to speak, but the words seemed to catch in her throat.

"Is it because," Kit asked, "you saw what happened?"

"How did you know that?" the girl said incredulously.

"I saw your footprints at the house," Kit said. "After I spoke to the gardener."

"The crazy man?"

"Yes. He is in a cell right now. But I had seen him before, and I know the thing he is crazy about most of all are his roses. You are the one who has been taking them, aren't you?"

The girl nodded, then her eyes grew dark. "It is how I eat. It is also because I hate them all."

"Who do you hate, Sarah?"

"The ones who did that to my father."

Something vague yet potent began to take shape in Kit's mind. "Is your father Dr. Lawrence Tanner?"

Sarah looked at Kit with wide eyes and a gaping mouth. "How did you know?"

"I am not sure, exactly," Kit said, trying to put comfort into her voice. "But it seemed a logical theory. Dr. Tanner had a daughter. You are about the right age. Your hatred for Mahoney and the *Gazette* is understandable. In your own way, you are trying to get them to pay by taking Mahoney's flowers and selling them. Is that about right?"

Sarah gulped in a tortured breath of air, then began to cry.

Kit and Corazón both moved to the girl, on opposite sides, and touched her softly. Sarah put her face into Kit's shoulder. Kit gently stroked her hair.

"I am so sorry," Sarah sobbed. "It is childish, I know, but all I could think of to do."

"Don't you worry," Kit said. "Do you feel well enough to tell me about the night of the murder?"

"Yes," Sarah said, fighting for composure. "But I must confess something to you."

Kit waited.

"I would have done it myself had I the chance."

Kit and Corazón resumed their chairs. "Go ahead, Sarah. In your own words. Tell us what you saw the night Gerald Mahoney was killed."

Sarah dabbed at her eyes with a napkin. "I went to get more flowers," she said. "I waited across the street, hiding in a doorway, until I saw the gardener leave. He generally goes out the same time in the evening. I don't know where he goes. But that's when I sneak into the yard to cut the flowers."

She paused, looking at Kit as if the lawyer were a policeman. Kit patted the girl's hand. "Go on."

After a moment's hesitation, the girl said, "I went in and as soon as I got to the window, I heard voices."

"From inside the house?"

"I don't rightly recall. I got scared. I dropped down behind the rose bushes."

Kit glanced at Corazón. Without a prompt, Corazón was writing the account on her pad.

"What happened then?" Kit asked.

"I heard a man's voice. Yelling something. It made me stand up. I don't know why I did. I just thought if I saw who was there, I could get my flowers and get away."

"What did you see? Were the curtains drawn?"

"Partly. There wasn't too much light, either. It was dim. But I could see them. The two men."

Kit felt her arms tingle with anticipation. Sitting before her was a camera, a human being who had witnessed the crime. Kit was about to get a verbal photograph. Finally.

"Can you describe the men?" Kit said.

"Mr. Mahoney I recognized, of course. He was wearing a green coat, like I'd seen him in before. But even if he hadn't I would know him. I'll never forget his face."

"And the other man?"

"He had his back to me. And the light was betwixt him and Mr. Mahoney. So I couldn't see him real well. Like I said, it was dim."

"Is there anything about the man you can describe?"

"All I know is he had a gun."

Kit wanted to go very slowly now. The exact picture and timing of events would be critical.

"What hand was holding the gun?" Kit asked. In her very first trial, when she'd had to take over for Earl Rogers, a key piece of evidence was what hand the killer might have used to cut with a knife. Since then she always wanted to know that information.

Sarah thought a moment, then held up her right hand. "His back was toward me. The gun was in his right hand."

"And did you see any other person in the room?"

"No one, Miss Shannon."

"What happened next?"

"Well, the two men were looking at each other, and Mr. Mahoney, he seemed to be angry. He said something, I couldn't hear what. And the next thing I knew the other man shot him."

"How many times?"

"I think it was two shots, Miss Shannon. One right after the other."

"And then what?"

Sarah looked at her hands. "And then I ran."

As if the photograph had been snatched from her hands, Kit blinked. "That was it? That was all?"

"Yes, ma'am. I'm sorry if—"

"No," Kit said. "No need to apologize. Just think clearly. Is there anything else you can tell me about that night, anything at all? Did you see any other people around the place?"

"No, Miss Shannon. I just ran. I was so scared. I didn't stop running till I got to town."

And suddenly, like an anchor tossed into a roiling sea, Kit felt something heavy plunge inside her. It was a plummeting disaster, something Kit had not seen coming. Sarah must have seen the look on Kit's face because she said, "What is it?"

"Do you have a place to stay?" Kit said.

"I have a room," she said. "It isn't much."

"Give us the number," Kit said. "And go there. Do not speak to anyone about this until I see you again."

EARL ROGERS WAS NOT at his office. Nor was he at home when she telephoned. Kit knew that his probable location was, unfortunately, O'Reilly's Bar.

Her former boss had fallen to the bottle again. There were many reasons Rogers drank, and Kit had tried without success to get him to quit. She would never give up on that, just as she would never stop praying for him.

But now she needed his legal advice. And she found him in the smoky bedlam of the saloon, sitting with two reporters. Tom Phelps was one of them. The other was a man named Harris, from the *Examiner*.

When Rogers saw her, he looked up with reddened eyes and smiled the half grin of the drunken man. "Why, look who's here, boys!" he said grandly. "It's the second greatest trial lawyer in the world!"

Phelps and Harris looked immediately interested. Harris, a thin dandy of a fellow with a pencil mustache, was first to question her. "What's the scoop on the Harcourt murder?"

"You got something for us, Kit?" Phelps asked hopefully.

"Now, boys," Rogers said. "You know we can't talk about a case while it is in progress." He drank a shot, then added, "Unless it helps us, of course."

The two newspapermen laughed.

Kit felt half like a mother, half like a student when it came to Earl Rogers. "Earl, I need to talk to you."

"Talk to all of us," said Phelps. "Have a seat."

The thick tobacco air and the smell of beer and whiskey were sickening to her. "Outside, if you please."

"Now, Kit," Earl said like a little boy not wanting to come in the house for dinner. "Can't this wait until tomorrow? Sit down and have a phosphate."

"This can't wait, Earl," Kit said. She reached for his white skimmer, on the hat rack next to the booth, and put it on his head. "Come on."

While the two reporters protested, Kit pulled Rogers out of the booth by the lapels of his jacket. At least in his somewhat inebriated state he did not protest. "Be back in a minute, boys," he promised.

Outside the saloon, Rogers began clumsily rolling a cigarette. "Now, what's so all fired important you couldn't wait?"

"Earl, I found a witness."

He paused a moment with the pouch of tobacco over the paper. "Well, that's a stroke of luck, isn't it?"

"You don't understand. She is not a favorable witness."

Rogers scowled as he pulled the pouch's string with his teeth. "What's she know?"

"It's what she saw. She saw whoever it was who shot Mahoney."

Now the trial lawyer licked the edge of the cigarette paper and rolled it up. "Did she say it was your client?"

"She isn't sure. The light was dim. The man's back was to her. She just saw this man fire a shot and Mahoney go down. And then she ran."

"An eyewitness to the crime," Rogers mused. "And she is of no help."

"Not without an identification."

Rogers nodded, took a matchbox from his vest pocket, and extracted a wooden match. He reached behind him and, with a broad arc, ignited the match on the bricks of the saloon's exterior. He lit his cigarette.

Kit was intent on the flame.

"What is the matter?" Rogers said.

"I'm not sure," Kit said. "What you just did reminded me of something."

"What was it?"

"I don't know."

"You're a fine specimen," Rogers chided. "Can I go back in now?"

"No!" Kit said. "I haven't asked you what I should do."

"About what?"

"The witness."

"You do nothing. This witness doesn't help you. You forget about it."

"But I can't," Kit said. Didn't he understand? Had the drink dulled his usually sharp senses so much? "She has to talk to the D.A."

Rogers' face became an open book, and the subject was Kit Shannon's stupidity. "Are you completely daft? The D.A. isn't going to know anything about her. You're going to keep her as far away from the D.A. as possible. And if she says she wants to talk, you're going to give her money to get out of town. The very idea of turning over an unfavorable witness to the prosecution!"

He dragged on his cigarette and blew out twin streams of smoke from his nostrils. He was a dragon now, and an angry one.

"Earl, I know how you feel about the D.A.," Kit said. "But the law is not about hiding the truth; it's about bringing it to light. If I hide what I know is relevant evidence, that is as bad as being a perjurer. The code of ethics teaches us—"

"Code of ethics!" Rogers spat. "This is a war, Kit. The prosecution is the enemy. Code of ethics be hanged. Do you want to win your case or don't you?"

The vigor of his protest hit Kit like a punch. He was the greatest trial lawyer in the land. He had not lost a case in years. Who was she to resist what he said? It had worked for him, hadn't it?

But deep inside her she could hear her father's voice, teaching her to trust in the Lord with all her heart, mind, soul, and strength—even when the world preached a different gospel. For

Rogers, the only gospel was winning. He lived it. But that was not enough for Kit.

Rogers' face was full of fury now. "Don't ever let me hear you talk that way again, Kit Shannon! If you find evidence that helps the D.A., you hide it. If you find somebody who talks against your client, pay him off if you have to. But don't you ever help the prosecutor convict your client."

That was not the advice she had come for. She scolded herself silently for thinking she would get it. She knew what Earl Rogers would say. And she knew she could not follow his line.

"Go home to Adela," Kit said, referring to Earl's young daughter.

He jutted his chin. "You're going to do it, aren't you?"

"You've had enough to drink."

"You and your blasted ethics! You and your blasted God! I'm done with you!"

Rogers turned his back on Kit. He stumbled slightly, then disappeared into the saloon.

————

"We just want some information," the man called Hill said. "If you talk to us, we may let you go."

Ted glared at him. "I told you, I'm not saying anything to you. What are you going to do, kill me?"

The man laughed. He was standing over Ted, who was sitting on the floor in the clammy warehouse. All Ted knew was he was somewhere in San Diego. They had blindfolded him, but the automobile had not taken him far.

The place smelled of horses and leather. The two men who had "escorted" Ted from the Hotel Del Coronado were playing mumblety-peg by the door.

Ted's wooden leg felt heavy and awkward on the ground. Hill, if that was the man's name at all, was not interested in his comfort.

"We have no intention of killing you, Mr. Fox," Hill said. His accent was stronger now and clearly German.

"And I have no intention of talking to you." Lack of sleep was playing havoc with Ted's mind. But he was not going to break.

In what had become his signature gesture, the German shook his head and folded his arms. "Let me try to help you along. We know you have met with men named Peter Garraty and Duncan Chase. We know that this was about your work. We know about your projects, Mr. Fox. You have gained a reputation."

Ted wanted to jump up and take them all on. If he'd had two good legs, maybe he would have.

"Look, boys," Ted said. "I'm an expert on aeronautics, and I'm an American. That's all I have to say."

"And what is your relationship to Chase and Garraty?"

"What's it to you?"

"I am the one asking the questions, Mr. Fox."

"Suppose you tell me your game."

"I could have my colleagues persuade you to talk."

Ted glanced over at the goons. One of them poised the knife they were using for mumblety-peg on the tip of his index finger. He smiled.

"Torture? You think you can torture an American citizen on his home ground? You Krauts are pretty cheeky."

"Ah, Kraut. Short for sauerkraut. A popular name for the Germans these days. Really an abomination of the language, don't you think?"

Ted waited. The man obviously liked to talk.

"But what makes you think I am, as you say, a Kraut?"

"You talk like one."

"A mere happenstance. What if I were to tell you I am a fully naturalized citizen of these United States?"

"I'd say you're a pretty bad liar."

The German heaved a heavy sigh. Then he turned toward his comrades. "What do you think?"

The larger of the two men looked at Ted. "I think he's too smart," he said. His accent was not German at all but perfectly American. Ted was more puzzled than ever. Was this an American who had gone over to the other side?

"And you?" the interrogator asked the second man.

"I agree," he said. This one also had an American accent.

The German folded his arms and shook his head slowly. "What are we going to do with you, Mr. Fox?"

35

SARAH TANNER LIVED IN what could only charitably be called a dive. It was a rickety, wooden rooming house just below Bunker Hill. It smelled of mice and dust. Here transients could get rooms for a dollar a week. And a girl without means could, if she was willing to do what it takes, make enough selling flowers to have a roof over her head.

What had happened to her father? Kit wondered as she and Corazón entered the small room. It was spare, dingy. The only window faced out over an alley to a building next door. The light that managed to filter in was muted at best.

Sarah looked as if she had not slept. Kit's heart went out to her even as it tore inside her own body. What she had to say was not going to be easy for either of them.

"Sarah," Kit began, "I have given a lot of thought to what you told me last night."

The girl nodded.

"And I am going to have to ask you to talk to the district attorney."

What little hope there had been in Sarah Tanner's eyes was immediately extinguished. Fear replaced it. "But no . . ."

Kit tried to comfort her by taking her hand. The girl snatched it away. "You have relevant evidence to a crime," Kit said. "You have to go to the D.A. and tell him about it."

"No," she said, with a wild shake of the head. "They will put me in jail."

"They won't," Kit said. "You have not been arrested for any crime. You are only giving testimony."

"But you said!" Sarah put a hand to her throat. "You said what I told you was a secret!"

Kit swallowed hard. This was the part she hated most. "What you told me was in the strictest confidence," Kit said. "I will not reveal it. But that does not mean you can keep it from the authorities."

Sarah thought for a moment. "But it hurts your client, doesn't it?"

Kit looked at the floor, at the small, faded throw rug. "It does not matter," she said quietly. "The law says that relevant evidence must be presented." She looked up at Sarah. "I believe in justice, Sarah. God will see to it."

Bitterly, Sarah shook her head. "If God was just, then they wouldn't have hurt my father."

Sarah's pain was palpable. Kit felt it. "Where is your father now?"

"I don't know," Sarah said. "I don't think he wants to have anything to do with me. He thinks I hate him. But I don't, Miss Shannon. I miss him." Tears crept into Sarah's eyes.

Kit took a kerchief from her pocket and handed it to the girl.

"All right, Miss Shannon," she said. "I'll go. But I will tell them something they don't want to hear."

"What is that?"

Behind the tears, a hardness came into Sarah's eyes. "I will tell them that Mahoney deserved to die for what he did to my father."

―――――――

Celia Harcourt had once believed that God planted a basic goodness in everyone. That was what Dr. Lazarus preached—that all men were basically good, not sinful. But the events of the last weeks had torn at those beliefs. In desperation, Celia turned to prayer.

Yet her prayers felt like empty breaths. This morning she had given one more outburst to God, challenging Him to bring some relief to her life.

And then she had, mercifully, fallen asleep on the sofa.

Now the opening of her front door awakened her. At first she thought it must be Truman, coming home as usual. But she remembered he was in a jail cell. The trial—the nightmare—was still upon them.

Then who could it be? She sat up on the sofa, her heart pounding in warning. Then she heard the voice. "Mama?"

"Louise?" Celia felt her breath leave her.

Her daughter stepped into the sitting room. Celia fought hard not to cry out. Louise looked as if she had been through several disasters and barely survived. She was dirty, distant.

Celia ran to her, enfolding her in her embrace. Louise felt smaller somehow, and in her hair was the unpleasant odor of fast living and slow death. But it did not matter. She was home.

John Whitney came in behind them.

Celia stepped back. "What is this?" she said. "What has happened?"

Whitney said, "Come. Sit." And with a firmness that Celia had never seen in him before, he led both women into the room to sit down.

"Celia," John said, "I want to ask your forgiveness for the way I have treated you and your daughter."

Celia, incredulous, looked at him. Somehow, he seemed to have aged. Matured. He was a man, not a boy. "Yes, John. But what of Louise? What has happened?"

Her daughter was looking away from her, silent.

"I have brought her home," John said. "This is where she needs to be."

Celia reached for her daughter's hand.

Louise shook her head. "I did not wish to come back."

Before Celia could react, John said, "I insisted that she come back. It was not her desire, but I would not leave until she consented."

"But where were you?" Celia said.

At first there was no answer. The look that passed between John and Louise was full of torment, some dark secret. But Celia sensed this had to be done by the two of them, in their own way.

Then a resolve came to Louise's face, as if she had been working up to this moment. She looked at her mother, and Celia saw a distance there that had never been between them before.

"I am not fit to live," Louise said. "I have given away my life."

"Things cannot be so bad." But Celia felt it. Something was very bad.

"Mama," Louise said. "I have given myself to men."

The cold statement and all of its implications hit Celia at once. Not her daughter. Not her Louise. But she knew it was true. She could tell by the look on Louise's face. It was a face that had aged in a short time.

"Louise," Celia said. "That does not matter to me. You are my daughter. I know you must think ill of me for hiding the circumstances of your birth. I am so sorry. . . ."

Celia Harcourt began to cry.

"Mama," Louise said. "Please don't. We have all failed in our way. I most of all."

"No," Celia said.

Louise turned to John. "You have brought me back. You must go now."

John Whitney shook his head. "No, Louise. I am not going to leave you. Now or ever. We are going to marry."

Louise stood up. "John. Please go."

Once more, John shook his head.

"You do not understand," Louise said.

"I understand everything," John said. "I love you and want to take care of you from now on."

"No," Louise said. "That can never be."

Blindfolded again. Hands tied in front of him with coarse rope. Walked to an auto. Placed inside.

Ted was being moved again. But where? And by whom?

He was no closer to answers about this man Hill and his cohorts than when he'd first been brought here. Hill had claimed to be a U.S. citizen, but that did not make sense. Or did it?

Ted listened to the engine as it fired up. It sounded large and efficient. Six cylinder, maybe seven liter. This baby could do some serious speed. Perhaps fifty. Ted knew it was not an inexpensive automobile. He also knew it was a two bencher. The hood was down in the backseat, where Ted was. Whoever was driving—and Ted guessed it was Hill—was alone in the front.

Another car engine started behind them. One of the goons was driving that one. That left one goon to guard Ted in the backseat of whatever they were in.

Ted figured the car to be a Benz or a Delauney-Belville. Something like that, anyway. Which meant a back bench door. With a latch.

They bumped along the road. Ted smelled dust and dirt and gas fumes. He sensed the big man next to him, complacent in his role as guard. And why not? What could a prisoner, especially with only one leg, do in this situation?

He was about to find out.

Ted prayed quickly. *Please, Lord, help me be free of these men.*

With a quick motion, Ted whipped the blindfold off with his thumbs. The bright light made him wince. He had to move fast.

He plunged his right elbow into his guard's stomach. He heard the *oosh* of the man losing air. Before he could recover, Ted reached across and flipped the latch.

The door swung open.

"Hey!" It was Hill, on the front bench and behind the wheel.

Ted jerked his body against the guard. With a wail, the guard was out the door.

Ted saw Hill fumbling for something in his coat and knew it had to be a gun. Ted did not think, only acted. He joined his hands to form one big fist and, with a roundhouse punch, slammed the side of Hill's head.

The driver grunted and slumped to the side. The car swerved

off the dirt road and onto a field. It was barren of crops, and Ted felt what had to be air-filled pneumatic tires keeping the auto's momentum going.

Behind him, Ted saw the other automobile close behind.

Hill, lying across the front bench seat, started to move. The car was slowing down. If that happened, the guy behind would be on Ted in short order. And maybe the driver would be shooting to kill.

Without another thought, Ted swung his bum leg over the bench and with a push from his right leg, he slid over into the front seat—and found himself sitting on top of Hill.

Ted reached for the ignition advance column. If this had been a model with the pedal on the floor, he would not have been able to increase the speed. But now he could by pushing the advance lever forward.

The engine spat. The car picked up pace.

Hill writhed beneath Ted, but his arms were pinned under him. "Let me up!" Hill shouted.

The car hit a bump, sending Ted and Hill up in the air, then down again. Hill grunted in pain.

Ted saw that the other car was gaining.

Ted pushed the advance lever all the way. He thought the car must be doing forty or forty-five now. And without a glass shield or goggles, his eyes stung from wind and dust. He wiped his watering eyes with the back of his hands.

Now what? Ted scanned his limited options. Unless the other car failed, he would be caught sooner or later. But even if he did get away, what was he going to do about Hill? He was sitting, almost literally, on a powder keg. He was sure Hill had a gun on him somewhere.

And where to steer the car? A grove of trees stood up ahead, maybe two hundred yards away. The car would not make it through. Should he try to get back to the dirt road?

"Get off!" Hill cried.

He couldn't do that. This was life and death. These men, some sort of German rivals of Garraty and Chase, would kill him.

Then he heard the shot. The other driver had his gun out. And

Ted was a sitting duck. With Hill underneath him, Ted was even higher up in the seat.

Another shot. It hit metal.

"You fool!" Hill shouted. "You'll get shot!"

Not exactly a revelation, Ted thought.

"You don't know what you're doing!"

Maybe not, Ted answered in his mind, *but I cannot stop now.*

"I am a federal officer!"

What? Before Ted could think anything else, the car hit a large gully. The front shot downward as the tires hit hard dirt, stopping forward motion.

Ted felt himself shoot outward and, for a moment, experienced the sensation of flight. But he was turning over, somersaulting in the air. Then he hit ground and felt himself fall into blackness.

36

CLARA DALTON PRICE CALLED Axel Bagby to the witness stand. To Kit, Mrs. Price seemed especially confident, as if some great fortune had just fallen into her lap. Was Bagby the pot of gold at the end of her rainbow?

"Mr. Bagby," Price said. "Can you tell the jury of your previous employment?"

The big man, whose gray suit did not fit well, nodded. "I was in the employ of Mr. Gerald Mahoney."

"In what capacity were you employed?"

"Capacity?"

Mrs. Price raised her eyebrows. "What was your job, Mr. Bagby?"

"Oh, yeah. I was his personal assistant." Bagby seemed quite pleased with himself.

"And in that capacity—in that job—were you with Mr. Mahoney a good deal of the time?"

"All the time, mostly," Bagby said. "At his house, outside the house. I went with him most everywhere."

"During that time, Mr. Bagby, did you ever know of anyone to threaten Mr. Mahoney?"

The witness smiled. "Oh, sure. If you're in the newspaper business, sometimes you rub people the wrong way. But mostly people called him on the telephone or wrote him letters, and that was all.

I never heard anybody as worked up as the defendant over there."

"Objection," Kit said. "That was not in response to a question. I want that answer stricken from the record."

"Now, Miss Shannon," said the judge, "I am certain that Mrs. Price will ask a follow-up question that brings out the same information."

He was coaching the prosecutor! Kit, livid, said nothing.

"Thank you, Your Honor," said Mrs. Price. To the witness: "What was it that you observed or heard about the defendant that made you think he was, as you say, worked up?"

"I was in the *Gazette* office on the afternoon of February 8. Doing some business for Mr. Mahoney like I did from time to time. And Miss Stringham got a call on the telephone from Truman Harcourt. Well, I could hear his voice screaming at Miss Stringham. He was saying—"

"Objection!" Kit said. "Hearsay."

Clara Dalton Price said, "Your Honor, we are only offering this conversation as proof of the defendant's state of mind, not the truth or accuracy of his statements."

"I will overrule the objection."

Mrs. Price nodded. "What, if anything, did you hear the defendant say to Miss Stringham?"

"I only heard him say, 'The man will pay.'"

The statement seemed to make an impression on the jurors. Kit saw their looks of rapt attention. Truman Harcourt put his hand on her arm and whispered, "That's a lie."

Clara Dalton Price paused a long time before asking her next question. She was letting the jury hear exactly what she wanted them to hear.

"Are you absolutely certain those were the defendant's words? *The man will pay*?"

"That's what I heard," Bagby said.

"Your witness," said Clara Dalton Price.

There was a jury instruction that stated a witness found to be lying in one part of his testimony could be discounted in all parts. It was with that instruction in mind that Kit began her questioning.

If she could catch Bagby in one lie it would taint everything else he said. And she needed to do it. His testimony had hurt badly. The problem was finding a lie that would stick. Price had no doubt coached him well.

"Mr. Bagby," Kit said. "You were, in fact, Mr. Mahoney's bodyguard, were you not?"

Bagby shrugged. "If you want to call it that." He looked singularly unconcerned.

"What would you call it, Mr. Bagby?"

"Like I said, I was his assistant."

"Oh? Did you assist him in setting policy for the newspaper?"

Axel Bagby blinked. "Well, no."

"Did you pay the bills?"

"No. I didn't have—"

"Did you keep the books?"

This time, Bagby shook his head.

"Did you clean the house?" Kit said.

"No, I did not."

"But you did push people away from Gerald Mahoney, didn't you?" Kit did not know of any specific instance of this. But the Rule of Human Probabilities told her it had to be true. And she hoped Bagby would think she did have a witness to corroborate the assertion.

The witness melted a little bit. "I am not a violent man, Miss Shannon."

Kit looked at the large man and nearly laughed. "Is that why you take boxing lessons?"

Bagby looked like he'd been hit with a jab. But he deflected it. "Boxing is a sport, Miss Shannon. I get my exercise in the ring."

Kit put her hands behind her back, looked at Bagby as if studying him. "You testified that you heard my client say the man would pay, is that right?"

"That's what he said."

"It sounded like a threat to you?"

"Yep."

"Tell us, Mr. Bagby, why you did not warn Mr. Mahoney."

Bagby turned his head a little. "How's that?"

"If you were sure Mr. Harcourt was threatening Mr. Mahoney, why didn't you, his bodyguard, warn him?"

Bagby tried to keep his face from twitching, but it did not fully cooperate. "But I did. I called Mr. Mahoney on the telephone, from the *Gazette* office."

Kit turned toward the counsel table and for a moment looked out into the packed gallery. In the back row she saw Harry Houdini, watching intently with his piercing eyes. What was he doing here?

Returning her focus to the witness, Kit said, "Mr. Bagby, isn't it true that on February ten you were involved in a bar fight at the Montoya saloon?"

Clara Dalton Price stood up. "Objection, Your Honor. Incompetent, irrelevant, and immaterial."

"What is the relevance, Miss Shannon?" Judge Quinn asked, less stridently than before.

"The witness has asserted he is not a violent man. I have the right to challenge that assertion."

After a short pause, Judge Quinn said, "Go ahead."

"Answer the question," Kit said.

"I might have."

"In fact, sir, you attempted to hurt a man who was defending a lady, did you not?"

Bagby looked cornered. "He was interrupting my business."

"He knocked you to the floor, did he not?"

"A lucky punch! While I wasn't lookin'."

Now Kit had Bagby where she wanted him, and she quickly changed the subject, like a fighter throwing a sucker punch. "Where did you go after your visit to the *Gazette* office on February eight?"

"I was with my pal, Sid Gates."

"The man who owns the alligator farm?"

"Yes, as a matter of fact."

"Where did you go?"

"Over to his place."

"No further questions."

Court was adjourned. As Truman Harcourt was marched back

to his jail cell, Clara Dalton Price approached Kit.

"Perhaps it would be better for your client to plead guilty at this point," she said. "Judge Quinn has told me he might spare his life."

"You have had discussions with the judge without my presence?" Kit said.

"Informally. You understand."

"Yes," Kit said. "I am afraid I do understand."

The prosecutor did not look at all perturbed. "Another witness has come forward, someone who actually saw the killing."

"Sarah Tanner," Kit said.

"Yes, she told us you sent her. Your ethics are commendable. Unfortunately, her account seals your client's fate."

Kit shook her head. "I heard her story first, remember. And the identity of the killer is still an issue. She was unable to describe the man who shot Mahoney."

"Oh, didn't she tell you?" Clara Price said, as if casually dropping a stick of dynamite in Kit's briefcase. "She can describe the coat the killer was wearing. It is the same coat your client was wearing when the police found him."

Kit barely had time to react before Clara Price turned her back and walked away. Then Kit noticed Harry Houdini at the rail.

"I must speak to you," he said. His curly hair was wild on his head, as if it wanted to shout.

"What is it?"

"I have it," he said. "The solution. I know what Kajar did to fool us. There is only one part of the mystery yet to be solved. Who would know about your aunt's wishes for her husband's memorial?"

"I think I know," Kit said. "Benjamin Stillwater. He was Aunt Freddy's confidante and got her to change her will. He would have known. And he would have had several written notes from her in his possession."

"Mystery solved!" Houdini said, sounding excited at the prospect of exposing another fraudulent medium.

"But how do we prove it?" Kit said. "Both of them can deny it."

"Miss Shannon, you and I are students of human nature. You, because you must learn to tell liars from truth tellers in court. I, because my living is based upon illusions, fooling the human mind. I propose we put our heads together to trap this man into an admission."

"However will we manage that?"

"Come with me."

———————

Ted woke up to dim light and a dank smell. His head felt like a punching bag. He took a deep breath and his lungs filled with flame.

He was on his back. On some kind of bed.

The wall next to him was gray and cold. He raised his head, pain shooting down his neck, and saw iron bars.

He was in a cell.

Outrage filled him. At least it helped dull the pain. His hands were free. What had happened? He remembered the car, sitting on Hill, the chase, the shots. And flying out of the car. They must have brought him here.

Who are they?

Ted pushed himself up on the hard bed and realized his fake leg was missing. That only added to his rage. He stood and hopped to the bars. So far as he could tell, he was the only one in what seemed like a block of four cells.

"Hey!"

His voice echoed off the walls.

"Hey, somebody get in here!"

No answer.

He thought of Kit then. If only she were here. She would give whoever was holding him a taste of an Irish storm, backed by the law of the United States. If only he could reach her.

Lord, bring her to me, he prayed.

Then he shouted three more times. Finally, a door opened and a small man with a set of keys came in.

"No need to wake the dead," the jailer said.

"I'll do more than that if you don't get me out of here now."

Shaking his head, the jailer regarded Ted as if he were a silly child. "You don't exactly have many cards to play. You're a prisoner."

"What for? Where am I?"

"You're in the hoosegow, is where you are."

"That much I know."

"That's all you need to know right now. I'll tell 'em you're up and around."

"Where's my leg?"

The jailer motioned with his thumb. "On my desk. First time that's ever happened. I'll go get it for you. Then we'll take a little walk."

"Where?"

"To see the man you tried to kill, I expect."

37

"WHAT IS THE MEANING of this intrusion?" Kajar said. He was without his turban, looking like any other American on the make. His voice trembled slightly, with either outrage or nervousness.

Anyone facing Harry Houdini's eyes would be nervous, Kit thought. She was just glad he was now doing the talking.

"You, sir, are a fraud," Houdini said.

The word toughened Kajar's resolve. "You are a slanderer, sir. I have already proven to you—"

"You proved nothing but your own cleverness," Houdini said. "Unfortunately for you, cleverness can be exposed."

Kajar looked at Kit. "Are you complicit in this?"

"I am here for the truth," Kit said. "As always."

"You are a troublemaker, is what you are," said the swami. "Do you not recall that the All Seeing Eye selected you?"

"Mr. Houdini has explained that part of the trick to me," Kit said. "It is called the magician's choice, for you can control the selection of the cards."

Kajar said nothing.

"You put out five cards," Kit said, "and asked me to be the first to touch one. There was one chance in five that I would select the card you wanted to force on me. And you know that most people do not select the middle card, nor the end ones, making it more of a one in two proposition."

"She's good, isn't she?" Houdini said.

"Had I not touched the eye card, as you wished me to, you would have told me to *eliminate* that card and touch two others. If the eye was one of those, you would ask me to make a choice between the two. And so on. You can control what card is selected."

"I can also control my premises," Kajar said. "You are trespassing. Shall I call the police?"

"We will leave," Houdini said, "after one simple request."

"And that is?"

"Remove your right shoe, if you please."

Kajar's pale cheeks drained of what color had been there. "I beg your pardon."

"Your shoe, sir," said Houdini calmly. "You see, your big toe is double-jointed, and you have the ability to snap with your toes. Quite loudly, I am sure."

Kit watched Kajar's face carefully, as she and Houdini had discussed. She would look for any twitch or hesitation that would reveal the truth. But Kajar remained impassive, save for his outrage.

"I will not do any such thing," Kajar replied. "Yours is a most ungentlemanly request, sir, especially in front of a lady."

"I'll hide my eyes," Kit said.

Kajar huffed. "I will not subject myself to this indignity. Please leave."

Houdini grinned. Like a shark, Kit thought, if sharks could smile. "Not before the spirits have spoken."

Kit could only admire the magician's sense of the theatrical. And Kajar was, finally, taken aback.

"What do you mean?"

"You are a believer in the spirits, aren't you?"

"Of course."

"Then you will not object if the spirits reveal the name of your confederate."

Kajar drew his thin frame to its full height. He raised his nose like a Russian count. "You are a mere magician," he said. "A trickster. A trafficker in artifice. I alone am a friend of the spirits here."

"Then you will have no objection," Houdini said. And before Kajar could say another word Houdini raised his right hand and snapped his fingers. Instantly, a deck of cards appeared.

Kajar's eyes opened like popping fireworks.

"An ordinary deck of cards," Houdini said, fanning them so the pips could be seen. "Observe. All different. But in the hands of the spirits, they become extraordinary." Houdini the showman closed his eyes. "O spirits!" he cried out, and Kit almost laughed. This was high comedy as well as serious business with a fraud.

Houdini held the cards up toward the ceiling. "Reveal to us the name of the man who was an aid in this fakery, who forged the message in chalk that purportedly came from Frederica Fairbank!"

"This is an absurdity," Kajar said.

"Shh," said Houdini. "The spirits wish to speak." Houdini fanned the cards out to Kajar. "Pick a card, any card."

"I will not," Kajar said. He folded his arms like a petulant child.

"Very well," Houdini said. "Then we shall have the spirits do it for you." Houdini held the fan outward, back toward Kajar, and waved his other hand over them. Nothing happened at first, adding drama to the act, and then, slowly at first, a single card began to rise out of the deck.

Kit watched as Kajar's face became paralyzed with awe. If this was a man of the spirits, he certainly was not showing it now.

The card rose, rose until it was suspended in the air, by itself—as if a ghostly hand held it there.

Houdini gripped the card with his thumb and forefinger. And then, with a theatrical *snap*, he flipped it so Kajar could read its face.

And Kit read Kajar's face. It was obvious. His eyes spoke more profoundly than any voice. What Kajar saw on that playing card was scaring the wits out of him.

On the card was written the name Kit had scrawled there earlier in black ink: *Stillwater.*

Though Harry Houdini had explained to Kit that the rising card trick was a simple one for magicians, the effect on Kajar was immense and instantaneous. He looked as if he was going to choke.

Houdini simply stood there, holding the card out like an indict-ment. Kajar could not stop staring at his own guilt.

But then, from the depths, the medium recovered his reserves. He breathed in deeply and stuck out what little chest he had. "That proves nothing," he said. "Despite your little trick, it is nothing more than your word against mine. And Benjamin Stillwater's."

"So you know him," Kit said.

"Of course I know him," Kajar said, "as your little ruse deter-mined. And we fooled you. We fooled the both of you! Harry Houdini, the great magician. Ha! You fell for the false chalkboard trick."

"No," Houdini said. "It was the handwriting that was the clever part. But then we determined Stillwater had samples of Freddy Fair-bank's writing and forged the message."

"But all of this is only our little secret," Kajar responded. "If you two try to spread this around, I shall only deny it. I shall tell every-one you are jealous and will stop at nothing to shut me down. Why, I may even consider a slander suit just to drag you two through the mud."

A voice from the shadows: "And the *Los Angeles Times* will print your confession."

Kajar jumped backward. Tom Phelps stepped into the parlor.

"How did . . ." Kajar stammered. "All windows and doors are locked, save the front!"

Harry Houdini reached into his vest pocket and took out a small skeleton key. He tossed it once in the air. "I am the master of escapes. That also makes me the master of entries."

"But you can't . . ." Kajar said weakly.

"He just did," Phelps answered.

Kit, ever the trial lawyer, sensed the moment was ripe. "Now, Mr. Kajar, I might be able to prevail upon my friend Tom Phelps to hold up this story."

Kajar looked as if the weight of the world had just been eased a bit from his shoulders.

"First," Kit said, "you will have to give me a story of your own."

"Story? About what?"

"About the time John Whitney and Louise Harcourt came to see you."

Kajar looked faint. And Kit knew that her hunch about his being the one that Whitney had referred to was correct.

Houdini slipped a chair from the round felt table and said, "Maybe you'd better sit down, old boy."

"I did not try to kill you," Ted said, "and you know it. So what's your game?"

He was seated across from the man called Hill, who looked like he came through the car mishap in better shape than Ted did. They were in the jailer's office. Along with the jailer was another man, thin and suited, who had not introduced himself.

Hill was his interrogator. "I repeat, Mr. Fox. Why did you try to kill me? After I told you I was a federal officer?"

"Why should I have believed you?" Ted said, his anger rising. "Why should I believe you now?"

"I think you know why."

Ted folded his arms. "Pretend I'm ignorant."

"Why don't you tell us about your friends, Garraty and Chase?"

"Why don't you tell me why I should be talking to you?"

Hill sighed and looked at the thin man sitting by the wall.

"You're a Kraut," Ted said.

"I assure you I am as American as you are," Hill said. "Though I am of German birth, I was naturalized five years ago, after being escorted here by the Army. Trained as a spy."

"A spy? You're joking."

"Germans are not known for joking, Mr. Fox. That aspect of my heritage I still carry with me."

"Even if I believed you, I've got nothing to say."

"You won't cooperate with us?"

"How?"

"By talking. Freely. Giving us as much information as you can."

"And that's why you had me locked up in a hole? So you could soften me up or something?"

"Or something."

"I have the right to speak to a lawyer."

"Mr. Fox, if you have nothing to hide, you have no reason to speak to a lawyer, do you? If you are a loyal American then surely you will want to tell us everything we want to know."

"I am a loyal American," Ted said. "And who is that?" Ted nodded toward the thin man.

"Allow us to ask the questions."

"I'm afraid not," Ted said. "Not until I talk to my lawyer."

Hill sat up stiffly. "What makes you think you need to speak to a lawyer? You haven't been charged with anything."

"Then I'm free to go?"

"Not until we get the information we seek."

"Then I'm a prisoner. You're not being logical, Hill. If that's really your name."

"Oh, hang it," the thin man said, standing. "My name's Collins. I'm the United States attorney down here. And we have a mind to charge you with treason."

"Treason?"

"We have your Mr. Garraty and Mr. Chase in custody."

"So?"

Collins, whose gaunt face carried no signs of mirth, looked taken aback. "So you had better talk to us."

"I told you, I'm not talking to anybody unless I talk to my lawyer. I've been manhandled and snatched and shot at. If that's how you want to handle things, then you'll get that back from me."

"Do you realize you will be charged with treason?"

"Do you realize you don't know what you're talking about?"

Collins' face very quickly turned red.

"Take him back to his cell," Collins said to the jailer.

———

Kit found Corazón waiting for her at the office. Her assistant seemed lit up by sunshine—in her face and bearing. Kit was observing, for the first time, a woman, not a mere girl. There was a blossoming about Corazón that was exceedingly pleasant to behold.

"I have news," Corazón said. "From Raul Montoya."

"You have seen him?" Kit said.

"Sí." And then Corazón's face became part smile, part shy attempt to hide the smile.

"And just what did he say?"

"He said that there is something about the man Bagby. His papa was once threatened by Bagby."

"But why?"

"Bagby says he is, what is the word, representing?"

"Representing, yes."

"Representing a man who wanted to buy the saloon. Señor Montoya, he said no. Bagby made a threat to him."

"I wonder if Bagby was representing Mahoney? Why would Mahoney want to buy a saloon?"

The two women pondered the question for a moment in silence. Then Kit paced in front of her window, as she often did when reasoning about a set of facts. "There are other things that trouble me, Corazón. The portrait of Mahoney that was hanging in the study. Bagby said it was out being repaired. I want to know why. Can you find all the portrait shops in town and give them a visit?"

"Sí, I will do it."

"And then there is the evidence in the study. McGinty did not do an inventory, which I find quite strange. But surely the evidence must be somewhere. It is either still in the house, as is, or someone has it. But when I looked in through the window, the room appeared to be empty. Where have all of the contents gone?"

Corazón thought hard about it. "The *Gazette* office?"

"That was my first thought, too. But I don't know if there is enough space there. So far as I know, Mahoney had no heirs. None were listed in the obituary. Which leaves another question—to whom did Mahoney leave his estate?"

"I will find out," Corazón said.

"Good. That leaves the broken glass. What was it and what does it mean? If we don't have an inventory of the contents of the room, it is impossible to tell. Davenport and McGinty know more about this case than they are letting on. I wonder . . ."

Kit removed from her coat pocket the black skeleton key Houdini had given to her.

"What is that?" Corazón asked.

"Maybe the key that will finally unlock this mystery."

––––––––––

"I must go away, Mother," Louise said.

"No! You have just come back." Celia faced her daughter in the drawing room. Outside the night was dark and still.

"I cannot stay in Los Angeles. I only came back because I weakened under John's insistence."

"But you and John can marry now, you can—"

"No, that can never be."

"Because . . . of what happened?"

"I did not want it to happen. I was taken in and fed and housed. By a woman called Lady Eve."

Celia listened with her hand on her swiftly beating heart.

"But a few days later Lady Eve told me it was time I earned my keep. That was the start of it." Louise's eyes filled with tears. "I was so weak. Dr. Lazarus used to tell us how strong we were inside, remember?"

Celia put her arms around her daughter, pulling her close. "Dr. Lazarus's god is the weak one. The God of the Bible is the one who truly exists and can heal anything, even this."

"No," Louise cried into her mother's shoulder. "I cannot do this to John."

"Have you talked to John about this?"

"He is trying to be noble, but it will not work. He will always look at me knowing I have been with other men."

"I saw the look in John's eyes when he brought you home. There was something strong and good there."

"And that is what I don't want to ruin."

"You won't," Celia said tenderly.

"I will."

"Your father and I want you to stay. At least stay with us."

"I've shamed you and Father." Louise looked at her hands, then up at her mother. "Do you think Father will go free?"

"I have faith in Miss Shannon."

"Then, when he does, I'd rather he not see me."

"But he will want to see you! He will want you to stay."

"You mustn't tell him I've been here."

Celia's heart jumped. "No, Louise. There must be no more secrets in our family. It is I who have brought all this upon us."

"Do not ever think that." Now it was Louise who embraced her mother as both wept.

38

TRUE TO HER WORD, Clara Dalton Price called Sarah Tanner to the witness stand the next morning. The girl was a wide-eyed doe, out of her element. Her plain, brown muslin dress was the sort worn by factory workers or day laborers. Her hair was crudely put up, strands falling haphazardly down the side of her face. Kit knew all of this would give Sarah favor with the men on the jury. She looked like a child needing protection.

And Clara Dalton Price questioned her as if she, herself, were that protector. "You have no need to be frightened," Price said after the oath was administered. "All we want is for you to give us the truth. Do you understand, Miss Tanner?"

Sarah Tanner nodded.

"You will need to answer aloud," Judge Quinn said, "so the court reporter can put it down."

"I'm sorry," Sarah said.

"No need," Mrs. Price said. "Just be calm and relaxed as I ask you these questions. The judge will see to it that no one hurts you."

Leaving the impression that I wish to hurt her! Kit thought furiously. Clara Dalton Price was as devious as she was smart.

"You live in a tiny room in a building near Bunker Hill, do you not?" Clara Dalton Price asked.

"Yes, ma'am."

"In a section the papers sometimes describe as the lower depths?"

"I don't know about that."

"It's not a wealthy section, is it?"

"No, ma'am."

"And you pay for your room and board?"

"Yes, I do."

"You sell flowers to make ends meet, do you not?"

"Yes, ma'am."

"This enterprise does not make very much money, does it?"

"Enough for me, I suppose."

"Where do you get your flowers to sell?"

"At the morning markets. There are castoffs. I take what looks good."

"And sometimes you don't have quite enough, isn't that true?"

"Sometimes."

"And in desperation, haven't you from time to time clipped flowers from private gardens?"

Sarah Tanner looked down, as if ashamed. "Sometimes. I am sorry for doing it."

Kit saw that Sarah was beginning to melt. Kit wanted to shout at Clara Price to stop. But the prosecutor was calmly going about her business.

"No one has ever pressed any charges against you?"

"No, ma'am."

Clara Dalton Price nodded approvingly. "Very good. Now, on the evening of February eight, did you go to the home of Gerald Mahoney?"

"Yes," Sarah said quietly.

"And did you clip some flowers there?"

"Yes."

"Roses?"

"Yes."

"And where were the rose bushes located?"

"Below a large window, ma'am."

"Were you able to see into this window?"

234 CE JAMES SCOTT BELL

"Yes."

Mrs. Price looked toward the jury. "Please tell the jurors what you saw."

Sarah swallowed, as if trying to get down a morsel of dry food. "I saw two men. I thought they were talking. Then I saw that one of the men had a gun in his hand. Then there was a shot, and the other man fell to the floor."

"Did you see anything else?"

"No, ma'am. I got scared, and I ran away."

"All right. Can you describe the man who shot the gun?"

Sarah quickly looked at Kit, then back at the prosecutor. "It was not very light inside. I couldn't see very clearly."

For the first time, Clara Dalton Price looked a bit perturbed. With a little more sharpness in her voice, she said, "Sarah, please relate to the jury what you related to me about the man with the gun."

The stern tone seemed to snap Sarah Tanner into a reluctant position. Her next words came as a struggle. "I saw the coat the man was wearing."

"Please describe the coat."

"It was a long coat, an overcoat I think, brown. It had a dark collar."

Kit tried to picture this in her mind. Did Truman Harcourt have such a coat? Clara Dalton Price, who walked to the prosecution table, answered the question. There she pulled out an overcoat exactly as Sarah had described.

There were gasps from the gallery and a few of the jurors. Price's theatricality was potent. Even though there was not yet a connection between Truman and the coat in Price's hands, it was a visual moment. Earl Rogers would have approved.

"Does this appear to be the coat?" Clara Dalton Price said, holding it up so the back of the coat was toward the witness.

"I think so," Sarah said.

"You see that the collar is a black velvet and the coat is brown, do you not?"

"Yes."

"Your Honor, I would like this coat to be marked as People's Exhibit Three, subject to the testimony of Detective McGinty that this is the coat worn by the defendant, Truman Harcourt, when he was caught outside Gerald Mahoney's house."

"Let it be so marked," said the judge.

And then Clara Dalton Price slowly turned the coat around so the front of it faced the jury. Kit could not see it from where she was sitting. She did not think much of the gesture, until the prosecutor said, "And I would note also for the court the stains on the front of the coat, subject to testimony that this is the blood of the victim."

Kit's objection was drowned out by the noise that erupted in the courtroom. Clara Price's statement was out of bounds, made solely to influence the jury. But the bell was rung, and as the saying went among trial lawyers, you cannot unring a bell. Kit decided not to follow it up, as it would only emphasize the matter to the jury.

"Your witness," Clara Dalton Price said with a smile.

Kit approached Sarah Tanner cautiously. Something about her testimony did not seem right. But she was fragile, like a vase. If Kit hit her too hard she might shatter.

"Sarah, you stated that the light was dim inside the house, isn't that right?"

"Yes, ma'am." Sarah seemed anxious to help.

"So dim that the man with the gun was almost a silhouette?"

"Yes. I could not see his face."

"When we spoke of this incident the first time, you did not mention the coat to me, did you?"

"No, Miss Shannon."

"Was your first mention of this coat to the prosecutor, Mrs. Price?"

Sarah looked over toward Clara Dalton Price and nodded. "Yes, it was."

"I'm curious," Kit said, giving her own glance at the deputy district attorney. "Did Mrs. Price ask you if the man was wearing an overcoat?"

The prosecutor stood up. "I object, Your Honor."

"On what grounds?" Kit said, before Judge Quinn could speak up.

Clara Price glared at Kit. "It is an improper inquiry."

"There is no such objection in the code," Kit said. "Is the prosecution trying to keep information from the jury?"

Quinn pounded on the bench with his gavel. "That is quite enough, Miss Shannon. What is the purpose of your question?"

"I want to know if Mrs. Price put the idea of an overcoat in the witness's mind," Kit said. "I want to know if she was the one who made the suggestion."

"What does it matter?" said the judge. "The witness has testified to it and is under oath. I will sustain the objection."

This was no surprise to Kit, but she hoped the jury got the message—Clara Dalton Price was capable of not playing fair.

"Sarah," Kit said, "you saw the man holding a gun. What hand was it in?"

"His right hand."

"You said you saw Gerald Mahoney fall?"

"Yes, ma'am."

"Can you describe how he fell?"

Sarah frowned. "I saw him fall to his knees," she said. "That was all. Then I got scared and ran."

"And at no time did you see any bloodstains on the coat of the man who fired the shot, did you?"

"I never saw the front of the coat."

"Nothing further, Your Honor."

Clara Dalton Price recalled Mike McGinty to the stand to testify about the coat. He said it was the same one worn by the defendant when he was arrested. He also verified that the coat had blood on it. On cross-examination Kit got McGinty to admit he did not know for certain whose blood it was. But that was all she got, and there was certainly not going to be much doubt in the jurors' minds as to whose blood it was.

When Kit sat down, Clara Dalton Price said to the court, "I have just one more witness to present."

39

"I CALL NORBERT STRONG to the stand," Clara Dalton Price said.

He was an older man, perhaps seventy, who used a rosewood cane to help him walk. Short and somewhat stooped, he had darting brown eyes under bushy white eyebrows. He was sworn in and took the witness chair.

"You live at 408 Laurel Street, is that correct?" Mrs. Price asked.

"Yes, sir," Norbert Strong said. Then he quickly added, "I mean, yes, ma'am."

"Were you acquainted with the resident of 406 Laurel Street?"

"You mean Mr. Mahoney? I knew him all right. Not to talk to, mind you. He was a standoffish sort of fella, and I have no use for such."

"But you knew him by sight?"

" 'Course I did. Everybody on the street knew Mahoney. Bit of a troublemaker, if you ask me."

"But we are not asking him," Kit objected to Judge Quinn. "Please instruct the witness to stick to answering the questions."

"How's that?" Norbert Strong said, putting a hand to his ear.

"Mr. Strong," Judge Quinn said loudly, "please answer only the question the lawyers ask you."

"That's what I've been doing," the witness snapped. "You think I'm deaf or something?"

Judge Quinn rolled his eyes, then nodded to Clara Price with a certain amount of resignation.

"On the evening of February eight, around seven o'clock, were you at home?" Clara Price said.

"Yep."

"What were you doing at that time?"

"Reading."

"What room were you reading in?"

"Bedroom."

"Your bedroom?"

"Yep."

"Were you by the window?"

"Yep."

"What is the view from your window, sir?"

"Outside."

Some of the people in the courtroom laughed. The witness was taking the judge's instruction a little too literally.

"Please tell us," Mrs. Price said, "what you could see of Gerald Mahoney's house."

"Well, why didn't you say so? I saw the west side of that big house of his. Only thing I like about it is that it keeps the sun off me in the morning."

More laughter, and a gavel from the judge. Clara Dalton Price looked exasperated.

"On this evening," Clara Price said, "did you have occasion to look out your window and see someone at the house?"

"You asking me about what you asked me about at my house when you came to see me?"

"Yes, Mr. Strong."

"I saw a man sneaking along the side of the house."

"I object," said Kit. "That is an opinion of the witness."

"Don't you think I know what sneaking is?" Strong shot at Kit.

The judge admonished the witness again to stick to the questions.

"What was this man wearing, sir?" Clara Dalton Price said.

"A coat."

"Would you recognize the coat if you saw it again?"

" 'Course I would. You think I'm blind *and* deaf?"

As titters scurried across the courtroom, Mrs. Price went to her counsel table and picked up the coat that was folded neatly on top. "I am holding the coat that has previously been marked at People's Exhibit Three for identification," she said. "I ask the witness if this looks like the coat he saw that night."

"Bring it closer," Strong said.

The prosecutor stepped toward him, looking as if she wished she'd never called this witness.

"That's it, all right," the witness said. "That's the coat."

"Thank you," said Mrs. Price. "Your witness."

Kit approached Norbert Strong. "When you said, 'That's the coat,' sir, you meant only that it looks like the coat."

"How's that?"

"You do not know if that is the exact coat you saw. You have no way of knowing that, do you?"

"Are you trying to get smart with me?"

"Please answer the question, Mr. Strong," Quinn said.

"I'm telling you that is the coat I saw," said Norbert Strong. "Can't make it any plainer than that."

Kit stopped there, knowing the jurors got the gist of the exchange. Besides, it was never good to go too hard on an older person in cross-examination. They were usually seen as weaker than the lawyers and easy subjects for bullying.

"Mr. Strong, it was dark at the time you made this observation, was it not?"

"Dark? I don't remember. I only remember what I saw."

"Can you describe the lighting outside at all?"

"Light enough to see that coat," Strong said.

Kit thought a moment, touching her lower lip with her index finger. "Sir, is it your habit to look out your bedroom window at night?"

"How's that?"

"Is it a habit of yours," Kit said patiently, "to look out your bedroom window at night?"

Norbert Strong got a twinkle in his eye, as if he had caught Kit trying to put one over on him. "No, ma'am. It is my habit to read by that window every night, and everybody knew it, too."

"What do you mean by everybody?"

"I mean that man Mahoney knew it." Strong leaned forward. "He was awful suspicious. Asked me if I was spying on him once. Said he didn't like people looking too close, and if I didn't stop he was going to write a story about me. I just laughed at him."

"What was his reaction?"

"Never heard from him again. I wasn't going to have somebody tell me what I could and could not look at. No, sir."

"Your house," Kit said, "is approximately how far from Mr. Mahoney's house?"

"Land sakes, I don't know. Why should I know that?"

"Was it as far as, say, from where you are sitting to the back of the courtroom?"

The witness glanced toward the back wall. He shook his head. "I don't sit around thinking about such things, missy. How do you expect a person to know?"

"You have been very precise about your observation of the coat," Kit said gently. "I would have thought you could be precise about this."

"Well, what you thought and what I think are two different things, now, aren't they?"

Judge Quinn slapped his palm on the bench, creating a loud rap. "That will do, Mr. Strong!"

"I have no further questions," said Kit.

"How's that?" Norbert Strong said.

"The prosecution rests," said Clara Dalton Price.

———

After a short recess it was time for Kit Shannon to begin. She was, as always, a little nervous, like a schoolgirl called up to the front of the classroom to lead the class in the good morning song.

"I call Lewis Muntz to the stand," she said.

A wave of murmuring voices seemed to ask the question, *Who is Lewis Muntz?* Certainly the look on Clara Dalton Price's face reflected the query. She was not a woman who liked surprises, and Kit had just dropped one.

The courtroom doors opened and in walked Kajar. He wore a plain business suit over his thin frame and looked far from the spiritualist he purported to be. Rather, he gave the appearance of a staid, if somewhat nervous, accountant.

Kit scanned the courtroom gallery as Muntz came forward. Allard and Edwina Whitney looked positively in shock, as did Jade Stringham. Kit knew why. Soon the whole courtroom would know, too.

Muntz was sworn in by the clerk. Kit said, "By what other name are you known, Mr. Muntz?"

He cleared his throat. "Kajar," he said.

"You have a business establishment?"

"Yes, I do."

"What is the purpose of your business?"

"I am a spiritualist, clairvoyant, and medium."

Kit left it at that. She was not going to use this moment to contest Muntz on his spiritualist claims. In exchange for the information he was about to give, and a promise that he would leave Los Angeles, Kit was going to leave him alone. There were larger fish to throw in the pan.

"Mr. Muntz, in November of last year, did you have a visit from two young people, John Whitney and Louise Harcourt?"

"Yes."

Kit felt the stirrings in the courtroom now, sensing the tension coming from certain interested parties. Clara Dalton Price looked ready to pounce at the mere hint of an objectionable question. Kit was not going to oblige.

"Can you tell us how that visit came about?"

Muntz grabbed the arms of the witness chair with both hands, as if riding a raft in a raging sea. "It was set up by Mrs. Allard Whitney."

A woman's voice cried out, "That's a lie!" Kit did not have to turn around to know it was Edwina Whitney.

Judge Quinn said, "Madam, you will refrain from speaking while court is in session."

"The very idea!" Mrs. Whitney said. "I am not used to—"

"Quiet!" said the judge. "Another outburst and I will have you removed."

Allard Whitney whispered something to his wife. She closed her mouth in a pout like a spoiled brat.

"Continue," Quinn said to Kit.

Nodding, Kit asked Muntz, "How did Mrs. Whitney set up the meeting?"

"She came to my establishment. She asked if I would do her a service. She offered to pay me two hundred dollars."

"That is quite a sum of money. Did you agree?"

"I am no fool," Muntz said, to the delight of the audience.

Kit waited for the laughter to die down. "What was the service she asked you to perform?"

"She said she was going to send her son and his fiancée to see me. She wanted me to find out if there was anything in the girl's past that they should be aware of."

"Did you get the impression that Mrs. Whitney did not approve of the match?"

"I object," a steaming Clara Dalton Price said. "That calls for speculation."

"Sustained," said the judge.

No matter. Kit had the idea planted in the mind of the jury now. She continued with Muntz. "Shortly thereafter, the couple came to see you."

"Yes."

"How did they seem to you?"

"Seem?"

"Yes. What was their demeanor?"

"Happy. Like a young couple in love."

Good. Kit also wanted that picture to be painted for the men in the jury box. "What did they say to you, if anything?"

"John Whitney said he had come on a lark, that his mother told him this would be fun. He asked to have their fortunes told, as they would soon be getting married."

"Did you proceed to tell their fortunes?"

Muntz drew himself up proudly. "That is what I do, yes."

"Now, during the course of that session, did you ask Louise Harcourt about her family?"

"I told her I sensed that there was a deep secret in her family's past and that she had to talk about it. This seemed to make her nervous, but she did tell me she was not aware of any deep secret, save one."

"Did she tell you what it was?"

"All she knew was that something had happened to her mother when she was young, in Baltimore. She said she thought that her mother had been abandoned as a girl and had no family."

Kit paused and looked at Celia Harcourt. She had her hand over her mouth.

"What did you do with that information, Mr. Muntz?"

"The next day, as was agreed, I reported it to Mrs. Whitney."

"Thank you, sir," Kit said. "No further questions."

Clara Dalton Price was up like a shot and approached the bench without asking permission. Kit joined her.

"Your Honor," Price said, "I ask that this testimony be stricken from the record. What Miss Shannon has done is to cast aspersions on someone who is not on trial here. What Mrs. Whitney may or may not have done on behalf of her son is of no relevance to the question of whether the defendant shot and killed Gerald Mahoney."

Judge Quinn's response was quick. "I tend to agree, Miss Shannon. While the law allows you to bring forth witnesses, they must have some relevant testimony to give. What is the relevance here?"

Kit had to think fast. "Your Honor, I am not content to cast reasonable doubt on the prosecution's case. I intend to show that the killer of Gerald Mahoney was someone other than my client."

Kit was now out on a very long, very delicate limb. She would have to connect Muntz's testimony to something relevant—and soon. But she was not at all sure what her next move would be.

There was a thread out there, waiting to be pulled. She had a sense of it. But where was it?

"That is quite a claim, Miss Shannon," Quinn said. "Are you prepared to go forward?"

"I am," she said.

"Then I'll let the testimony stand for the moment. But I warn you. If you don't show some positive proof that there could be another person involved in this killing, I will strike all of the testimony and admonish the jury, in the strongest terms, to disregard this waste of their time."

Judge Quinn instructed Clara Dalton Price to cross-examine.

"Mr. Muntz," the prosecutor began. "You did not know the deceased, Gerald Mahoney, did you?"

"No, ma'am."

"So you didn't kill him, did you?"

Laughter in the courtroom. Kajar tugged at his collar and said, "Of course not."

"I was just asking," Clara Dalton Price said in a voice dripping with sarcasm. "Miss Shannon certainly thinks it was someone other than her client. So far as I can determine, she is the only one."

"Objection," Kit said.

"I withdraw the question."

"What question?" Kit challenged. "You were making a speech for the jury."

"That's quite enough," Judge Quinn said. "Any further questions for this witness?"

"No, Your Honor," said Price. "We don't see that he has offered anything of value to the trial."

Kit bit her lip to keep from saying something she might regret. Instead, she turned toward the gallery. "The defense calls Edwina Whitney."

"I won't do it!" Edwina Whitney cried. "I won't!"

Judge Quinn did not look inclined to grant her any favors. "Madam, are you Edwina Whitney?"

"Yes."

"Then you have been called. Walk right up here to the witness stand, or I'll have a deputy sheriff escort you."

With a huff that could have been heard for miles, Edwina Whitney—dressed in cascades of yellow taffeta and a matching yellow hat with white feathers—strode forward. Her angular features were pinched in disdain.

"The very idea," she muttered as she swept by Kit. Edwina plopped herself in the witness chair, was told by the clerk to stand up so she could be sworn, stood up and took the oath, then plopped right down again.

"Mrs. Whitney," Kit said, "you heard the testimony of Lewis Muntz, did you not?"

"You know I did, young woman." Edwina was going to give no quarter. Kit was content with that. A furious witness made mistakes.

"So you sent your son, John, and his fiancée, Louise, to see him?"

"Why not? I needed information."

"Dirt is what you were looking for, isn't it?"

"Whatever do you mean by that?"

"You did not want your son marrying Louise, isn't that true?"

Edwina became a picture of wrath. "Why, I . . . nothing of the kind!"

"And when Lewis Muntz, also known as Kajar, reported to you that there was a family secret buried back in Baltimore, you went to the one person you knew could help you find out what it was." In fact, Kit only had a hunch about this, but it made so much sense she was sure she was right.

"What do you mean?" Edwina said, clearly stalling.

"You went right to Miss Jade Stringham and the *Gazette*, didn't you?"

"What if I did? I had a mother's right to know."

So it was true. And another piece of the puzzle had fallen into place. But what was the picture?

"What was your relationship with Gerald Mahoney?"

"I knew the man's name," Edwina said. "I had seen him at some social gatherings. But I never spoke to him."

"You were familiar with the *Gazette*?"

"A little. One cannot exist in this city without seeing it."

"Did you read it?"

"No. That is not my kind of reading matter."

"But it was just right for getting dirt on your son's fiancée?"

Clara Dalton Price objected, and Judge Quinn sustained her.

Kit thought for a moment, then said, "No further questions."

"Cross-examine?" said the judge.

"No questions," said Mrs. Price.

Kit had no more witnesses.

"Perhaps it would be a good time to adjourn," the judge said. Kit did not protest.

"DID I RECEIVE ANY MAIL TODAY?" Kit asked when she returned to the office.

"No," Corazón said. "Nothing today."

"Strange," Kit said. "Ted has been writing daily. I wonder if he has gotten busy. I have not had a letter in three days."

Corazón looked up with concern. Kit patted her arm. "I'm sure all is well. We'll hear something soon. What news do you have?"

"I have been busy," Corazón said. "I found out about the Mahoney estate. He has no will."

"He died intestate."

"What is that?"

"To die without a will is to die intestate," Kit explained. "That means the estate is distributed according to the law. First to the surviving spouse, but Mahoney, so far as we know, was not married."

"No."

"Next come children. Do we know if Mahoney had children?"

"I do not know."

"If there is no spouse, and no children, parents come next. I would doubt that Mahoney has parents still living, though that is certainly possible. After that, brothers and sisters have a claim. And then next of kin. We will need to do a little more digging."

"I will dig!" Corazón said enthusiastically. "And I have been to the portrait shops. I have asked. No one has had a painting of Mr. Mahoney."

Kit mused about this. "I suppose it could have gone to a private individual, but that is unlikely."

"But one man, he knew Mahoney."

"Really? What did he say?"

"He did not like him, is what he said. He said that Mahoney was not a nice man."

"That is certainly consistent. Did he say anything else?"

"That Mahoney has cheated him of money. But he did nothing because Mahoney is a man who is ruining other men with his paper. But he once tried to steal something from Mahoney."

"He admitted to this?"

"He seemed to be happy to talk, because I told him I am working for you. He said that he hopes the man who killed Mahoney is getting a medal."

"What else?"

"He told me that he followed Mahoney and his man—I think he is meaning Bagby. He followed them to the alligator farm."

Kit began to pace. "Did he see anything?"

"He saw them go into a shack. That is all. Then they came out and went to the Montoya saloon."

"Anything else?"

"No. That is the last time he saw him. He saw that Bagby is a big man and decided to do nothing more. But he says something funny is going on."

———————

"How dare you speak to us this way!" Allard Whitney's face was flushed with anger.

John did not back down. For the first time in his life, he was going to defy his parents.

"I am speaking plainly," John said. "That is all. I am going to marry Louise Harcourt."

Edwina Whitney let out a fresh whimper. She was sitting on a divan with a fan in front of her tear-streaked face.

"Look at what you are doing to your mother!" Allard motioned toward Edwina as if she were an exhibit. "And after what she went through in court!"

"It is not my wish to upset either of you. Nevertheless—"

"Nevertheless you will give up this wild notion. The very idea of marrying a strumpet."

"She is *not* a strumpet!" John was standing, his hands gesturing wildly.

"Would you prefer I call her a harlot?"

"You will call her my wife!"

Edwina yelped again.

Allard patted his wife's shoulder as he glared at his son. "That is something we shall never call her. If you insist on disobeying my wishes, we will no longer call you son."

John's heart swelled. At the same time, he felt resolute. And he knew he was a different man. Transformed. That was the word Miss Shannon had used.

"I am sorry you feel that way, Father. But I will not change my mind."

"Then you will leave this house and never return."

Edwina stopped her sniffling and looked up at Allard. Her eyes were wide with a fearful certainty. But Allard's face was set. John had seen that look many times before. His father would not change his mind.

"And you will see nothing of the fortune I was planning to leave to you," Allard Whitney added.

For a moment John hesitated. Money. That had never been a concern for him. Growing up he had always had the best things handed to him, fed to him. His future as a comfortable man was assured. No more. Was he being the world's biggest fool?

The thought passed as quickly as it had come.

"I don't care about your money," John said. "I am going to marry Louise because I love her and because we are partly complicit in what happened. I let her down when she needed me most. I intend to spend the rest of my life making up for that."

"Don't be a fool," Allard said.

John shook his head. "I am not a fool. For the first time in my life, I am a man. I shall always honor you and Mother. I pray that someday you shall see things as I do."

He started for the door.

"Don't walk out on me," Allard said. "I order you!"

John opened the door and walked out.

———

The sun had just set under the Pacific rim when Kit and Corazón approached the Gates Alligator Farm. They came from the back side, via a dirt path. The white clapboard shack jutted into the path like a wayward arm. In the dimness Kit could make out the larger structure just beyond, where she had seen the alligators come out.

She felt her way along the side of the shack, with Corazón close behind. A wind whipped the trees, giving off a hiss. But still the voices of children out front could be heard.

Kit found the side door and, as she had expected, a padlock. Corazón whispered, "What do we do?"

"Magic," Kit said. From her dress pocket she pulled out Houdini's skeleton key. It was designed to open any known lock, he had told her, if one only gave it some good jiggling time. Kit put the key in the lock and commenced jiggling.

The key hit something, but the lock did not give way.

She heard the crunch of footsteps, just in front of the shack.

Corazón grabbed her arm.

"Easy," Kit said and listened. It was a man humming a tune. She saw only his shadowy form pass by, not twenty feet from them.

The humming stopped momentarily, then began again and faded as the man walked on.

Kit tried the lock again. The key was not working. And then, like the snap of a dry twig, the lock was open.

Kit took a deep breath. Corazón still held her arm. Kit removed the lock and opened the door. It creaked loudly.

Corazón squeezed harder.

"Don't worry," Kit whispered. But she was worried herself.

As soon as there was enough of an opening to slip in, Kit and

Corazón entered the shack. Kit let the door close quietly behind her.

The room was black. Kit took out a box of matches from her skirt pocket and lit one. The small yellow glow revealed a set of tools—rakes, hoes, shovels—and coils of chicken wire. Nothing of interest.

Until Kit turned around.

There, like hoarded treasure, was a collection of furniture and goods that came from a well-appointed home. Mahoney's?

The flame of the match burned Kit's fingers. She dropped the match. Darkness enveloped them again.

"We must be quick," Kit said, lighting another match. "Look at as much as you can."

She and Corazón stepped carefully toward the compilation. Fine chairs with ornate woodwork sat haphazardly around a rolltop desk and two end tables. A glass Bordeaux lamp leaned against a wicker cage that might have held, at one time, a fashionable canary.

Kit lit a series of matches as the two of them searched. When she found a candle and ceramic holder, Kit illumined the place in a permanent fashion.

Kit fixed her eye on several items—a circular sofa, a clock sitting on top of it, a wraparound chair with cabriole legs, and a mahogany armoire. Nothing much of interest here.

Except for the frame. A large frame leaning against the end of the sofa. Kit grabbed the candle and held it out so she could see what was in it.

Nothing.

The door to the shack slammed open. Kit spun around so fast the candle flame trembled.

"What are you doing?" It was Sid Gates. He held a gun.

"Come on out," Gates said. "There's no other way."

Kit reached for Corazón's arm. "Let's go. It will be all right."

Outside the door, Gates's face and bearing could be seen in the light of a lantern hung on the exterior of the shack. He did not lower the handgun.

"Just what do you think you're doing in my shack?" Gates said.

"Put the gun down, Mr. Gates," Kit said.

"I don't see as you have anything to say about this. I caught you on my land. I could have shot you."

"But you didn't because you have more sense than that. If you shoot now, you're a murderer. Put the gun down before you do something you'll regret."

The gun stayed where it was. "I'll take no orders from you. You tell me what you're doing here, or I'll hold you for the cops."

"The cops will be interested to know why you have Gerald Mahoney's property in your shack."

"How did you get in there? It was locked."

"Answer the question," Kit said, as she would if she were cross-examining a witness in court.

"I don't got to answer anything from you, missy."

"What did you and Axel Bagby have on Mahoney?"

Gates did not answer. His face tensed.

"Were you blackmailing him?" Kit said.

"I've taken all I'm gonna take from you," Gates said.

"You going to shoot? With witnesses around?"

"I just might," he said. "It's dark. I could say I thought you were thieves. And I'd be real sorry for what I did."

For a moment, Kit thought he really would shoot. She stepped in front of Corazón. "Listen to me, Mr. Gates. I don't know what the connection is between you and Bagby and Mahoney. Frankly, I don't care. What I care about is my client. I need information that will shed light on his case. If you will cooperate with me, I give you my assurance I will not talk to the D.A. about any of this."

Across Gates's face came a crooked smile. "And what if you find out I shot Mahoney?"

A chill ran down Kit's arms. "Did you?" she heard herself say.

Gates let out a nasty laugh. "If I did, do you really think I'd tell you? It doesn't matter, anyway. Your client is going to swing, and there's not—"

A dark flash from behind, and suddenly Gates was on the ground. The man on top of him had Gates around the neck with one arm and with the other, grabbed him around the stomach.

The two men rolled once around. Kit saw the gun still in Gates's hand. The other man's hand gripped Gates's wrist, freezing it.

Both men grunted. Kit smelled the dirt they kicked up.

And then, like the crack of a whip from an expert coachman, the gun fired.

41

DETECTIVE MIKE MCGINTY obviously did not like being called away from his dinner. He said so numerous times, around the stub of an unlit cigar in his mouth, and his scowl was deep.

"Trouble sticks to you like pomade sticks to my hair," he said to Kit.

"You're all heart, Mike," she said. They were standing over the dead body of Sid Gates, three lanterns on the ground lighting up the scene.

"Well, you got me here," McGinty said. "Now, you want to tell me what happened?"

"I will tell you what you need to know," Kit said.

McGinty's scowl deepened. "None of your shenanigans, Kit."

"Corazón and I came out here to try and get some information."

"What information?"

"That is confidential." Before McGinty could protest, Kit added, "Suffice to say that Sid Gates did not look kindly upon us."

Looking down, McGinty said, "He won't look kindly on anybody again," he said. "Who shot him?"

"Allow me to continue," Kit said. "Gates had a gun on Corazón and me and made threats."

"Why should he threaten you?"

"Again, confidential."

Whipping his cigar butt out of his mouth, McGinty fairly shrieked, "Now listen, you. I don't care if you are a lawyer and a woman, I want to know everything that happened here tonight."

"But I am a lawyer," Kit said, "and my being a woman is not relevant, is it?"

The detective shrugged and replaced his cigar. A sign he was calming himself.

"I will tell you what happened," Kit said, "but it must be in my own way. You will understand when I finish."

"I don't understand my own wife," McGinty said. "And I don't think I'll ever understand you. But go ahead. I didn't need to eat dinner anyway."

"You'll be back in no time. Gates had a gun on us, as I said, and then he was attacked from behind. In the struggle, the gun went off. That's what killed Sid Gates."

"Begging your pardon, Miss Shannon, but might I, being the head detective in the city of Los Angeles, ask one little question at this point?"

Kit put her hands on her hips. "Of course."

"Who did it?" he said.

"I cannot tell you."

"Kit!"

"Listen to me, Mike. The man who shot Gates did it in defense of Corazón. And me. He is not guilty of any crime. At the proper time he will give you a full statement."

"Proper time?" McGinty spat. "What kind of bird feed are you handing me here?"

"I represent the man."

Now McGinty looked as if he might hit the wall of the shack with his fist. Kit did not like to upset him, but she was resigned to this fact of life. As a criminal defense lawyer in Los Angeles, she was often going to butt heads with McGinty.

"Do you mind telling me," McGinty said, "how you can be representing somebody who just killed a man? The body isn't even cold yet!"

"He asked me to help him. I told him I would."

"And where, may I ask, is your client?"

"I don't know."

McGinty stared.

"That's the truth," Kit said. "He got up and ran off in the darkness, but as he did he cried out for me to help him. I said I would and told him to stop. But he did not."

"Just ran off?"

"I suspect he is scared."

"What's he got to be scared about? You said he's an innocent man."

"Sometimes," Kit said, "the innocent are more scared than the guilty. This is Los Angeles."

Mike McGinty looked down again at the body of Sid Gates. Then back at Kit. "I wonder if I should believe you."

"When have I ever lied to you, Mike?"

After a long moment, during which the world seemed not to turn at all, McGinty said, "All right. I'll let this slide this one time. But if I ever catch you not being square with me, or in some place you're not supposed to be, or doing something you're not supposed to be doing, I'm going to do my job and slap some cuffs on you."

"I would expect no less, Mike," Kit said.

———

At home, Angelita was waiting with a wire for Kit. It was from the Hotel Del Coronado.

MR FOX WAS CHECKED OUT TUESDAY LAST STOP MGT

Kit's next breath came hard. She felt Corazón's warm hand on her arm.

"Is bad?" Corazón said.

"It's Ted," Kit said. "Why would he check out of the hotel? Why hasn't he written in days?"

"You are worried."

"Yes."

"The Book says, 'Cast thy burden upon the Lord.' Yes?"

Kit felt a comfort pass through her, something from on high.

She smiled and kissed Corazón on the cheek. "Yes, my friend. 'Cast thy burden upon the Lord, and he shall sustain thee: he shall never suffer the righteous to be moved.' Book of Psalms. We will hold to that promise, yes?"

Corazón nodded.

"I will inquire further tomorrow. Now let's make tea and talk about the case. And what to do about our new client."

"The man who ran?"

"I suspect it is your own Mr. Martin, the man who worked at the alligator farm. But we don't know where to find him."

"I think I know who can help," Corazón said. "Raul Montoya."

"You think he can?"

Corazón nodded. "I will ask."

They went into the kitchen and Kit set out a pot of water to boil for tea. "If it is Martin, he's the one you talked to in Montoya's saloon, correct?"

"Yes."

"We must find him quickly. Is there a possibility that he is the one who shot and killed Mahoney? There seems to be a connection to Gates and Bagby, and therefore Mahoney himself."

"I wonder," Corazón said. "I do not think."

"Why not?"

Corazón said, "I only think of what I saw in him when I talked to him. He said something that is strange. I wrote it down. He said, 'What is done is done.' And then he said, 'The devil has his due.' I think he was saying this of Mahoney."

Kit pondered this as she started to pace around the kitchen. "A lot of people thought that of Mahoney. I wonder if Mr. Martin was just talking or if he had a personal interest in Mahoney. We simply have to find him. Tomorrow I must call Truman Harcourt to the stand. I don't have anything to connect anyone else to this murder. It seems as if I've given the jury a button. Now I must sew a vest on it."

Corazón looked at her quizzically.

Kit said, "We have no way of knowing if Gates was telling the truth or not about his killing Mahoney. Now that he's dead, I cannot question him. Is there anything else you can think of?"

"I saw the Mahoney neighbor again. He did not want to talk to me. But a little girl, she did."

"What little girl?"

"She ran after me as I was going down the street. She said she likes the way I look. She asked me about the killing. I told her I worked for you. She said she saw a curious man go into the Mahoney house one day. And then there was yelling."

"Yelling?"

"Men yelling at each other. One man said he will not pay any more. And another man said yes he will. And the curious man ran out."

"What was it that made this man seem curious to the girl?"

"His hat," Corazón said. "It was a funny hat, like the cowboys have. But one side of it was up."

"Gates!"

"Oh!" Corazón cried out. "I forgot!" She shoved her hand in the pocket of her walking dress and pulled out a small leather-bound book.

"What is it?" Kit said.

"I do not know," Corazón said, handing it to Kit. "I found it on the rolltop desk. It looks important."

Kit began to breathe faster as she looked over the pages of the journal. "Important! I would say so, Corazón. This could be the very thing we—"

The teakettle began to whistle.

As Kit entered the courtroom for the morning session, the tension in the air was almost a physical presence. The reporters seemed more like circling sharks, waiting to be fed, than men of the press. Would this be the first loss for Kit Shannon? And a major victory for the "other woman," Clara Dalton Price?

The morning papers, both the *Times* and the *Examiner*, had stories that painted a bleak picture of Truman Harcourt's chances. Even Tom Phelps, who would normally give Kit a break in his stories in the *Times*, could not hold back the damaging information.

The only thing Kit had now was what she held in her hand. It was the item Corazón had found in the rolltop desk—Gerald Mahoney's appointment book. It was dynamite, but Kit would have to tread most carefully. If Clara Dalton Price got wind of what was in it, she would move heaven, earth, and most of Los Angeles to stop its admission into evidence.

Judge Quinn gaveled the session to order and told Kit to call her next witness.

"The defense recalls Axel Bagby," Kit said.

The big man, who had been sitting in the back of the courtroom, looked dazed as he made his way forward. Clearly he was not expecting this. Nor was Clara Dalton Price, who studied Kit with all the concentration of a cobra.

"You are still considered to be under oath, sir," the judge said to Bagby. "Take the stand."

Kit approached the witness, holding Mahoney's leather appointment book in her hand. "Mr. Bagby, you have testified that you were Mr. Mahoney's assistant, correct?"

He nodded pugnaciously. "Right."

"Did you ever post letters for him?"

"Sure."

"I take it, then, you would be familiar with his handwriting?"

"Of course," Bagby said.

Kit opened the appointment book to the first page, labeled *January 1, 1905*, and laid it on the rail of the witness-box. "I am placing before you a journal, Mr. Bagby, and ask if you recognize Gerald Mahoney's handwriting."

Bagby leaned over, his eyes homing in on the page. Clara Price said, "Your Honor, I should like to see this journal before the witness answers."

"And I object to that," Kit said. "When my question is answered, I will make an offer of proof to the court."

Judge Quinn said, somewhat reluctantly, "That is the proper procedure. Let Miss Shannon attempt to lay a foundation."

Mrs. Price sat down with a disdainful sweep of her dress.

"You may answer the question," Kit said.

Bagby said, "Yes, that's Mr. Mahoney's handwriting."

"Do you recognize this journal?"

"It appears to be Mr. Mahoney's appointment book."

"Where did you get that?" Clara Dalton Price demanded.

"Your Honor," said Kit, "I don't believe I heard an objection."

"Proceed to the bench, Miss Shannon, Mrs. Price." Judge Quinn turned to Price. "Is there an objection?"

"Yes!" the prosecutor said.

"On what grounds?" Kit asked.

"This isn't proper evidence. That should not be in your possession!"

"Your Honor," Kit said, "how relevant evidence came into the possession of the defense is not before this court. If the D.A. wishes to prefer some charge against me, and has the evidence to back it up, I am quite certain Mr. Davenport and Mrs. Price will pursue that particular course and, I might add, with gusto."

Kit paused to allow Clara Dalton Price's steam to rise, like the teakettle from last night.

"But," Kit added, "since the only issue before the court is relevance, and since the witness has identified the handwriting, there is nothing to bar this evidence from entering the case. The code provides that *all* relevant evidence shall be admissible."

"I have not even seen this book," Clara Price pleaded to Judge Quinn.

"I shall show you the portions that I intend to use as the basis for questioning," Kit said. "That is also what the code provides."

"But you have not made any offer of proof yet," Judge Quinn said. "What is the relevance of this particular book?"

"I intend to show that my client was framed."

The look of shock on the judge's face must have been clearly visible to the gallery. No one could hear their words, but Kit realized the reporters were suddenly writing with a vigor more in keeping with covering a three-alarm fire. They would be after her to tell them what went on at the bench. Of course, Kit would not tell them.

That was not her concern now. Her entire case was, and it hinged on the judge's ruling.

"Is there any ground to keep from admitting this piece of evidence?" Judge Quinn asked Mrs. Price.

The prosecutor was, for the first time Kit had seen, speechless. She slowly shook her head.

"Very well," the judge said. "But Miss Shannon, you will show Mrs. Price every page you intend to base questions upon. Is that clear?"

"Yes, Your Honor."

Kit turned the appointment book to the page for February 10. There were two notations in Mahoney's handwriting. She showed the page to Clara Dalton Price, who could only nod.

Kit showed the book to Axel Bagby. "Sir, do you see the page that is marked February ten?"

Bagby looked at it. "Yeah. I mean, yes."

"And do you further see notations made in the handwriting of your employer, Gerald Mahoney?"

"Yes."

"Next to nine A.M., what is written there?"

Reading, Bagby said, "Jade."

"Who do you understand that to be?"

Bagby looked at Kit with chagrin. "That would be Miss Stringham, of course."

"Editor of the *Gazette*."

"You know that."

"I am interested in what you know, Mr. Bagby," Kit said. She had him back on his heels and was not going to let him regain his balance. As she had learned in jiu-jitsu class, the one who controls the balance is the one who wins the match.

"What name is listed next to four P.M.?"

"Gates," Bagby replied.

"Who do you understand that to be?"

The big man's eyes almost misted over. "Sid Gates, may he rest in peace! A finer friend never—"

"Thank you, Mr. Bagby, you've answered the question."

He looked at Kit like he wanted to strangle her. That was good. She had struck a nerve and knew she was on the right track.

"Tell me," Kit said, "what was the purpose of this meeting between Sid Gates and Gerald Mahoney?"

"It never took place," Axel Bagby said, "because Truman Harcourt shot Mr. Mahoney."

"That is not what I asked you, sir. I asked you what the purpose of the meeting was."

"How should I know?" Bagby said defiantly.

Kit stepped up to the rail, a blaze in her glare. Bagby actually shrank back in the chair a little. "Because you proclaim to be Mr. Gates's true friend and the closest associate of Mr. Gerald Mahoney.

Do you want us to believe that you had no idea about the meeting between these two men?"

"Listen here," Bagby said. "That is to say . . . I mean, why can't you leave the dead alone?"

"Is it not true, Mr. Bagby, that Gerald Mahoney was blackmailing Sid Gates and receiving payments from him, and you were the go-between?"

Axel Bagby's chin dropped like a brick. That was answer enough for Kit.

"And isn't it also true that you were skimming from those payments yourself?"

"That's a lie!" Bagby erupted.

"Wasn't it your plan all along to play Gates and Mahoney against each other?"

"No!"

"And when a man named Martin, who worked for Gates, found out about it, you threatened to kill him if he talked?"

"All of that is a lie. All of it. I don't know anyone named Martin."

Kit paused a moment. Bagby's breathing was audible to the hushed courtroom. Kit turned toward the courtroom doors and pushed a strand of hair behind one ear, her signal to Corazón, who stood at the door.

Corazón opened the door, and into the courtroom stepped Martin.

Everyone looked at him. Bagby's eyes became saucers and his lip started to tremble.

"Do you have anything further, Miss Shannon?" the judge said.

"Not at this time," Kit said, "unless Mr. Bagby wishes to change his answers."

Bagby, looking mesmerized, shook his head.

"Your witness," Kit said.

Clara Dalton Price said, in a subdued voice, "No questions."

Kit said, "I call to the witness stand Dr. Lawrence Tanner."

43

THE MAN WHO HAD CALLED himself Martin took the stand. He was dressed in a suit and tie, though they were a bit worn. His deep-set eyes bespoke a troubled life. Kit hoped that would give his testimony credibility with the jury. Men with nothing to lose have little reason to lie.

Raul Montoya had indeed found Martin—hiding in a shack near his father's establishment. Kit had spent a late hour asking him to testify, but she did not need to persuade. He was anxious.

"You are a doctor?" Kit asked the witness.

"Not anymore," Tanner said bitterly. "I was an ophthalmologist. A good one."

"What happened to your practice?"

Tanner looked out at the gallery, in the general direction of Jade Stringham. "The *Gazette*, that's what happened. They lied about me in their paper and I had to . . ." Suddenly his voice choked. He looked down, trying to recover.

Kit waited a moment before continuing. "Did you have to give up your practice?"

Tanner nodded. "I couldn't stay in this town. I went away. But the story followed me."

"You came back to Los Angeles?"

"To see my daughter."

"Sarah is her name?"

"Yes. But they ruined her, too. I haven't helped her much. I'm beholden to the bottle, ashamed to have her see me."

Kit looked at the jury. Tanner's admission was a brave one in open court, further helping his credibility.

"Where have you been working as of late?"

"At the Gates Alligator Farm."

"What were your duties?"

"All the dirty work, the things decent people wouldn't do."

"Can you tell us why you stayed on in this job?"

"Gates knew who I was. He said he'd keep my presence a secret so long as I worked for him and kept my mouth shut. If I made trouble, he'd tell the papers about me. I didn't want that. I wanted to stay so I could make enough money so Sarah and I could get away together, start over again somewhere else."

Kit looked at the jury when she asked, "Did you know Mr. Axel Bagby?"

"Yes," Tanner said forcefully.

"How?"

"I saw him many times out at the farm. He and Sid Gates seemed to be very good friends."

"Why did you conclude that, sir?"

"Because they liked to talk to each other, push other people around."

"Can you explain that last answer?"

"I mean, they liked to show people who was boss. Bagby, he was the muscle. He liked that part of it most of all."

"Did you have an occasion to get on Mr. Bagby's bad side?"

"Yes. Once. I was out in back of the farm working the manure pit when he came up behind me and started trying to get my goat."

"In what way, Dr. Tanner?"

"Calling me a rummy. Telling me I must feel pretty good about the way my life turned out. He laughed when he said it."

"Did you retaliate?"

"I lifted the shovel I had and told him to back away. He just laughed and walked on. I followed him. I was going to show him who was boss, all right. I still had the shovel."

"What happened next?"

"I came to the shack and stopped. The door was open. I heard Bagby and Gates talking in there. They were talking about Mahoney."

"Can you tell us what was said?"

"Objection," Clara Dalton Price said. "That is hearsay."

"No, Your Honor," Kit said. "This statement is being offered to impeach Mr. Bagby. He testified that he was not part of any scheme involving money and Gerald Mahoney. This is testimony to refute that." This was the law, and it was clear. Kit waited for the judge to overrule the objection.

But he did not. He sat for a long time, leaning back in his chair. Then he said, "I sustain the objection."

"You what?" Kit said.

"That is the court's ruling, Miss Shannon. Move along."

She would move along all right. To the Court of Appeal. But that would be later, if Truman Harcourt was convicted.

"Very well," Kit said. "Then without telling us what words were actually spoken, Dr. Tanner, what was your impression of what was being said?"

"I got the impression Sid Gates was on the run from the law, in both Arizona and Mexico. A poacher is what he was, and that's how he got most of his gators, too. He had people working for him, a whole network. And Mahoney found out about it and threatened to spread the story in his paper. So Gates started paying him off."

"Did you ever see any money changing hands?"

"I saw Gates give Bagby a satchel one night, and I saw it had bills in it. I don't know what happened to the money, but no doubt it ended up in Mahoney's bank account."

"Objection—"

Tanner said, "Less the cut Axel Bagby took for himself!"

"Objection!"

"There has been an objection," Judge Quinn said. "The witness's last remark will be stricken from the record."

Kit was not concerned. They could strike it from the record but not from the jurors' minds. A seed of doubt had been planted about Bagby's credibility.

"Thank you, Dr. Tanner," Kit said.

Clara Dalton Price was quick on her feet—and with her questions.

"You botched an operation on a young woman, leaving her blind, did you not?"

Tanner looked as if he'd just been attacked by an angry dog. "That's a lie!"

"Is it? Isn't it true that you sued the *Gazette* for libel and lost?"

"Objection," Kit said. "This is irrelevant and immaterial. And Mrs. Price is simply trying to badger the witness."

"The witness can handle himself, I am sure," Judge Quinn said. "And the questions are relevant to Dr. Tanner's credibility. I will allow them."

"You lost that case, didn't you?" Mrs. Price snapped.

"A lousy jury," Tanner said. The moment the words were out of his mouth he winced. Kit did, too. She saw several scowls from the jurors in the box. With that one statement Tanner had undone any sympathy he might have had with the jurors.

Clara Dalton Price smiled. "So it was the jury's fault, eh? You don't think they did their job?"

Tanner tried to regroup. "It was a lie, I tell you. They were out to get me. Mahoney took my life away from me!"

"And Truman Harcourt took Mahoney's life from him, didn't he?"

"I object to that question," Kit said. "Dr. Tanner is not here to speculate. Mrs. Price is already arguing to the jury."

"Unlike Dr. Tanner, I have confidence in the jury system," Mrs. Price said.

Kit looked at the judge but knew he wasn't going to do anything about this. Clara Dalton Price owned the courtroom. Kit was the intruder and was being treated as such.

"I think we have heard enough from this witness," Mrs. Price said dismissively. "I have no more questions." She returned to her chair like a conquering monarch.

"Call your next witness, Miss Shannon," Judge Quinn said.

The case had unraveled. Kit's defense of Truman Harcourt lay like broken glass on the floor of the courtroom. That momentary thought ran through Kit's mind, and at the same time a cog clicked into place. Puzzle pieces. It was not exactly the voice of God but something very much like it that seemed to whisper, *That's it.*

And then Kit knew that Truman Harcourt's life rested upon the next few moments. She was about to make the most audacious request of her legal life. But she had to do it. There was no other choice.

"Your Honor," she said, "the defense has but one or two more witnesses to call. I assure the court I will be brief. But these witnesses must be called at the proper time and place."

Kit walked to the center of the courtroom and faced the judge as if giving a final argument. "There is a crucial piece of evidence that can only be appreciated by the jury at the scene of the crime. I request that we convene tonight at the home of Gerald Mahoney, jury and all, for the final session of the trial."

In the stunned silence of the courtroom, as everyone seemed poised on the edge of shock, a single voice arose from the reporter's section. "I'll be a monkey's uncle." Kit recognized it as the voice of Tom Phelps.

————————

Louise Harcourt took a last look at the city she had once loved. From the train window it looked smaller, distant, even though the train was still at the station.

Had Los Angeles ever been a part of her? Had it ever been home?

Leaving it meant sorrow beyond words. But there was no choice. A clean break was the only way.

What would she do in San Francisco? She had decided to try to find work as a schoolteacher. That was the best a woman who would never marry could hope for. She loved children. Perhaps being around them would rekindle some hope that her life could be salvaged. A penitent life educating the young offered some hope.

But inside her was also the fear that she was beyond salvation. She had sinned greatly in the sight of God and man, had hurt too many people. Maybe it was just too much to—

She sensed someone sitting down beside her.

"John!"

"Hello, Louise."

"What are you doing?"

"Not letting you go."

Louise felt the sting of tears in her eyes. "Please don't make this harder on me."

He took her hand. She let him. His grip was sure. "In the sight of God, I made a pledge to you."

"No, John. We did not marry. I will not hold you."

"Don't you see that I am holding *you*?"

She shook her head. "I cannot go back. I am not getting off this train."

"That is quite all right, darling." John smiled and squeezed her hand. "Neither am I."

44

"MR. FOX," THE SHORT, squat man in the tight suit said. "I have been asked to provide you with legal representation."

Ted looked up from the corner of his cell. "And just who are you?" he said.

"Wilkins Little, sir. Attorney-at-law." He stood outside the bars, the jailer by his side. The top of his head was smooth, the light from a single light bulb shining off it. Tufts of thinning black hair sprouted from behind his ears.

"Who sent you?" Ted said. He was unshaven and dirty. They had kept him incommunicado for the last forty-eight hours.

"I am here at the request of the United States attorney for the district of San Diego," Little said. "It is his opinion that you should be afforded the services of an attorney."

"How big of him."

Little forced a chuckle. It was the most inappropriate response Ted could remember seeing outside of drunken men at proper social gatherings.

"Get out of here," Ted snapped. "I already have a lawyer, and I want to contact her."

"Her? Am I to understand you are referring to a woman as a member of the bar?"

"That's right."

"And her name?"

"Kathleen Shannon of Los Angeles. I demand the right to contact her."

Little glanced at the jailer, who had a bemused expression on his face.

"Mr. Fox," Little said, looking at the nails of his right hand, "you do not quite understand your predicament. You are not in a position to demand rights. I, your lawyer, am the one who can speak for you."

Ted stood up. "Listen, whoever you are, I'm not going to turn my life over to you or anyone else around here. I want to contact my own lawyer, and I will not talk to anyone until I do. And when I get out of here, I'm going to spread this story around. Is this how you treat citizens of the United States?"

Little puffed his cheeks a couple of times in a gesture Ted took to be indignation. "Leave us a moment," the lawyer said to the jailer. When the jailer closed the door, Little said, "Mr. Fox, you are being accused of treasonous acts against the government of the United States."

"Certainly. I am a one-legged spy."

"Mr. Fox—"

"Get me Kit Shannon."

"It is not what I—"

"Get out of here!"

The short lawyer almost hopped backward.

For a tense moment, the two men stared at each other through the bars. Then Little brushed the front of his suit as if to remove a layer of dirt.

"I feel sorry for you, Mr. Fox. There is nothing more I can do for you. Recalcitrant clients almost always end up on the end of a rope. Good night."

He went to the end of the corridor, rapped on the door, and left.

A hole opened up in Ted Fox, like a grave. He turned and went back to his cot, falling face down upon it.

What was the Scripture that Kit was so fond of quoting? He

listened for her voice in his mind. And then he heard it, lilting and lovely, his Kit.

"God is our refuge and strength, a very present help in trouble. Therefore we will not fear. . . ."

The moon over Los Angeles was as bright as a Chinese lantern. There was a crowd on the street just outside the Mahoney house, a large gathering for this fashionable part of town. Word had spread from the courtroom to the meeting halls and saloons. There was a festive air, as often happened in the city when there was news in the making. The curious crowd was kept under control by a small squad of L.A. policemen.

Officer Ed Hanratty was stationed at the swinging gate. He tipped his police hat as Kit walked by. "Go show 'em, Miss Shannon," he whispered.

Kit hoped she could. It was to be a show, indeed. And she could not afford a single mistake.

Truman Harcourt was in the company of a deputy sheriff, who kept a watchful eye on him. The jurors, who seemed most interested by this strange turn of events, lined up along the pathway to Mahoney's front door.

Judge Quinn and Clara Dalton Price stood at the edge of the stairway, both looking strangely quiet. To Kit, the mood seemed like the quiet at a gathering storm. Clouds were rolling in. She was the clouds, and she needed some thunder.

The press were afforded their own special section of grass to the left of the walkway. Tom Phelps nodded at Kit as she passed him. He had a face that was ready for a big story. She intended to give it to him. To all of them.

"All right," Judge Quinn said when all the principals had gathered. "We are back on the record in the case of People against Harcourt."

The court reporter had a special chair given to him with a writing desk and kerosene lamp. He scribbled his shorthand as the proceedings continued.

The house itself was a dark, brooding presence. It watched over the strange assemblage like a quiescent ghost.

"Miss Shannon," the judge said. "Call your next witness."

This is it, Kit thought. *Be with me, Father, in great strength.*

"I wish to recall Sarah Tanner," Kit said.

"Sarah Tanner!" Judge Quinn's clerk barked. At the gate, Sarah came forward, Corazón holding her arm. Kit silently thanked God that Corazón had been able to find her.

"Miss Tanner," said the judge, "you are still under oath. Please take the—" He stopped suddenly. "As there is no witness chair, just stand over here by me."

She did, then looked at Kit.

"Sarah, you testified about seeing a shooting inside this house, isn't that true?"

"Yes," the girl said.

"And you were standing outside that window"—Kit pointed—"when it happened?"

"Yes."

"And you said you saw a man in a coat, like the one that has been admitted into evidence, holding a gun in his right hand, with his back to you?"

"Yes, ma'am."

"Sarah, I would like you to go to the window and assume the exact position you were in when you saw inside the house."

Tentatively, Sarah turned and walked toward the window. All eyes were watching her. The newspapermen were jostling among themselves to get a closer look.

Sarah Tanner paused a moment, looking at the rose bushes, then placed herself between them and the house, exactly where Kit had seen her footprints. She was slightly to the left of the window.

Kit turned to the judge, choosing her words carefully. The next few moments would be played to the newspapermen. The judge would have to feel their keen interest, their rabid desire to capture this exciting story. She wanted Quinn in a position where he wouldn't dare stop the show.

"Your Honor," she said, "may the record reflect that the witness is currently in position to reenact exactly what she saw for the jury?"

Quinn cleared his throat. "Well, I will certainly have the record show she is standing behind the rose bushes beneath the window, and that is her testimony, but I certainly would not call this a reenactment."

"If there was a reenactment," Kit said, "surely the jury should be entitled to see that."

"Surely," said the judge. "But that is not possible."

"Oh, but it is," Kit said. "May I continue now?"

Quinn looked around as all heads gathered turned toward him, awaiting his ruling. "Continue, by all means. But be very careful."

"I intend to, Your Honor. Step by step." To Sarah Tanner, Kit said, "Now, Sarah, you testified that you witnessed the shooting through a slight opening in the curtains and that the lighting was dim. Is that correct?"

"Yes, ma'am."

"Then I ask if this is the way it appeared." Kit stepped to the window and rapped on a pane of glass three times. Someone inside drew the curtains a few inches.

An immediate eruption of voices rose from the lawn. The knot of reporters pressed forward to see what was happening, while a lone cop, caught off guard, tried to push them back.

Clara Dalton Price's voice rose above the clamor. "Objection! Objection! What is going on here? Objection!"

"Your Honor," Kit said quickly, "there is no such thing as a 'what is going on here' objection. You have given me permission to proceed so long as I lay the foundation."

"But that house is supposed to be locked," Mrs. Price insisted. "The district attorney's office did not give permission—"

"If the D.A. wishes to prefer charges," Kit said, "he may do so at a later time. Right now we are in an official court proceeding, the jury is here—in fact, Your Honor, it looks as if the entire city is here—and the witness is testifying to facts. Let us not waste the court's or the jury's time with irrelevancies. Your Honor, may the witness continue?"

Judge Quinn's face told Kit that he understood he had little choice. He was up for election later in the year, and the newspapers would not be his friends if he blundered here. "Yes, yes," he said finally. "The district attorney may deal with Miss Shannon on the matter of the house later. Let's just get this evening's entertainment over with."

"Thank you, Your Honor. Sarah, is that approximately how far the curtain was drawn?"

"Yes," Sarah Tanner said.

"May I have the jury stand behind the witness, please? I want them to have the same viewpoint."

At this point, Judge Quinn looked in no mood to argue. He motioned for his clerk to gather the gentlemen of the jury in position behind Sarah Tanner. Clara Dalton Price and the judge also joined them. The grouping looked like a crush of children trying to peek into a circus tent.

When all were in place, Kit said, "I will now ask the witness to observe the following reenactment of the crime and tell us if it is substantially correct."

Kit rapped on the window again.

A moment passed when all of the people outside the house seemed to take a collective breath. And then, from inside, a flicker of light. An orange hue filled the room. And two men were suddenly visible inside, one with his back to the window. The one with his back to the window wore a long brown coat with a black collar. In his right hand was a revolver. He pointed this at the other. And fired.

A woman in the crowd screamed. Several of the men shouted in surprise.

The man who was shot fell.

The curtain closed.

Before anyone could say a word, Kit faced Sarah Tanner. "Is that approximately what you observed?"

"Yes, it is," Sarah Tanner said.

"Cross-examine," Kit said to Clara Dalton Price.

The prosecutor seemed more than a little annoyed at this. "I do not see that this proves anything, Your Honor, other than that Miss Shannon has taken on Earl Rogers' penchant for theatrics. I would ask that this whole display be stricken from the record. Let's go home, get a night's sleep, and return to sanity—and the court-room—in the morning."

"But if Mrs. Price says this does not prove anything," Kit countered, "then why strike it? Permit me one more witness to show the relevance."

"Get on with it," Quinn said.

"The defense recalls Jade Stringham," Kit said.

45

THE EDITOR OF the *Gazette* was in the mood for a fight. Her anger radiated outward toward the crowd. The reporters had smiles on their faces, as if this were the front row of a boxing match between Jack Johnson and Jim Jeffries.

"You recall our meeting at the *Gazette* offices, Miss Stringham?" Kit asked.

"Sure," Jade Stringham said.

"You lit a cheroot in my presence."

"What of it?"

"I was fascinated with how you struck the match. Would you demonstrate that ability to the jury?"

To Kit's surprise, Clara Dalton Price did not object. Perhaps she saw it would be folly now. In any event, the bemused witness shrugged her shoulders, took a match from her pocket, and held it. "There is nothing to strike it on," she said.

"Just show us, then, without igniting it."

Jade Stringham made the grand gesture Kit had seen in the office.

"You are left-handed, then?" Kit said.

The witness looked around like a bird on a low limb, then quietly said, "So what?"

"I show you Gerald Mahoney's appointment book, which has

previously been admitted into evidence. Please turn to the page marked February ten."

Jade Stringham did so by the light of the kerosene lantern the bailiff held. When she got to the page, she looked at Kit.

"Do you see your name there, marked in Gerald Mahoney's handwriting, indicating a meeting at nine in the morning?"

"Yeah, I see that."

"What was the purpose of that meeting?"

"It was our regular Friday business meeting. We always discussed the upcoming issue of the paper."

"And you see he had a meeting scheduled with Gates for later in the day?"

"I see that, sure."

Kit took the book back and held the open page toward the jury. She wanted them to see it, even if they could not read it.

"But Miss Stringham," Kit said, "you told Truman Harcourt, on the morning of February eight, that Gerald Mahoney was leaving town on Friday, didn't you?"

"Why . . . why would I do that?"

"Did you or did you not tell that to Truman Harcourt over the telephone?"

"I don't recall any such thing."

"You are acquainted with Valerie Amman?"

"She used to work for me. I fired her."

"What for?"

"For listening to . . ." Jade Stringham's eyes became saucer-size.

"For listening to conversations over the telephone, isn't that right? And if she were to testify that this is exactly what you said to Truman Harcourt, would you accuse her of lying?"

"I don't recall what I said; I told you that."

"Is it not true, Miss Stringham, that you said that to Truman Harcourt so he would go to Mahoney's house? And isn't it also true that you were there at the house, waiting for him, that you had left the door unlocked, and when Truman Harcourt entered, you hit him over the head with a blackjack?"

"No," Jade said, but her voice was getting weaker.

"You then took the gun that Truman Harcourt had and took off his overcoat and put it on."

Jade Stringham stared at Kit, silent.

"You knew from Mahoney that his neighbor, Norbert Strong, liked to sit in his bedroom window overlooking the house. For good measure, you ran alongside the house, to the back door, which you had unlatched from within. Gerald Mahoney must have arrived home at just that time. He went into his study, where you confronted him and shot him."

"That is not true," Jade Stringham said, but her tone was weak.

"You shot him."

"No."

"Objection," Clara Dalton Price said. She had an oddly satisfied smile on her face. "This entire line of questioning should not be allowed, Your Honor, because Miss Shannon has already precluded it."

"How so?" asked the judge.

"She has gone to great lengths to reenact a crime, to show the jury that Gerald Mahoney was shot by a man holding a gun in his right hand. Then she established that the witness—a woman, I might add—is left-handed. Her presentation is hopelessly confused."

"What about it, Miss Shannon?"

"Your Honor," Kit said, "let me introduce you to the players in my little drama." She rapped on the glass of the window sharply, and the curtains opened in full. The room was full of light, revealing two men there.

"The role of the shooter was played by Harry Houdini," Kit said. "Mr. Raul Montoya was Gerald Mahoney. But what Sarah Tanner saw was not the actual people but a reflection."

She gestured to Houdini, who stepped over to the wall and pointed to a huge framed mirror.

"This was what was hanging on the wall, Your Honor. Not a portrait, as we were told. Sarah Tanner could not have seen it in any other way, as the demonstration proved. From where she was standing, the position of the drapes allowed only a view of the wall, not the room. And because Jade Stringham wore a long coat and has short hair, Sarah assumed she was a man."

Kit looked at Clara Dalton Price. "But Sarah also saw Gerald Mahoney fall to his knees. How, then, did he get the cut on the back of his head? Because he did not die immediately. He got up, struggled with Jade Stringham, leaving blood on the coat, but she was able to wrestle him to the wall and push him into the mirror, which broke. The blow knocked him out, and he fell and died on the floor."

It seemed as if a silence had fallen over the entire city. Not even a cricket chirruped. Kit said, "Are you aware, Miss Stringham, that a pistol discharges a gunpowder residue when fired? It is a matter of record that Truman Harcourt is right-handed. Now, we may ask an expert to examine the left sleeve of the coat, or you can tell us right now why it is you killed Gerald Mahoney."

Kit faced the witness again. "Why did you kill him, Miss Stringham?"

In the flickering of the lamps, Jade Stringham's face twitched. The silent crowd watched her. Even Clara Dalton Price seemed interested in the answer.

"Why did you shoot your employer, Gerald Mahoney?" Kit asked.

"He wasn't my employer," Jade Stringham said. "He was my husband."

Kit caught sight of Clara Dalton Price. For the first time Kit saw on that face a look of absolute confusion and loss.

"We were without benefit of clergy," Jade Stringham spat, "but he had pledged his troth to me! He promised me everything. But then he got mixed up with another woman." Stringham looked at the crowd of people just inside the property fence. "He betrayed me! After I did his bidding! It was Gerald who told me to get the story on Celia Harcourt. I did because I thought he would come back to me. But he was not going to do it! He told me so. He was not going to leave me anything in his estate. Don't you see how evil that was? I had given him my best years!"

"So you paid off Axel Bagby," Kit said, "to help you get Mahoney's property. Bagby played both sides, but you hoped Gates would be the one to kill Mahoney. Isn't that true?"

"You know it is," Jade Stringham said. "And I hope you rot."

"Your Honor," Kit said, "I ask that all charges against Truman Harcourt be dismissed."

Judge Quinn seemed relieved all of a sudden. "Does the prosecution have anything to say?" he asked Mrs. Price.

Clara Price glared at Kit. "No."

"Then the motion to dismiss is granted," said the judge. "Someone take this woman"—he pointed at Jade Stringham—"into custody. Gentlemen of the jury, you are herewith dismissed. And the rest of you? Let's all just go home."

THE NEXT MORNING at the Bible Institute, Kit spoke to a group of clergy from the churches in Los Angeles. Reverend Macauley, who was to have spoken, asked Kit if she would step in at the last moment. He said it was about time they heard from the true benefactor of the Institute. Far from being tired from last night's events, Kit was invigorated and happy to comply.

Notably absent at this august gathering was Dr. Edward Lazarus. He had made his feelings known about the Bible Institute from the start. And they were not favorable.

Notably present was Tom Phelps of the *Times* and a reporter from the *Examiner*. They had tracked Kit here and wanted comment on the Harcourt case. Well, she was going to make them sit through her lecture before giving any comment.

"The Word of God," Kit said, "stands as the light of authority for our religion. It is not interested in playing second fiddle to the fashions of the age. No matter where we are, what we have invented for ourselves, or how much money we manage to acquire, there are principles that remain in place for all time.

" 'Thou shalt have no other gods before me' is the first commandment. When you look at the Old Testament in its fullness, you see that it is a battle of the gods. The gods of Abram's home, the gods of Egypt, the gods of the pagans. The message is that our God is a jealous God. He is the one and only ruler. That is, as we lawyers like to say, nonnegotiable.

"Our city is full of false gods, gentlemen, and I say to you that our task is to speak up as never before. We are on the verge of becoming a great and mighty city. But we will never be truly great if we are not truly good. That means that frauds and charlatans must be rooted out—and only the Truth will do it. Preach the Truth in your pulpits and in your social gatherings. Live a life worthy of the Gospel, that men may look upon your good deeds and give praise and honor to the Lord. That is the mission of this institute, and that is why we ask you all to join with us in the noble enterprise of God's Kingdom."

The pastors applauded. Even Tom Phelps almost—almost—dropped his pencil. But then he regained his equilibrium and folded his arms.

After the lecture, and after receiving kudos from several of the pastors, the room cleared and Kit was left with the reporters.

"You owe us a comment," Tom Phelps said.

"Certainly," Kit said. "Are you ready?"

The two reporters nodded and readied their pencils.

"My comment is this, and you can quote me. The Word of God is quick and powerful and sharper than any two-edged sword—"

"Come on!" Tom Phelps whined. "You know what we mean!"

Kit smiled. "Oh, you're not interested in my lecture?"

"Kit!"

"All right. The trial. What do you want to know?"

"How did you figure it out?" Tom Phelps asked. "This was the most sensational trial we've ever watched. And that includes those with Earl Rogers."

"Boys," Kit said, "here it is on the level, and I want you to print it just as I say. Are you ready?"

"Shoot," said Phelps.

"I believe that God guides me in everything I do. I pray hard and use whatever reasoning power He has given me to plead my cause. I do not know how the mind works, but I do believe that

God is the creator of the mind. And He promises to lead those who truly and earnestly seek Him."

Both men stopped writing and looked at Kit.

"Write it," she ordered.

They did.

And then a voice behind the men said, "Arrest her."

Kit looked up and saw John Davenport walking toward them, Clara Dalton Price and Detective Mike McGinty by his side.

"What's going on?" Tom Phelps asked.

"I am putting Miss Shannon under arrest for criminal trespass," Davenport said with a happy lilt.

"She knowingly violated a crime scene," Clara Dalton Price added.

"I'm sorry to have to do this, Kit," McGinty said.

Kit said, "You are making a mistake, Mr. Davenport. I advise you not to continue."

"The day the D.A.'s office takes advice from you," Davenport said, "is the day I join the circus."

"Get ready for the animal act, boys," Kit said to the reporters. "If you want a story, come down to the station. Oh, and do me one favor, Tom. Call Corazón Chavez at my office and have her meet us there. Tell her it concerns the Mahoney house."

For the slightest moment Davenport appeared to hesitate. But then he waved his hand at McGinty. "Let's go."

The judge glowered at the United States attorney. He was a magisterial presence, this judge, whose name was Porter. The bench on which he sat looked about ten stories high to Ted. This was federal court, after all, and everything seemed bigger.

"Are you telling me you've held this man in jail since *Tuesday*?" Judge Porter said. He had flowing gray hair, like some Civil War general, and a large patrician nose. He looked like he could smell injustice—and didn't like the scent in his courtroom.

Collins cleared his throat. "This is a matter of some importance to the government, Your Honor, as it involves possible treasonous activity."

"Why haven't you brought this man before me sooner?"

"He refused a lawyer," the attorney said.

The judge looked down at Ted, who was standing behind a large oak table where a federal marshal had positioned him. "Is that right, son?"

Ted said, "I refused the lawyer they sent me. I want to pick my own counsel."

"Do you have someone in mind?"

"I do."

"Who is it? We'll send for him."

"Her," Ted said.

Judge Porter scowled. "A woman?" He scratched his head. "I don't know of any gentlewoman who practices criminal law in the federal courts. What is her name?"

"Kathleen Shannon. She practices in Los Angeles."

The judge suddenly seemed pleased, folding his hands over his stomach and leaning back in his chair. Then he laughed heartily. "Oh my, but isn't that something?" he said. "Kit Shannon, who has been making news all over. Tell me, son, is she as good as they say?"

"Better," Ted said, looking at Collins. The lawyer did not look impressed.

"Well," Judge Porter said, "the law says you are entitled to a lawyer, and you are free to choose one. How long will it take her to get down here?"

"I don't know," Ted said. "I have not been allowed to send her a wire."

The judge snapped his head toward the U.S. attorney. "You've held him incommunicado to boot?"

Collins cleared his throat again, loudly, like a steam engine trying to climb a mountain. "Like I said, Your Honor, this is of great importance."

"The U.S. Constitution is of great importance, too, sir. I hereby remand this man into custody pending the arrival of his lawyer. I also order that he be taken forthwith to the nearest telegraph office and, at the government's expense, be allowed to send a wire that is any length he chooses. Is that clear?"

Before the U.S. attorney could respond, Judge Porter said, "Good. Next case."

47

ON THE STEPS OF THE POLICE STATION, John Davenport faced the group of reporters before him. He stood rather still, in deference to the photographic camera that a *Times* man stood behind.

To Davenport's right stood Detective Michael McGinty. On McGinty's right was Kit. Clara Dalton Price, eager to get in the photograph, squeezed close to Davenport's left side.

"Gentlemen," Davenport said in his courtroom voice, "I am here to announce the arrest of attorney Kathleen Shannon for criminal trespass. While this office respects Miss Shannon as a lawyer, it will not allow her to trample the law as she pursues her ends. We intend to put a stop to these tricks by defense lawyers."

"I second that," Clara Dalton Price stated.

"Give us a statement, Kit," shouted a reporter.

"I will in a moment," Kit said. She saw Corazón walking briskly toward the gathering and waited until she made her way to where Kit was standing.

"I applaud the district attorney's zeal for the law," Kit said. Davenport and Clara Price looked at her with chagrin and puzzlement. "That is why I am prepared to walk back to my office and get to work on my next case."

The reporters looked at each other.

"What's this about, Kit?" McGinty whispered.

Corazón handed Kit a piece of paper. "I hold in my hand a telegram from one Blair Mahoney, Gerald Mahoney's brother. He lives in Pennsylvania. My assistant, Corazón Chavez, tracked him down. Because Gerald Mahoney died without a will, Blair Mahoney is the sole heir of Gerald Mahoney's estate. Blair Mahoney was more than happy to have a lawyer secure those premises pending his arrival. Especially since the lawyer offered to do it for free."

She handed the wire to Davenport, who snatched it. Kit said, "That is a grant of full authority to me to enter and maintain the premises. Of course, this means entry onto the property by me or my agents is not trespass at all. It is simply good work."

Like a hungry tiger, the collective heads of the newspapermen swung toward Davenport. His eyes were desperately scanning the telegram. *A lawyer looking for a loophole*, Kit thought. She knew there was none.

"What do you have to say, Davenport?" Tom Phelps said.

The chief prosecutor of the county of Los Angeles cleared his throat and straightened his tie. "As I said, this office respects the law. It appears Miss Shannon is correct. We shall investigate further. Pending that, she is free to go."

Mike McGinty whispered to Kit, "You're a slippery one, all right."

"Maybe next time," Kit said.

The reporters wanted to ask more questions of Clara Dalton Price and John Davenport. But the duo quickly jumped into a waiting carriage and hurried away.

"How about you, Kit?" Tom Phelps said. "You want to say anything more about the D.A.? You have the floor."

"No more today, fellows," Kit said. "Never hit a man when he's down. That is the way of jiu-jitsu."

"Huh?" Phelps scratched his head.

"No further comment," said Kit.

———

Sarah Tanner threw her arms around her father. "I do not want to be apart from you ever again."

Lawrence Tanner could not keep the tears away. "I am so sorry." The feel of his daughter in his arms was overwhelming. "You have every right to hate me."

They were alone now at the top of Bunker Hill, looking out over the city. The sun made the Pacific sparkle. Sarah, looking out at the scene over her father's shoulder, saw it as a sign of new hope. She would spend the rest of her life helping her father regain his dignity and worth.

"No, Papa. I would never hate you."

Tanner shook his head. "I told many lies. I did not provide for you."

Sarah pushed back so she could look him in the eyes. They were wet but clear now. "That is all over now, Papa. We will go on together."

"Do you really mean that?"

Sarah nodded. "We need each other."

"I must face a charge that I killed a man."

"Miss Shannon says no charges will be filed."

"I would like to believe that."

Sarah Tanner, feeling an inner strength she could not have imagined before, stroked her father's wet cheek. "Papa, there is one thing I know with certainty. You can always believe Kathleen Shannon."

And then Sarah saw her father smile. He reached out for her, pulled her close, and did not let go for a long time.

———

Truman and Celia Harcourt met Kit and Corazón at Kit's office at four in the afternoon. Celia insisted on giving Kit a huge basket of baked goods—biscuits, cakes, cookies. "It feels so good to bake again," Celia said. "It is the least I can do after what you have done for us."

Kit nodded and accepted her compliment. As always, she gave God the credit for seeing justice done. But she also knew that Celia needed to give thanks, that it was her gift.

"And what of Louise?" Kit asked.

Celia and Truman exchanged glances and two wry smiles. "John and Louise eloped and were married last night in San Francisco," Celia said.

"I am so happy for you," Kit said, just as a blossom of sadness opened in her chest. She and Ted had almost done the same. Now she did not know where he was.

"It was your doing, Miss Shannon," Celia said.

"My doing?"

"That John had the gumption to stand up to his folks. He told us, just before he and Louise left, that you had talked some sense into him."

"I was rather presumptuous," Kit said.

"Good," Truman Harcourt said. "The boy needed it. But the most important thing is that there is hope for Louise now. She could have been lost, Miss Shannon."

"God has His hand on her life," Kit said. "My father loved to talk about the Good Shepherd who leaves the ninety-and-nine sheep to find the one that is lost."

After more expressions of thanks the Harcourts left, but only after getting Kit to promise to come to dinner the next evening. As the afternoon light began to give way to dusk, Kit sat in her swivel chair and let out a tired breath. "What a week," she said.

Corazón agreed. Just then Earl Rogers entered the room, giving only a cursory knock.

"Well done," he said, rather sheepishly. "Even though you danced with the devil."

"Earl," Kit admonished. "The D.A. is not the devil."

"He only acts like it, then." He put his head down. "I must apologize for my outburst outside O'Reilly's. It appears God is on your side after all. Can you find it in your heart to forgive your old friend?"

"Done."

"Oh, this came for you." Rogers pulled a telegram from his coat and handed it to her.

Kit ripped open the message and read it. After each line, her heart quickened. When she finished, she could tell her face was drained of color. She looked at Corazón, whose eyes were wide with curiosity.

"It appears we are going to San Diego," Kit said.

"What for?" Earl Rogers said.

"My fiancé has been arrested."

48

"YOUR HONOR," KIT SAID. "The government is accusing Mr. Fox of treason, which is a very specific crime."

"Go on," Judge Porter said. He seemed to be one of the good ones, open to a sound legal argument.

"It requires either an overt act to overthrow the government to which the accused owes allegiance. Or an overt act betraying one's country to a foreign power. The government alleges the second."

Collins, the United States attorney, nodded from his table.

Ted sat at the opposite table, watching Kit with what seemed to be calm eyes. In the courtroom a few spectators had come in out of the San Diego heat to get cool in the well-ventilated federal court-house.

Kit continued her argument to dismiss the complaint. "The government faces two problems, Your Honor. The first is that we are not at war with any foreign power, which means the act of betrayal cannot be shown."

"Might there not be an argument that certain foreign powers are engaged in acts that are against the interests of the United States?" the judge asked.

"Too flimsy an argument for a charge of treason, Your Honor. But the second problem with the government's case is fatal. Even if we accept that Germany is a foreign power opposed to our interests, my client, Mr. Fox, never committed an overt act that was an aid to

Germany or harmful to our nation."

The judge thought a moment, then looked at the government lawyer. "What is your response to that, Mr. Collins?"

Confidently, the attorney stood. "If I may call a witness?"

"Proceed."

A man Ted had pointed out to Kit earlier came forward and was sworn.

"State your name," Collins said.

"Hobart Hill," the man said.

"What is your occupation?"

"I am an agent of the United States Army."

"In what capacity, sir?" Collins questioned.

"Espionage."

"You are a spy?"

"Some call it that, yes," Hill stated.

"Do you have a special area of operations?"

"I do. Germany. It is where I am from."

"You have been a United States citizen for how long?"

"Five years."

Collins paused. "Can you tell us how you came to be aware of the accused?"

Hill nodded. "My operatives and I were on the trail of two German spies, who used the names Duncan Chase and Peter Garraty. We suspected they were looking for military information, in particular the use of aeronautics for warfare. During the course of our observations, we found that they had made contact with Mr. Fox. We followed Mr. Fox to San Diego, where he met with Chase and Garraty."

"What happened then?"

"We observed for a period of time, until we could place our hands on evidence of wrongdoing. Finally, we did."

Collins walked to the counsel table and took out a sheaf of papers from his briefcase. He then placed those papers in front of the witness.

"Can you tell the court what these documents are?"

Hill leafed through the papers quickly. "Yes. These are detailed plans for the design of an aeroplane, specifically a monoplane. We recovered them from the room of Duncan Chase. These are plans that Mr. Fox worked on with the Germans."

"Thank you, Mr. Hill. I have nothing further, Your Honor."

Kit stood to address the witness. "Mr. Hill," Kit said. "When you took Mr. Fox into custody, you held him incommunicado, isn't that correct?"

"Yes," Hill said, crossing his arms. "We have to do that sometimes."

"You did not inform him of the charges against him, did you?"

"Not at first. We wanted him to talk."

"Through coercion."

"Persuasion," Hill corrected.

"And all because of this?" Kit snatched the design papers off of Collins' table and waved them in the air.

"That is the evidence, yes."

"Evidence of what?"

For a moment, Hill looked confused. "Why, evidence of treason."

"Your entire case is built upon these plans, isn't it?"

"Well . . ."

"It is not a crime to associate with people, even spies, is it?"

"I suppose in some cases."

"Unless there is an overt act of treason, that is."

"Correct."

"And these documents, then, are the only evidence of an overt act that you have. If they were to disappear in a puff of smoke, you would have no case, now, would you?"

Collins stood up nervously. "But they won't disappear, Your Honor. I want those documents to be introduced as evidence."

"So do I," Kit said.

Now Hill, Collins, and the judge looked puzzled.

"May I call a witness, too?" Kit asked Porter.

"On this matter?"

"Oh yes."

"Then you may."

"I call Ted Fox."

Collins almost fell over in his chair.

Ted came forward and took the oath. Kit handed him the papers. "Mr. Fox, will you take a look at these documents, please?"

Ted took the papers and glanced at them.

"Are these papers the result of your meetings with Chase and Garraty?"

"Yes, they are."

"These are, in fact, detailed plans for a monoplane, is that correct?"

"Correct."

Kit paused and looked at the judge. He looked at her as if she were crazy.

"Mr. Fox," Kit said, "what kind of monoplane could be built from these plans?"

"The kind that crashes," Ted said.

"What was that?" Judge Porter asked, leaning toward Ted.

"Your Honor," Ted said, "these plans will not build a plane that can fly. Anybody who tried to build and fly this plane would be a fool. Most likely a dead fool."

"Objection!" Collins said.

"On what grounds?" Porter asked.

"I don't know." The lawyer scratched his head. "Something is not right here."

"If I may?" Kit said.

The judge nodded.

"Tell the court what happened when you met Garraty and Chase in San Diego."

"It was at the Hotel Del Coronado," Ted said. "We had dinner the first night and spoke of many things."

"Were you at all suspicious about these men?"

"I was being careful. But then Chase said that he was raised in Pittsburgh. That's where my mother's family was from. I tried to talk more about it, but Garraty interrupted. That's when I really got suspicious."

"And what did you do?"

"Near the end of the meal, I asked if either one of them had anything to do with the capturing of that German spy in New York, Honus Wagner."

"Honus Wagner?" Judge Porter said. "He's the shortstop for the Pittsburgh Pirates."

"As all good Americans know," Ted said. "But Garraty and Chase both said they did not have anything to do with that case. That's when I knew they were frauds."

Judge Porter burst out with a laugh.

"Now, if you will have these plans examined by an expert in aeronautics," Kit said, "you will see that what Mr. Fox states is true. This plane will not fly, and neither will the government's case."

The judge looked at Collins. "Have you had these plans examined by an expert?"

Collins, red-faced with indignation, said, "I . . . we . . . Not yet."

The judge shook his head and thought for a long time. "I have to say this is a new one on me. Here is what I am going to do. I will take these papers myself to someone who can be trusted and who is working in the science of aeronautics. If I confirm that these plans are bogus, I will dismiss the government's case."

"But that could take weeks," Kit said.

"I am aware of that. So I am going to release Mr. Fox on his own recognizance. And if I dismiss the case, I will order the government to pay your client suitable damages for his unlawful detention."

"Objection!" Collins said.

"Oh, be quiet," said the judge.

———

The train rattled along the coastline toward Los Angeles. Outside the window of the dining car, the blue of the Pacific was as deep as Kit had ever seen it. Aunt Freddy had once called it "my little pond." Now it was Kit's. She felt as much a part of it as if she'd been born here.

"That may be your lot in life from now on," Ted said. "Getting me out of scrapes."

"Are you planning to get arrested again?"

"No need. I'm already a prisoner. Of love."

"Oh, brother." Kit rolled her eyes. "You are going to have to do much better than that if you wish to get back into my good graces."

"How about a long, lingering kiss?"

"How about ordering dinner?"

"You prefer food to Ted Fox, aviator?"

Kit stroked her chin. "Depends. What's on the menu?"

Ted crossed his arms and shook his head. "Kathleen Shannon. I have to wonder what marriage to you is going to be like."

She smiled. "And you thought flying was an adventure."

Author's Note

The history of the early twentieth century continues to fascinate me. So many crosscurrents were happening at once as the American imagination moved from the country to the city. The great majority of citizens, of course, still lived in that great middle between California and New York, but the call for progress was being hailed in Chicago and San Francisco, Manhattan and L.A. In 1905, as Teddy Roosevelt took office for his second term, he preached a doctrine of "self-reliance and individual initiative." Hundreds of thousands of Americans listened and were eager to sign on.

This was the year that construction on the Panama Canal commenced. Wilbur and Orville Wright flew twenty-four miles. Movies as a commercial enterprise were in their bare beginnings. All production was based on the East Coast. No one had yet thought of Los Angeles as a base of operations.

Even though Los Angeles was at this time searching for an identity, it didn't care what its snootier (and sootier) sister cities to the east thought. It proceeded to act like a major city even as it was trying to find a distinctive style. (This it would never find; Los Angeles was, and remains, the most eclectic of municipalities.)

But throughout its history a parade of colorful, controversial, and sometimes just plain crazy people passed through its portals.

Harry Houdini was a real person, of course, and the illusions described in the novel are exactly as he performed them on stage.

In 1905 he had just returned from several years touring Europe. For the next three years he would crisscross America, performing the daring escapes he had perfected while across the Atlantic.

Houdini was also a famous debunker of spiritualists and mediums. When he was just starting out in magic, in the 1890s, he actually performed a mind-reading act, including fake séances, in small towns up and down the East Coast. His results were amazing to the small populations. How could he know such intimate details of the people in the audience?

Simple. A week ahead of the show, Houdini would slip into a town posing as a salesman. He would loiter in barbershops to pick up gossip, read the papers, and slip a few bucks to locals who would provide intimate details of prominent citizens. By show time, he had a wealth of material supposedly picked up from "the spirits."

But Houdini never pretended this was real. He was an entertainer and told people so. The fun was in trying to guess how he did it. That was his philosophy for his entire performing career.

Thus, when he would encounter spiritualists who took money from people under the pretense of actually being able to contact the dead, he reacted with outrage. These frauds were doing what he did, only they were bilking those who suffered and filling them with false hopes. He reveled in exposing their tricks and did so whenever he could. The episode in the novel is modeled after some of his actual encounters.

Spiritualism in America began in the 1840s, when two sisters in upstate New York, the Fox sisters (no relation to Ted!), claimed to have received messages from the dead in the form of rapping noises. P. T. Barnum even signed them up for a tour. Years later, one of the sisters admitted the noises from beyond the grave were actually produced by a peculiar skill—the sisters could crack their toes loudly under the table.

But by the turn of the century spiritualism was on the rise. Going through the Los Angeles newspapers of the time, one finds numerous ads for clairvoyants, spiritualists, mediums, and others of similar ilk. What Kit was fighting in 1905 was very real.

After World War I, spiritualism hit a new wave of popularity, due in part to the efforts of Arthur Conan Doyle (author of the Sherlock Holmes stories). All of this produced a sad longing in Houdini. Every medium he had encountered in his career was a fake; yet he wanted desperately to be able to contact the ghost of his beloved mother, Cecilia. He never did. In 1924 he published *A Magician Among the Spirits*, detailing the long history of spiritualist frauds. He lectured on the subject widely.

At one such lecture, a spiritualist stood up and shouted, "Christ was persecuted, and now we spiritualists are being persecuted!"

Houdini shot back, "But Christ never robbed people of two dollars, did he?"

Houdini's efforts helped hasten the decline of the medium industry in America—for a time, at least. How ironic that in our own day spiritualism seems on the rise again. As I write this, there is a hit television show on the air featuring a "medium" who helps audiences get "messages" from their dearly departed. Books by those who claim they can communicate with the dead climb the bestseller lists. Houdini would have had a field day with these folks. One wonders why such spiritualists don't channel any useful messages, such as, "The money is buried in the backyard."

The fad for jiu-jitsu was described in the February 11, 1905, *Los Angeles Examiner*. The writer reports that the Japanese have "won the women by telling them if they only know how, no matter how big a man is, they will be able to subdue him."

The *Examiner* reported that jiu-jitsu's usefulness was apparently demonstrated by a woman who subdued a burglar and, with application of hand to chin, nearly dislocated the man's spine. As he writhed on the ground she used another hold to keep him from escaping until a constable arrived.

Even President Theodore Roosevelt became enamored of the ancient art. In February 1905, Roosevelt arranged for a White House exhibition between a Japanese jiu-jitsu master named Yamashita and the U.S. champion middle-weight wrestler, named Grant. Within one minute, Yamashita had Grant in a choke hold; within two, he had an elbow lock on Grant that could have broken the champion's arm. Roosevelt was amazed that a small Japanese could subdue a bigger, stronger American.

The city of Los Angeles was still rather "wide open" when compared to its more genteel cousins in the east. And that was how many citizens liked it.

Harrison Gray Otis, the publisher of the *Times*, was an incessant supporter of the city. But he wanted only a certain kind of citizenry. In one of his editorials around the turn of the century, he wrote:

> *Los Angeles wants no dudes, loafers and paupers, people who have no means and trust to luck, cheap politicians, failures, bummers, scrubs, impecunious clerks, book keepers, lawyers, doctors. The market is overstocked already. We need workers! Hustlers! Men of brains, brawn and guts. Men who have a little capital and a good deal of energy—first class men!*

There was never any mention of women in his promotions, by the way. Though women like Kit and Clara Dalton Price were beginning to make headway in formerly male-only professions, the day of full opportunity was still a long way off.

Kit, in other words, has plenty of challenges to come.

Don't Miss

A Higher Justice

Book Two in THE TRIALS OF KIT SHANNON
Coming in Fall of 2003!

As Kit Shannon defends a down-and-outer named Mousy Malloy on the charge of attempted murder, she also takes on the case of a woman whose young son is tragically killed by a Los Angeles trolley. Was the death of little Sammy Franklin an accident? Or could it have been avoided?

The trolley case pits Kit against a powerful coalition of railroad men and politicians—all of whom seem to have something to hide . . . a secret Kit must uncover in order to win.

As these two cases move forward, it becomes clear there is some sort of connection—one that could blow the lid off a conspiracy of corruption. As Kit continues her pursuit of justice, it becomes evident that some powerful people will stop at nothing to keep her from finding the truth.

July 04
July 16
June 2021